Wyler's Wager
A tale from the Great Mountain

Troy Barrington

FOWARD

I met Troy some years back, when I joined his team in a major financial organization. I had made an accidental career change into a field about which I had little knowledge. I enjoyed the people I worked with, who were all very kind and helpful, but it was Troy, ever the storyteller, who spun for me surprisingly interesting tales about how High-Finance worked. He helped me develop the comfort level I needed to ask the sorts of questions that would allow me to succeed in my new endeavor.

It wasn't long before I realized what the rest of my tight-knit group already knew: Troy was a natural storyteller, who would regale us with usually hilarious stories about his childhood, people he had worked with before, his dog and his kids. Troy and I often exchanged story ideas; he told me he was going to write; I had complete confidence that he would, and that he would do it well.

So it was that sometime later Troy came to me and offered me a surprising honor, that of reading an early draft of the book you are about to begin. It was unpolished, seemingly worried about how long it was becoming…and completely captivating. So I resolved to use my red pen for Good, because I LIKE Troy, and I LOVE this story. I wanted to contribute my little part towards helping it meet its full potential.

Almost as good as the story between these pages is the story outside them. Lots of people are lucky enough to live their dreams. Some people even begin doing so long after a logical person would say it is prudent. This is what Troy is doing here, pursuing a dream when it was not prudent, logical, or, in a world of mortgages, college tuition and car payments, safe. But the fact that he is doing so speaks volumes about how important following your dreams is. Troy looked ahead and decided that NOT doing this crazy thing would be the cause of more regret than being "crazy" and doing it. We should all be so brave.

I know there are a lot of things out there competing for your time, but there is nothing like a cracking good old-fashioned adventure story to make you ready to go back out there and tackle the real world. Wyler's Wager is just that. There are kings and magic and monsters and beautiful princesses. There are long difficult journeys, across the land and within the heart. There are young men and women whose strengths surprise even themselves. The Mantoo will bet on anything and everything, but I am only willing to take the safe bet - that you will love this story as much as I do.

DEDICATION

First, to my father, who taught me the value of expressing oneself through writing; and to my mother who taught me to strive for excellence in everything I do.

To Kyle, Bria, Troi and Tai (my children), who have taught me that there is no expiration date tied to our ability to imagine.

To Betsy, Kim, Dexter and Sean for listening to my crazy stories about a mountain-planet filled with gamblers and fallible kings.

Lastly, to Lynn, who taught me the most valuable lesson a man could learn… to love.

Wyler's Wager

CONTENTS

TROY BARRINGTON

ACKNOWLEDGMENTS

Edited by Elizabeth Freeman
Art by Dexter Samuels
Graphic Art by Troy Toorie

PREFACE

They say the mountain has always been here. It gives us life, water, food, everything we need. It is all we know, and all we can see from its edge or highest peak. They say it is blessed with both good and bad magic because it takes care of those who dwell under its peak, but no one has ever left the mountain that was ever seen again. No one knows exactly how big it is, but it is so big that it sustains many very different races. There are three that above all others have dominion over the mountain. Little is known of the other two races, except for what Wyler and his brother have told in their stories, or what little the prophecy scrolls have reviled. Our borders on the Great Mountain are sealed; Mantoo is protected by a great gate that no one enters or leaves, so we rely on those stories and the scrolls for information outside of Mantoo.

Of what we know, those from Alkotten live on the highest part of the mountain above the clouds. I do not know how they survive there, for it is cold and bright, and as far as we know, nothing grows there. Their skin and hair are as white as the snow, which is everywhere. Their eyes are the color of the water under the ice before the spring thaw. They do not feel the cold as we do. They wear long gowns of white, to cover their long thin bodies. They say some of them are eight feet tall, and have very long feet. They are able to walk on the snow without leaving a single mark, and are so light and white, if they stood still in the midst of a snow fall, you would never see one of them in front of you. They experiment with magic and alchemy, which are not permitted here. They believe their physical placement above all else on the mountain, to be sign from the gods. Such an arrogant lot; they walk in the belief that they are above all other mountain folk in every way. Well, that's what they say about the Alkotten.

The Alusta live along the base of the mountain, in the great darkness. They say they have a great fear of the light, and live in the hot sweltering mist, and fire below. Their skin is dark and thick like fine leather. They can withstand great heat and can breathe under water for long periods. They say that their homes are built into the very mountainside. There is little to eat there so they feed on rock. They say the Alusta have curly dark hair. Their bodies are heavy with muscle and their eyes are as the emeralds and sapphires. They see very well in the dark, and some say they can leap great distances. They adorn themselves in the jewels that are plentiful in their land, and they care nothing for the other races on the mountain. Well, at least that is what they say about the Alusta.

Now the Mantoo are the greatest of the three races on the mountain. We live in the middle where the grass is green and lush, and the water is fresh and clear. We have many different types of animals and grow many varieties of food. Our houses are made of river wood. They are built the same; usually two levels. The lower level has a kitchen, eating area, a study and a relief, while the upper floor has the sleeping quarters. We are a strong and proud people, although not as tall as the Alkotten or as well- muscled as the Alusta. Our clothes are not as simple as the Alkotten, or as pretty as the Alusta. We dress in fine, colorful fabrics; the color of many flowers in the region. Mantoo males almost always wear a large tie around their necks and long tailed jackets with many buttons. Our females dress in wonderfully colorful gowns for every occasion. We are farmers and millers, and smiths, and bakers. Most of all, we are gamblers. Yes, we gamble day and night; it is in our blood. We spend many hours gambling each day, and will make a wager on just about anything; anything at all. It is said that once, two young men wagered on which blade of grass would outgrow another. And they both, not trusting the other, stayed next to his blade of grass watching it grow for three seasons. At the end of the third season, the great frost came and killed many of the crops. They both nearly caught their deaths staying there trying to keep their blades of grass warm. It was the first tie in Mantoo history. You see, when we gamble, there must be a winner.

Our king Wyler Wantoo is the greatest of the gamblers, or else he is the luckiest. Why, he even won the throne by gambling with the former king. Wyler's kept the throne for almost 200 years. Oh, did I mention we Mantoo have very long life spans. Most live to be the grand age of 500 or so years before we pass to the great beyond and King Wyler Wantoo is the oldest Mantoo. They say he is sick with age, and his son, Ringo may soon inherit the kingdom. Ringo, the King? What a laugh that one is. When he's not doing something as honorable as gambling, he passes the entire day sleeping, or drunk, or womanizing. That lout! He does not dress like the rest of us. His trousers and boots are made from the leather of a giant black cow he won in a wager. His shirts are all white and colorless. He refuses to wear a tie, or a long jacket. They say the day he becomes king, will mark the first of the dark times prophesied eons ago. The say the elders are gathering at the request of the king. Wyler wishes to have his son assume the throne. The elders hold fast to prophecy, and believe that Ringo will lead our people to darker days. Speaking of our people, we are a people of many laws. We adore order, even in the gambling houses. I believe it is the fear of disorder that drives the elders to move against Ringo. Yes, yes I bet it is. King Wyler will have to perform a great feat of magic in order to pass the throne to his son.

The elders know of Wyler's intention to crown his eldest son as King, and do not like the idea. They met in secret to ensure the vote would not favor Wyler's crazy notion that Ringo could be handed the crown while Wyler was still alive. But Wyler Wantoo is clever and wise. Knowing all the members of the council as he does, Wyler will not come unprepared. If one were the betting sort, he would wager that Wyler would find a way to again sway the council despite his odds. If one were inclined to wager.

The house of Wyler was to be the one that united our people. Wyler built and trained our army. They keep the peace and are the reason no enemy was dared to attack our borders. Ringo is their captain. Despite his poor habits and bad manners he is a great soldier, but that will not be enough to secure him the throne. His younger brother Wesley is being trained to take his place in the elite guard. Our army has ensured our security for many years. The youngest of the lot is Princess Dionne. She is a tough one. She is just a child, but she is as feisty as the elders. She spends her time running against the Mantoo lads. Having two older brothers has undoubtedly made her to desire rough-housing and fisticuffs. Hardly the behavior expected from a princess, but she helps to keep her brothers in line, so everyone overlooks it.

They say Wyler Wantoo has been the wisest king of all time, and when he passes; there will be no way to fulfill the prophecy. But there are other prophecies that are darker still. The prophecy scroll told a dark tale of deceit, betrayal and even death. The dark days will soon be upon us all, and all that dwell on the mountain will be touched by this ageless force of darkness. The days of the great mountain will soon come to pass. Well, at least that's what they say.

1 THE GATHERING

A soft wind was blowing from the west on the morning the elders came to gather at Mantoo castle. The tall green grass outside the finely crafted stone walls swayed to and fro as the gentle wind changed direction. The morning dew was still on the beautiful blue lilies that adorned the king's garden as the elders began to arrive. The sound of the grand waterfall in the distance filled the air and the mist formed a rainbow near it that lasted most of the day. The roar of the falls could not be overtaken by the noise made by the horse-drawn carriages.

The morning sky was unusually bright and clear, which made the castle look that much brighter. The Mantoo castle was always immaculate. The staff was always cleaning, polishing, pruning and sweeping.

Just outside the main door, King Wyler Wantoo was adjusting his crown and belt, while waiting impatiently for the elders to arrive. He pulled the brown leather belt up toward his chest, and shifted the crown to the left side of his head. His short and stout frame was adorned with a gleaming white outfit that was lined with gold trim and silver buttons. His crown was simple, yet elegant. It had one large diamond in the center and two smaller diamonds on either side. There were gold leaves on the top of the crown that pointed toward the heavens and a thin line of silver wrapped around its base. Wyler's beard and hair were completely white. His eyebrows were thick, but neatly trimmed. He looked at his well-manicured finger nails and nodded his head in satisfaction before looking out toward the gate. He smiled as he saw his daughter, Princess Dionne, approach him. He studied her beige lace dress and frowned.

"Young lady, you're not dressed," He said, annoyed with her appearance.

"I'm not naked father. I threw this on so that I could walk the garden with Wesley. I came here before changing." She answered in a very delightful and playful tone.

"Here first? Why would you need to do that?" he began.

"Oh father, indeed." She said adjusting his crown to the center of his head and lowering his belt. "We can't have the king of Mantoo looking as though he can hardly dress himself, can we?" She smiled.

"No," he smiled back. "We can't have that. We also cannot tolerate the scandal that would arise if the Princess were to be seen in last year's lace and no matching bonnet."

Dionne's mouth opened and her face was lit with shock as the realized the gravity of her father's words. "Goodness!" she yelled running into the castle.

Wyler smiled as he looked out toward the gate. His smile grew larger as Dionne unexpectedly ran back to him and planted a kiss on his cheek before running back inside. Once again he fixed his eyes on the Castle path and watched as the carriages containing the elders began to arrive.

Each elder was met at the gate by one of the royal greeters who were always over-dressed for the occasional elder council meetings. The Royal Callers met each elder at their carriage and escorted them inside the castle, and to the great hall. The elder council was made up of the nine oldest members of the kingdom. Wyler, by virtue of being both the eldest and the King, chaired the council. Like Wyler, each of the members was short and stout. Age had made many of them bitter and stuck in their ways, which often made business difficult to manage. Despite their differences, Wyler was always able to sway them to vote one way or the other, so that decisions concerning the Mantoo people could be handled as quickly as possible.

Their gathering in the great hall was a common occurrence in the governing of Mantoo, but today was different. It was the first time that the other members of the elder council were united to oppose Wyler. As with all such meetings, the thunderous sound of the elders arguing rang through the great hall. Wyler sat at the head of the long table and looked around the hall with a look of disdain.

"To order. Come to order," Wyler said pounding his gavel to quiet the council members.

The elders sat on large pillows around a long, low granite table and quickly became quiet. Some were eating, while others looked at notes written on fine parchment. Wyler began the meeting as he had done so many times before with prayer, and gave each member an opportunity to discuss the matters of the district they governed. The meeting went on for many hours with the usual arguing jockeying for position or favor, and as with any Mantoo gathering, a wager or two was made.

After a long lunch, Wyler looked around the table and noted a change in the mood across the great hall. The smiling faces and warm fellowship being expressed was not unexpected. Wyler knew a good meal could mellow the disposition of the most disgruntled Mantoo.

"Now, that we are finished with the business of days prior, it is on to new business. As many of you know, I intend to relinquish the crown to my son Ringo."

The chamber was immediately filled with shouts of protest. Wyler pounded the gavel violently.

"To order! Come to order!" He shouted. Wyler stood up, which caused the others to pause. "We will have order," he said calmly as he looked around the room.

Dugan Shipnor stood up and placed both hands on the granite table. His long red beard almost touched the floor. "Wyler," he started. "We are not just members of the elder council; we are your oldest friends. I believe I speak for all of us when I say how much we respect you, and cherish the friendship we have. Each of us took a position in this council because we seek the best for our people."

"Even though we may not always agree on what that is," Wyler interrupted.

"Yes that's right," Dugan continued. "Wyler your reign as king will be considered the greatest of all. It will be written into the archives as such, and all others have and will pale in comparison." Wyler took notice as Devonsire rolled his eyes and frowned as Dugan said these things. "The next king will have to be equally regarded to maintain order and prosperity throughout Mantoo. I fear your son's reputation for sport, and other things have made it impossible for him to succeed you." Dugan said with some concern.

"Sport?" Wyler asked.

"You know of what I speak. His drinking, womanizing, havoc-reeking..." Dugan began.

"His two-timing, heart-stealing, debt owing, tax-cheating." Lady Arna of Mortortown interjected.

"Don't forget trick-playing, game hording, and public intoxication." Devonsire of Lumdoren added.

The room became loud with everyone speaking at the same time. Rather than pond his gavel, Wyler simply began to speak and room fell silent.

"My dear friends I know of what you speak, and though my heart is troubled by your words, I assure you I speak in the best interest of all of Mantoo."

Devonshire sighed. "Were you to pass to the great beyond, his succession would be incontestable, but to appoint a successor while you live is against our laws Wyler."

Wyler sank into his seat. "There is no doubt I will pass to the great beyond Devonsire, as we all must one day, and when that happens Ringo will be king. I ask that he take the thrown now, and would not ask this if it were not necessary. I would not seek to defy a law written before most of our recorded history if I knew another way. Hear me now, as you never have before."

Wyler pulled a scroll from behind him and unrolled it. He laid it on the table and carefully spread it out. Everyone looked with anticipation as Wyler laid out what appeared to be a blank scroll.

He looked across the table and nodded. "An ancient evil is upon us. It threatens to destroy all that we know and love. As you know, the Haurookena scroll is our oldest and most valued scroll. It's revelations about our future have saved us three times during my reign."

Wyler paused as everyone nodded their heads in agreement.

"Its latest premonition appeared two days ago and must be shared with each of you. I can only assume that as with each premonition before, we will have sixty-four days before the event it displays happens."

Wyler touched the center of the scroll with his index finger. All were amazed as picture of stars and distant galaxies took shape within the scroll. The image of a blue comet speeding through space captured their attention. Their faces filled with terror as they watched the comet slam into the Great Mountain from the west. A cloud of fire and ash was all that remained of the Great Mountain and each elder wore a look of horror and despair.

"I don't understand" Said Swoggle of Bedlahm. "The original elders told tales of a dragon with a long fiery tail devouring the mountain with but one swallow."

Wyler pointed to the tail of the comet as the scroll replayed the images again. "Behold your fiery tail Swoggle. Surely this beast will devour anything that lay in its path."

"We must flee to the east side of the great mountain." One of them said.

"And go where? We know nothing beyond our side of the mountain." Another answered.

Wyler pointed to the scroll, which kept replaying the moment of destruction over and over. "If the destruction to the West end of Great Mountain is imminent we have nothing to fear, because the destruction will occur despite our best wishes. We can do little more than prepare for the end, but I do not think this is our fate."

"What?" Dugan snapped. "We all just saw the end; the end of all things. How can you say that Wyler?"

Wyler sat down. "The scroll shows our destiny if I do nothing. It is the outcome if there is no action on my part, and so I must act. As I have three times before, I must commit to an action that preserves our way of life. Now I must say that the end you see is not the end that is upon us. The images are a metaphor for the real danger."

"What does that mean?" Devonsire asked angrily.

Wyler flashed a look of anger at Devonsire, but quickly caught himself and manufactured a smile. "See the darkness around the comet; there are no stars. I take it to mean that destruction approaches from an unseen location. It will be marked by the passing of a comet, but whatever it truly is will mean nothing less than the utter destruction of all we hold dear if I fail to act. And so, I must do something to stop it."

"Yes, you must do something Wyler." Lady Arna demanded.

"Yes I must." Wyler said playing with his beard. "Now, I am trying to do just that, but the members of this council seek to oppose me."

"Surely you have another solution. After all we've said about Ringo, you must know that he not capable of saving us. What plan can he devise to destroy this dragon?" Swoggle asked.

"I have taken two days to contemplate the best course of action. We now have Sixty-two days to change our fate and the fate of every living thing on this mountain. We have no time to argue and bicker; there is only time to act. I am too old to do what must be done. I believe that not only is he capable of saving us, he is the only one that can." Wyler said confidently.

The loud protests filled the chamber once more. This time, it went on louder and longer than before.

Devonsire pounded his fist on the table. "Mantoo cannot do this alone!" He yelled. Alusta and Alkotten must help!"

"That is in fact part of the plan," Wyler said calmly. "But they must be convinced if they are to work together. Brutus and Meccah are still at odds despite the peace between their nations. I believe that collectively, the three nations can save ourselves, but only if we work as one. Ringo can bring them together to aid us in our endeavor. They will aid us in doing this if it will preserve us all."

"Then we are doomed!" Swoggle began. "They will never come together, even for the sake of their lives or their kingdoms."

"They must and will do it," Wyler shouted back.

"This is your plan? This is our salvation?" Devonsire asked loudly.

"What reason do any of you have to doubt me? I have never failed Mantoo before. It has been my judgment and careful planning that has saved us in the past, so why do you doubt me now in this dark hour? If I were struck down this very hour, you all would have to bow to Ringo in the next. So why now when it is so important that we agree do you seek to oppose me at every turn? What is it that bends your will so?" Wyler asked as he looked into each of their eyes one by one. He knew at that moment that a great evil had reached his kingdom, and touched the minds of the elders. Wyler knew they were beyond his ability to reason with, but he had one last chance to get his way.

"I know what I ask is against our bylaws, but I am determined to see this through," he fired.

Once again, the chamber was filled with protests and yelling. Wyler took a deep breath and dropped his head. When it looked as if he could take no more, Wyler climbed on top of the table and yelled a single phrase that caused the room to go silent immediately.

"Maisha-Vad!" he screamed.

"You cannot be serious." Devonsire said.

"Oh I am serious. As it is my right to do so in accordance with our laws, I invoke the Maisha-Vad."

"We cannot refuse the Vad. Wyler you risk all of our lives, not merely your own if you do this," Swoggle said angrily.

Wyler made his way off of the table and sat by the window on the north wall. Everyone was completely silent in anticipation of his next words. He looked out the window and let out a deep breath. The heat from his breath made the small panel foggy. "You each act as if your actions require your gaze through this fogged pane of glass, but the next thing that must happen is very clear to me. You have all seen the prophecy of the scroll. Our lives are at greater risk if I do nothing. As we have no time to debate I must act, and so I have. The life bet must be honored."

"Under the law, we must attempt to win the bet Wyler. You wager all of our lives on the abilities of your son. You condemn us to die," Dugan Shipnorr responded.

Wyler continued to stare out of the window. "The entire world sees your children for what they believe to be their true measures of character and sprit. In truth, what they see may be all that the child truly is at that moment, but a parent sees his or her child for their potential; all they can be or could become. Being his father does not blind to what he is, it allows me to see him in ways that you cannot. You've not seen his courage, his intellect, or his wisdom at work. I have taught him all that I know. He is all that I am and more, and not even half my age. He uses his abilities for personal gain, and because of that you see in him the sum of his past actions and not the promise of his future. I cannot do what must be done. I am too old for the journey. It is too late to begin anew with someone all of you would deem worthy. Time; we simply have no time. Ringo can save us. He must. He will," he turned to face them. "And for the sake of all we hold dear, I am betting my life on it."

2 PARLOR GAMES

There were many gambling houses throughout Mantoo, but the main gambling parlor was huge. It was a long stone structure with large windows that had thick frosted glass. The main door was heavy, and took quite a bit of force to open. The gable roof was covered with red hand-made clay tiles and had eight windows on each side that operated like skylights to capture and make use of the sunlight during the day. At night, a series of mirrors were used to bounce the light from the moon and quite a few candles throughout the room. This made the parlor almost as brightly lit at night as it was during the day. There were over a thousand tables, each filled to capacity with gambling Mantoo. Every table hosted a different sort of game where the Mantoos could wager with one another. Each of the Game smiths was bald and dressed in long blue robes. The robes had a long, white stripe that extended from the center toward the left side. The thickness of the stripe on the robe was an indication of the seniority the smith had.

The smiths presided over all of the parlor games. There were games of cards, games of chance, arm wrestling, thumb wrestling, dice throwing, wheel spinning; contests of every kind. The hall was filled with gamblers from every village in Mantoo and the best gambler was its prince, Ringo Wantoo. Ringo was very skilled at all of the parlor games, and even showed skill at the games the folks made up on a whim.

His dark hair and eyes seemed to draw the attention of every Mantoo female. He was rugged and slim. He stood a few inches taller than the average Mantoo his age, and had confidence and cunning beyond his years. His skin was tanned from his morning exercises in the sun. There were many who would attribute his tan to the position of his table in the main parlor. Ringo made certain the table was in the center of the room, where more sunlight shined upon it than any other table. The young women of Mantoo delighted in his handsome features. Many of them did very odd things to get his attention, but there was one girl who often ignored him. And it was her, above all the women of Mantoo that he desired. Her name was Ayana. She was the youngest daughter of Grand Parlor Master, and was keen to every trick Ringo used. Ringo often stopped whatever he was doing to watch her as she walked by. Her dark hair, olive skin, and green eyes drew him in whenever she looked in his direction. When she was not working in the parlor, she could be seen with a book or an armful of scrolls. She was always dressed in a color of blue that reminded him of the water near Orlander

Falls. She was thinner than many of the other girls her age, but had a confidence that demanded attention.

Ringo took a small piece of bread from his plate and popped it into his mouth. He sat at the black slate table listening to the cheers and jeers from the winners and losers that filled the parlor. He was patiently waiting for his next challenger when a tall, thin woman approached and dropped a small sack of silver on the table.

"I bet you cannot beat my husband Norfas in an arm wrestling contest" she said pointing at a small skinny elderly man standing in front of a large nearby column. Ringo smiled and gave her a nod. She looked delighted and yelled, "NORFAS!" A large, muscular Mantoo made his way from behind the large column and walked toward the table. While all eyes were set on the large man, Ringo lifted the pepper shaker from the table and sprinkled a tiny bit of the black pepper on his gloved knuckles. The dark gloves hid the pepper perfectly, and Ringo was careful not to be seen. As Norfas took his seat in front of Ringo, all eyes turned to their table. The room fell silent in anticipation of Ringo's next words.

"Now this is will be fine wager indeed," Ringo said smiling. "So... Norfas is it? That name sounds northern. I heard they grow quite large out there and you my friend certainly fit that description." Ringo leaned back in the chair and lifted his head. "A big match calls for a big wager," he yelled.

Ringo looked around the table at the crowd. "I'll give three to one odds!" He said loudly. Suddenly a large crowd that wanted to accept his wager engulfed the table. The sea of gamblers were yelling and pushing against each other in a desperate attempt to bet against him. When all of the bets were collected, the game-smith gave a nod to begin. A table hand quickly removed the dishes and condiments from the table and the two combatants joined hands.

"Rules?" Ringo politely asked the smith.

"No outside interference, no one may stop until the contest has been decided; there must be a winner." The smith shouted.

Ringo stared across the table into the eyes of the much larger man.

"Is this to be a starring contest as well?" Norfas asked.

"You might have better luck if it were. I'm afraid this won't last that long." Ringo replied confidently.

"Why is that?" Norfas asked angrily.

"Your height tells me that you are probably related to the Mantoo of Gilderren."

"What of it?" Norfas quipped.

"Gilderren is on the high ground, and the Mantoo there have limited exposure to the river rock from which this table is carved. They are quite allergic and will often sneeze in its presence."

"I've never heard of that!" Norfas belted.

"GO!" The Smith yelled

Ringo began to breathe deeply as soon as the match began. The cheering from the crowd was deafening to his ears, but he had to concentrate. The strain of keeping his arm from touching the table was almost too much to bear. He waited until Norfas' face was close enough and he blew the pepper from the top of his knuckles as he took another deep breath. Norfas' eyes began to water, and he sat up straight. He could not maintain the strength in his arm as he let out a roaring sneeze. Ringo easily pinned his arm as the crowd roared with disbelief.

He began to collect his winnings and placed them in a black sack. Norfas kept sneezing long after it was over.

"I told you; allergies." Ringo said as Norfas' was led away from the table by his wife who was shouting and throwing up her arms in anger.

In that same moment, one of the royal callers made his way through the crowd of disappointed gamblers. He removed his hat and bowed once he reached the table.

"Prince Ringo," he started. "The king desires council with you."

"Tell my father I will be there shortly. I am having a streak of fortune."

"He said you would say that my lord. He says I am to remove you with force if you hesitate."

The entire parlor was silent for a moment. Someone shouted "two to one he goes without force," and the parlor came alive with a fury of mad gamblers. After a few moments, the game-smith blew the horn and all eyes were fixed on Ringo. The entire crowd waited eagerly to see what happened next. Ringo looked up at the game-smith and managed a slight smile.

"What are my odds?" he said calmly.

The smith looked at his notes. "Three to one you'll leave sire," the smith answered.

Ringo walked to the door closest to the table and waited at the doorway as the Royal caller opened it. He paused and turned toward the Game-smith. "Pity," Ringo said looking adjusting his gloves. "Under different circumstances, I would have taken those odds."

As Ringo walked out, the room behind him was again filled with the deafening sounds of gamblers screaming over each other to make their wagers.

"What is this about Buxhorn?" Ringo asked stepping into the Royal carriage.

"As usual sire, I am without cause or reason. Mine is a simple task; retrieve you at the kings' calling."

Ringo ignored Buxhorn's comments and watched as Ayana walked out of the parlor with a book in her arms. She began to walk west past the carriage and Ringo saw an opportunity to speak with her.

"Ayana," he called while jumping out of the carriage.

"Yes your Highness," She replied while turning to face him.

Buxhorn noticed the prince jump from the carriage and let out a deliberate cough to make Ringo aware of his presence.

Ringo ignored him and kept talking to Ayana "Please dispense with the formalities; we've known each other since we were children. I have a carriage, could I take you somewhere?" he asked politely.

"That is very kind of you Prince Ringo, but it's so lovely a day that I think I shall walk."

"Walk?"

"Yes. It's what we did before we discovered the horse or carriage," she said laughing."

Ringo was captivated by her laugh and returned a smile.

"I ah...very well then milady; I do hope you enjoy your book," he said climbing into the carriage. She turned to walk away when he quickly thought of something else to say to her. "Ayana what is your book about?"

She turned to face him once more and smiled. "It's a book about an Ogre that turns into a handsome Prince," She said smiling at the fact that he expressed interest.

"I've read that one. It's very sad," he replied.

"I've read it three times myself. Is it sad because the Ogre dies, or because the maiden has lost her one true love?" she asked, trying to test him.

"For both of those reasons," he replied, unsure of his answer.

Ayana turned away feeling dissatisfied with his answer, but stopped as he began to speak once more.

"The real tragedy was that they waited too long to find each other, and had very little time before the end. The maiden is not just sad for the love she lost, but for the loss of a love that could have been."

She placed her hand on her heart and turned around to face him, but all she saw was the carriage pulling away from the parlor. She watched it for a moment and turned the corner toward the bakery.

Inside the carriage, Ringo began to nervously rub his hand together. He looked back in Ayana's direction, but did not see her. He huffed in disappointment and pulled off his gloves.

"Am I an Ogre or a Prince?" he asked himself. He turned back toward the caller and took a gold coin out of his pocket. Ringo began to flip it into his hand and call the side while his fist was closed. "Eagle," he said before looking at it. He flipped it again and caught it. "Gate," he said before opening his hand. "Oh," he grunted in disappointment. He kept flipping the coin, but turned his attention to the caller. "Buxhorn did he really say to use force if necessary?" he asked unconsciously playing with his left ear.

"Yes my lord, he did." Buxhorn replied.

"Humph." Ringo sighed. "I bet he did."

3 THE APPOINTMENT

Ringo jumped out of the carriage as it arrived in the main courtyard. He caught a glimpse of his younger brother Wesley training his falcons and stopped to greet him. Wesley looked like a younger version of his brother, but was dressed in the traditional royal clothing. His dark blue trousers and white silk shirt were adorned with beautiful gold buttons. His pants were neatly tucked into black leather boots, which had three gold buttons on each side. Ringo ran up to the stables and stopped as he saw his horse. He stroked her mane for a moment then turned to find Wesley approaching him.

"Still training those retched creatures brother?" Ringo asked as he hugged him.

"These creatures are far smarter than that smelly horse you love so much. Where are you off to?" Wesley asked.

"Father calls; I must not keep him waiting," Ringo said, while looking toward the castle.

"Not unless you desire a visit from the Buhmann."

Ringo laughed. "We are far too old to be coaxed into doing father's bidding by using that old trick. Remember how he used to use it to make you do your studies?"

"Or whenever he wanted you to run an errand," Wesley laughed.

"Oh, it was cruel to do that to two young lads, and he would dare to call us his sons."

"It kept you in line." Wesley quipped.

"It kept me awake; the idea of some vile, dark creature haunting your dreams."

"How did you get past the nightmares?"

"I don't think I ever did. Even with the magic muffin that somehow kills him."

"Do you remember the recipe? Mantoo iron, Alkotten Ice, Alustan fire, and dead zone spice….'

"The magic muffin recipe, are you serious? Wesley, you're practically a full grown Mantoo now. It's ridiculous to hold on to the demons of our youth; the scary things father used to tell us to keep us in line. We were babes then, but we're grown up now, and Princes no less. Promise me you will let go of that silly youngling fodder," Ringo pleaded. He looked at the falcon perched on the pole nearest the doorway to the barn and smiled. "Although I doubt that I could get you to let go of that wretched thing," Ringo said gesturing toward the bird.

Wesley whistled and the falcon immediately took flight and landed on his arm.

"Neat trick for a dinner in waiting," Ringo quipped.

"Hey not fair," Wesley protested. "I've had Tara for a long time. She's my most trusted bird. If I asked her to journey to the stars, she would do so out of loyalty.

"Really?" Ringo said while folding his arms in disbelief.

"Alright then," Wesley said facing a large tree in the distance. "Watch this," he said confidently. He pointed to the tree and softly said "Find Yulok."

The bird immediately flew from his arm and into the tree. They both laughed as the falcon began screeching and the sounds of someone screaming suddenly came from the tree. The next moment, Devonsire's youngest son Yulok fell out of the tree amongst a few dozen leaves. He stood up and pumped his fist at Wesley and hollered "That's not funny!" before running down the castle path. They both laughed again as they watched him run into the distance.

"You knew he was there?" Ringo asked.

"He's always there. Spying on us for his father no doubt," Wesley answered.

Wesley looked to the tree once more. "If you think that was nice, watch this," he said as confident as before. "Find Ringo!" Wesley yelled.

The bird flew from the tree and on to Ringo's shoulder.

"You see, I told you. I could send her anywhere and she goes without question." Wesley said proudly.

"Well, send her to the sun. Maybe she'll come back as roasted and stuffed. If nothing else, she'll make for a good meal. Now get this infernal creature off of me before she relieves herself on my shoulder," Ringo said nervously.

Wesley held out his arm and made a clicking noise with his teeth. Ringo tried not to show how impressed he was as the falcon flew onto Wesley's padded arm.

"Father will have my hide. I'm off," Ringo said runny toward the castle entrance.

"Roasted and stuffed" Wesley said mocking him. "That's not funny," he said looking at Tara. He gave the bird a treat and rubbed her head. "He didn't mean it," he said kindly. "He never does."

Wyler sat on his throne in the great hall and studied the beautifully painted ceiling and columns that lined the pathway from the throne-room door. He looked at his hand and straightened his ring. The royal caller entered the room through the far door and approached him.

"The Prince has arrived sire," he said bowing.

Wyler nodded and began pacing the floor. From a distance, a girl's voice could be heard. Princess Dionne entered the room from the other side with two young ladies behind her. One of them was writing down everything she said, while the other tried to keep the train of her gown from touching the floor. They each took turns answering "yes Princess" to everything she said. Her mauve colored gown was lined with fine white lace. She carried a small fan that was finely detailed with lace and beads that she fanned her face with as she walked.

"And the flowers in the meditation garden are not the right color," she began. "Please have the gardeners use the violets; they are exquisite this time of year."

"Yes Princess," they both said as the practically ran to keep up with her.

"Oh Father." she said as she embraced Wyler. "I'm glad I found you."

"I was not aware that I was lost," Wyler smiled as her returned her hug.

"I am having the cook prepare a goose for dinner with an elderberry glaze. I hope that is to your liking." Dionne said.

"That my dear is Ringo's favorite. He will be pleased; excellent as always." Wyler said rubbing his hands together.

"Well Father, Wesley will no doubt protest the consumption of any bird, but the cook will prepare fish just for him. We wouldn't want his allergies to get the better of him"

"You are a wonder in intellect as well as beauty. You've thought of everything. Run along now. I must tell your brother his task," he said as Ringo entered the room.

"Hello raindrop." Ringo said as he kissed Dionne on her cheek.

"Hello rain storm." she said and hurried off with the two ladies.

The two young ladies giggled aloud as they hurried off. Dionne paused for a moment, which caused them to straighten up and abandon their smiles. Dionne glared at both of them for a second and stormed away furiously fanning herself.

"Father, you called for me?" Ringo asked as he hurriedly walked in. He took notice to the far-away look Wyler had in his eyes.

"Come walk with me, son," he said gently.

They exited through a door on the side of the room, and entered the palace garden. Wyler raised his hand to stop Ringo who was about to ask a question.

"Ringo, when you were a child you had many questions; Day and night you asked question upon question. I did as any father would and answered them in as much truth as I thought you could stand to hear. One day, you stopped asking questions. I cannot pretend to remember exactly when it happened; over time I would imagine, but I learned something the day I realized that you no longer asked those questions. It was not that you knew all you needed, or that you no longer needed me to answer them. No. I learned that you had a greater need to discover the answers for yourself. You once asked me who you were that everyone would bow when they greeted you. I said you are the prince; heir to the throne of Mantoo; the son of King Wyler Wantoo of Mantoo and all its' lands. I was proud and boastful back then."

"Father I…. I am trying to understand why you are telling me these things," Ringo interrupted.

"You know, one day you will have to wear the crown."

"Yes father. You've told me that all of my life."

"And what if it were not to simply be handed to you? What if you had to earn the crown rather than inherit it as a privilege of birth?"

"Father?"

"The elders are opposed to your taking the crown before my death."

"What? Those pompous windbags. Surely you don't…" Ringo began.

"Those pompous windbags are the elders of this land and are to be respected," Wyler said in an intense tone.

"Yes father," he said, dropping his head. "But, if I do not take the crown then who? Wait! I just realized what you said a moment ago. Why would I need to take the crown before your death? What is this about? I'm confused."

"The crown is yours after my departure to the life after. They dispute my right to make you king while I still draw breath. My child, none of that may matter soon. In fact, it is possible that there may soon be no kingdom to govern."

"What? Father you ….you speak in riddles. Why would I become king if you live? Moreover, why would there be no kingdom to govern? I do not understand."

"Ringo a grave matter that affects all of Mantoo has come to my attention. The only riddle is whether any Mantoo will survive it."

"All of Mantoo? What save war could affect every being in the Mantoo lands, father?

"The scrolls have shown us a disastrous end. A comet will plunge from the stars and destroy the great mountain."

"A comet? Aren't comets supposed to be a good omen?"

Wyler touched the scroll's center and Ringo watched in amazement as the scroll replayed the images of the comet arrival and the mountain's destruction.

Wyler watched his son view the moving images and took note to the horror on his face.

"As you can plainly see, this is no good omen. This comet marks the second coming of the enemy in this age."

"This comet approaches from the west, opposite the rising sun. This is a problem for Alkotten father".

"No Ringo, this is not just a problem for Alkotten, or even Mantoo, or Alusta. I fear all of the people on the great mountain will perish if this comes to pass. The comet you see on the prophetic scroll marks the destruction of the Great Mountain as we know it; none would be sparred."

Ringo looked amazed. "Mantoo, Alusta and Alkotten, all destroyed?" he said in horror.

"You know well the tales of the scrolls from the past. They prophesize in metaphor. Whatever danger is before you, its' true nature will not be known until it is upon you."

"So the comet…"

"Is merely the sign of something to come from the distance, but no less dangerous I assure you. Something is coming that will mean the destruction of all that dwell on the Great Mountain. I have told no one else what I am about to share with you."

Ringo looked at his father with the eagerness of a child awaiting candy.

"I fear it marks the return of the great destroyer, the bringer of chaos and destruction."

Ringo was puzzled by his father's words. "Yes, you called him the enemy a moment ago, but if it is not a direct reference to Alusta or Alkotten, then of what enemy do you speak father?"

"Alusta and Alkotten have ever only been our friends. The enemy I refer to goes by many names, but in our last meeting it called itself Aubaultmor."

Ringo looked on in disbelief. "Father this is absurd. Aubaultmor is the demon from our stories as children; he is little more than a fairy-tale," he said looking around to see if anyone was near.

Wyler returned the look of disbelief. "You believe me to be mad then?"

"No father," he said slowly dropping his head.

"The stories I told you…. they were true. I…" Wyler paused and sighed. He placed his hands behind his back and walked to the window. "As with all such things, time has a way of molding the lives of men into the fantasies of children. He is as real as I am. He was as deadly and as evil as any tale you've heard. He was…locked away into the very heart of the mountain through the gallant efforts of the three kings of the mountain. Alkotten lost many soldiers that day. King Brutus went into seclusion for many years, and took to using science to revive his numbers. We foolishly thought Aubaultmor's confinement was to be forever, but in our journeys, we found another scroll; one that told us of his return, and the signs of his coming. My son, it took all of us, Alusta,

Alkotten, and Mantoo to defeat Aubaultmor and it will take no less than that effort to bind him once again."

Ringo folded his arms and looked back at the scroll. "A monster that breathes fire and raises dust? This is ridiculous father!" he said raising his voice in frustration.

"He is counting on your disbelief, your skepticism, your…doubt, because it means you will be ill-prepared for the carnage he will bring. You will be weak and caught sleeping while your enemy destroys your home and those you love. Aubaultmor is the darkness that causes men to hate and kill. He is the embodiment of all things destructive and callous. He is the spirit that brings about war and murder and the whisper that divides and separates. The Great Mountain is filled with such wondrous life and goodness throughout, and he is its antithesis in a physical form. He will stop at nothing until all life is destroyed, and the Great Mountain is little more than a heap of ash and cinder," Wyler said out of breath.

Ringo was bewildered. "And you believe that I can defeat him?"

"No one being can defeat him Ringo. It will take the united effort of all countries on the mountain to defeat him once more."

"And I assume you were not forthcoming with this information to the elders?"

"I tried to tell them once many years ago. They did not believe me. They called it mountain sickness," he laughed. "They laughed at me," Wyler said sadly. He quickly grew angry as he thought about the memory and yelled "THEY LAUGHED AT ME!" with great intensity a second time. Wyler folded his arms and looked to the floor. He grew quiet, and cleared his throat. He spoke softly when he said "I knew at that very moment… I knew then that was how Aubaultmor would take his revenge. Through doubt and deceit he would put one against the other until we were all gone. The only other Mantoo that saw him was Troldomen, and you know well that a Mantoo will never believe what he does not see with his own eyes. No, I could not tell them, though I wish I could."

"So what do the elders actually know Father?"

"They know what I have shown them. As always they turn to what their eyes see and ignore what their hearts tell. They believe a comet is upon us. Now I am too old, and too weak to make the journey that is needed. You know the law of the mountain; only a King can address another king. So you must take the staff and the crown to seek out the lords of the Alusta, and Alkotten. You must convince Meccah and Brutus to help. Every life on the mountain depends on you accomplishing this task."

"Father what you ask of me is impossible. Both sides were at war for ages and despite the peace for over a hundred years, neither side trusts the other. They hardly trust us. And what of the elder council, they will never approve of me taking power, even for this. You just said so yourself."

Wyler smiled. "They had no choice. I have elected to use the Maisha-Vad."

"The life gambit? Father you never gamble any more, much less a Maisha-Vad."

"Precisely. And as you know every Mantoo is entitled to one Maisha-Vad and cannot be denied. I have gambled on the premise that you can save us all, but only as king. Now, the time grows short for you to prove me right."

"Father, the Maisha-Vad is conditional. And the conditions set are designed to bring failure to your opponent. They will try to win the bet at the cost of your life and mine." Ringo paused to think about his plight. "What conditions did the council set?"

Wyler signed, and scratched his head. "You know, they do not like you, and therefore do not trust you, so they have made this exceeding difficult, but not impossible. First, you must do this alone; no citizen of Mantoo may accompany you on this task. Second, because they are a very superstitious lot, no Alustan or Alkottenian may know of the impending danger until they have agreed to help."

Ringo looked confused. "Are they mad? How can I get them to help me if I don't tell them why I need help? They won't even help their own brethren, much less a Mantoo. Is there no other way?" Ringo asked as he rolled the scroll and placed it back into its case.

"Perhaps you miss the gravity of our plight. You cannot take any Mantoo citizen with you, which means you may only employ the services of Alusta and Alkotten. Only the combined resources of all three cultures can win the day as it has in the past. My son if you fail to convince them there is but one outcome; death. We will all die."

"Humph. I would think that with all that is at stake, they would at least try to lose this once. So, I will need to gain the trust and the assistance of two kings that refuse to trust each other? They do not know, and therefore will not trust me. Then I must somehow convince them to help me, but cannot reveal to them why they should help until they both actually agree to do so?"

"Yes." Wyler said nodding. "In forty days".

"I am supposed to figure out how to get up and down, and back in forty days? And find a way to …avert this coming destruction with the help of two Kings that cannot stand the very sight of each other?"

"In a word…yes."

"I just said it and don't understand it, how do you understand it so clearly?"

"My son, you just require some time to digest it all. And so there you have it; those are the terms."

"They'll never do it father. Eventually they will know of his coming."

"Of Aubaultmor's return," Wyler said, correcting him.

Wyler rubbed his beard. "By then, you would have united the mountain against him."

"What if I cannot? What if I fail?"

"That is what the Elders are counting on. If you fail to come back within the forty days, I will lose the life bet. The elders will elect someone else to be king and we will all certainly meet with our doom then. But they believe that they can use the remaining twenty days to solve the crisis with the new Mantoo King. So, that is the wager, and those are the terms. Now then, do you have any other questions about your task before we celebrate?"

"Celebrate? What do we have to celebrate? No Mantoo has ever left the gate that has returned. You send me to certain doom father."

"Not so. I left, and as you can see, I did return."

"Yes, but you did not leave through the gate alone." Ringo quickly caught himself, but it was too late. Wyler was clearly hurt by his words. He took a deep breath and sat down on nearby chair. He gently stroked the tips of the lilies next to him. "These were her favorites," he began. "I never wanted her to come. She said my long adventures would worry her, but I spoke of the wonders of the mountain with such passion that she longed to see for herself what kept pulling me away. I lost her too Ringo. I carry the burden of watching her pass to the great beyond as I held her. The mountain is filled with a great many horrid things outside of our gates. Things that I have not spoken of; things that come for you in the dark; and things that you will not see until they are right before you. I survived, and you will survive. The scrolls will guide you as they did me."

"The scrolls?"

"The scrolls have helped us before."

"And yet we don't even know where the mystic scrolls come from."

"Come with me." Wyler said leading him into the castle to the secret room behind the throne. He opened a dusty trunk and began to shuffle through the contents.

"I've not been in this room since I was a child," Ringo said looking around.

"I made many trips away from Mantoo in my youth. I had many adventures, and I have mapped almost the entire mountain. Ah, here it is," he said lifting it high.

"What?"

"I knew I would have a need for such a thing one day," he said handing it to Ringo.

Ringo opened it and looked at it in wonder. "It's a map; a map of the entire mountain. How is that possible?

"The map and the scrolls will guide you. They have shown us our way for some time now. That's the problem with you children; always looking for useless information."

"I do not," he said in protest.

"You don't do you?"

"Not me. Maybe Wesley, but certainly not me," he mumbled.

"Both you and your brother are guilty of this Ringo. You gossip like young girls, but you need to remember one thing on this quest. Do not wish for success. For it does not come without deliberate action. You must plan, then execute against your plan to attain your objective."

"We are taught that in our honor guard training. I…have said that hundreds of times to the men in the war games."

"Ringo, whether you are aware of this or not; you have spent a lifetime preparing for this very moment. . I would not have committed to the Vad unless I felt so with every fiber of my being. You've been Captain of the Guard and leader of the Army before you were Wesley's age" He said patting Ringo on the back.

Ringo lowered his head and passed his hand through his dark hair. "I am not ready for this father," he said full of self-doubt.

"You are your father's son Ringo. You will rise to the occasion".

"So, you wager all the lives on the mountain on the soldier that you've trained for this very moment?"

"No. I place all the lives on the mountain in the hands of the son that I've raised. A son, who in addition to being a great soldier, is also a very capable prince, and gambler. You will need all of your skills and a bit of luck to succeed in your task. Now, tonight we dance in the great hall and we have a celebration like no other."

The festival in Ringo's honor was the biggest celebration in years. Fireworks lit the night sky, and the Mantoo people filled their bellies with delicious food and vintage wine. Wyler lit a special rocket from the palace that was not like any of the others. When it exploded, a green star appeared through the mist that lasted for almost a full minute. It marked the end of the celebration, but while the people cheered at the stunning display, another spectator off in the distance knew it had a different meaning. A few miles above Mantoo, a dark figure, dressed it a brown cloak was looking down on the celebration from his cave, and saw the green star. He rubbed his hands eagerly and grabbed his pointed hat before heading down the mountain in the darkness.

In the early morning, Ringo gathered what provisions he could muster, and rode his horse to the giant gate at the entrance of the city. The citizens of Mantoo and the elders lined both sides of the cobblestone road, and one by one, wished him well. He turned his gaze on the colorful flowers and dark green grass that covered the plains. Then he looked up toward the castle's tallest balcony where his family was standing and smiled. "You cannot tag along this time dear brother." Ringo yelled.

Wesley leaned over toward Wyler and whispered. "Can I have his room if he dies?"

Wyler smiled and tried to ignore him. Wesley continued. "Oh that was a bit brash father; I didn't mean it that way. I do get the crown though, right? I mean, if he dies I am next in line."

Wyler gave him an odd look and rolled his eyes in frustration. As he made his way down the spiral staircase he looked over his shoulder. "You'll be first in line when I start handing out lashings," he fired.

Wyler made his way outside the main door. Ringo stopped his horse in front of Wyler and bowed his head. He extended his hand to his father who squeezed it while fighting back tears.

"Do you have any final words of wisdom for your son on his great quest Milord?"

Wyler continued to hold his hand and looked to the mountainside next to them.

"Life on the mountain has always been a gamble my son. The Mantoo people have always thrived by having the greatest nerve, the steadiest hands, and the greatest luck. You go forward today to represent us all. You are a Mantoo, and you are from the house of Wyler. You already possess all you need to complete your task....no matter the odds."

Ringo turned to Wesley, who had made his way outside behind Wyler, and gave him a quick nod. "And you my brother?" He asked.

Wesley thought for a moment. "Be steady, like your horse. She will take you wherever you need to go as long as you hold the reins."

"Hold the reins?" Ringo asked uncertain of his meaning.

"Remain in control at all times. Hold the reins." Wesley assured him.

"Indeed." Ringo said looking behind them. "And where is Dionne?"

They each looked in different direction for a moment. Ringo dismounted and handed the reins to Buxhorn. He ran into the castle and quickly made his way to the Castle's highest point, which was Wyler's meditation chamber. As he entered the room, he saw Dionne being consoled by Ayana. He slowly approached and touched Dionne on the shoulder. He exchanged a quick glance with Ayana. She began to swell with emotions and walked out of the room. Ringo took notice to her slow and tearful exit, which quickened the pace of his heart. He fought the urge to follow her and turned to face his sister. He bent to one knee before Dionne and smiled.

"I could not leave without a goodbye from my favorite sister." He said still smiling.

"I am your only Sister." She said wiping a tear and trying to smile. "I am afraid Ringo. And living in this Castle, for all my life, I have never had a need to be fearful before."

"You are thinking of Mother?"

She returned a quick nod and wiped her eyes again.

"I have done that every day since her passing. You look like her more each day," he said lifting her chin with his finger. "I will be back in time to share your birthday dinner with you."

"Do you swear?" she cried.

Ringo hugged her and kissed her head. "I do. There is an entire world outside of that gate. It will be a wonderful adventure. I'll no doubt have plenty of stories to tell you when I return…Rain drop."

Wesley walked into the room and stood beside them. Ringo reached out to him, and the three of them hugged each other tightly.

Ringo broke their embrace and removed his sword, then held it out toward Wesley. "Here," he said handing him his sword. The mystical singing sword of Hooglieed is Mantoos' most prize possession. Its gleaming gold handle had a large diamond in the pommel. The grip was wound in leather, and the guard was meticulously crafted with fine symbols and writings. The blade was long and sharpened on both sides. Despite the amount of usage over the ages, it appeared new.

"What are you doing?" Wesley asked. "Algriot was forged from the irons near the whispering lake. It is the only one of its kind. It belongs to the presiding prince."

"It belongs here with our people as our greatest weapon and symbol of hope. Give me your sword, and we'll trade until I come back," he said

"You will come back, won't you?" Wesley asked holding back tears.

"Until I do, you are the prince. You now lead the honor guard. Take care of my sword and each other, but above all else, take care of father."

The three of them hugged once more. Wyler looked on from the door way and summoned enough courage to let out a cough.

"It is time my son," he said.

Ringo walked over to him and hugged him. Wyler was caught by surprise at first, but quickly closed his eyes and returned the hug.

"A father was never more proud of his son." Wyler whispered.

Ringo took a step away and looked at his father. He turned to Wesley and Dionne and gave a nod. "Take care of father," he said as he quickly turned and walked out of the door. As he made his way to main door, Ringo saw a figure from the corner of his eye. He turned to see Ayana holding a flower with a sad look on her face. He moved slowly toward her and pulled the flower from her hand. He smelled it and looked into her eyes.

"Of all the flowers in the royal garden, the Yandi is the most beautiful, and yet the beauty of this one pales in comparison to its bearer."

"Thank you Prince Ringo," she said as a lone tear fell on her cheek.

"Have you finished your book?"

"I've now read that story four times."

"You hope to change the ending?"

"I realized some time ago that I could not possibly change how thing worked out for the maiden or her Prince, but perhaps if I..."

Ringo passed the flower over her cheek and wiped her tear with it. "Fair maiden am I an Ogre or a Prince?"

Ayana thought for a moment. "You are a Prince," she said softly

"Then do not despair. I leave as your Prince, and will return as your Prince."

He turned and walked down the corridor and grabbed the door handle, but paused as he pulled it open.

"Ayana, when the prince left to fight the Ogre, what did he say to the fair maiden?"

"He bowed before her and said "for your honor milady." Ringo there is so much unsaid that I..."

"It will not go unsaid for long," he whispered.

Ringo took a step toward her and bowed. "For your honor milady," he said.

She ran into his arms and kissed him softly. He smiled as they parted and pulled her closely for one more kiss before he quickly exited the castle and mounted his horse.

The crowd roared as he waved to them. He looked up at the meditation room and saw Wyler, Wesley and Dionne. He waved and gave a nod as he rode toward the gate. Ringo turned to look at Ayana, who was standing on the steps outside the castle door. She ran toward the gate as he exited. As the large gate doors slammed shut, Ayana reached them and touched the large brass sign. It read "None that passed through these gates unto the mountain have ever returned." She took a deep breath and whispered "Oh Ringo" as she turned back toward the castle.

4 THE PATH

The secret path behind Vannet Falls led Ringo through a small tunnel that let out on a side of the great mountain he had never seen before. He continued on horseback down a steep edge and carefully made his way to level ground. He continually checked the map provided by his father and was careful to stay on course. After a few hours, he stopped by a stream to rest and to give his horse a drink. He heard a strange sound coming from behind him and turned to see large lizard-like creatures walking upright in the distance. Their clothes were dull and torn, and some of the larger ones appeared to be leading the others. Ringo squinted and placed his hand above his eyes to block the sun as he looked in their direction. He noticed that they were marching in a straight line away from his position. "Crocodons," he told the horse. "If my father's tales were not exaggerated, these things are very dangerous. We best not linger," he said climbing back on the horse.

Ringo allowed his mind to wonder back to the conversation he had with his father the night before. He replayed the images and words over and over again before pulling the reins for the horse to stop near a lake. He filled his canteen and allowed the horse to drink for a moment before looking back toward Mantoo. He was surprised to see that the entire kingdom was hidden from view on the trail. He placed the feed bag over the horse's mouth and gently stroked her mane.

"We're on a fool's errand my dear. I know my father means well, but I fear he has told us the tale of Aubaultmor so much, that he believes it himself. We will make the best of this trip by getting Meccah and Brutus to extend the treaty. That is a sign of unity that will allow father to win the Vad. See that? We extend the treaty, and win Vad. We catch two fish with one lure."

Once the horse was finished eating, Ringo laid out a few blankets and built a small fire. He looked up at the stars in the night sky and stretched out his hearing to pick up any noises around him. When he heard the sound of the water falls in the distance, he smiled. He rubbed his ears and yawned before settling in for the night.

In the early morning, Ringo quickly packed up and continued down the mountain. He traveled for a few hours along the route laid out by his father until he came upon a large dry clearing just outside the land of Fricke. He noticed a lot of dust being kicked up in the distance, and extended his hand to feel for wind. When he realized that the wind could not be responsible for what he was seeing, he decided to take a closer look. He rode the horse around the clearing, taking care not to be seen. Doing his best to remain down-wind of the ruckus, he made his way to the small band of trees not far from the dust.

Ringo tied his horse to a tree and moved through the thick patch of trees toward the dust cloud. He heard loud laughter as he approached, and stepped carefully toward it. The dust was being made by two Fricke giants, who were wrestling in the clearing. There were three other giants looking on with their backs to the trees. They were laughing while they cheered the other two on in their match. The giants were odd looking, and clumsy. In addition to their enormous height of twelve-feet or more, they had thick bodies, thin hair, and enlarged feet and hands. Their noses were long, and round, which did not match their small eyes, mouth, and ears. Their clothes and faces were dirty, and they carried a horrible smell that Ringo likened to the Mantoo stables.
They were bare-foot and filthy, which gave Ringo pause as he approached them.

He held his breath as he positioned himself behind a large tree to get a better view of the combatants. "Wrestling?" He whispered as he looked on.

The wind shifted and blew softly around Ringo. One of the giants named Gongo was looking on with his arms folded until he caught a strange scent in his large nose. The giant turned his head from the wrestling and looked toward the tree patch.

"Gongo, what's the matter?" The giant standing next to him asked in a raspy voice.

Gongo continued to smell the air around him. "Nothing," he replied. "Thought I smelled something in the wind."

"Probably a dead crocodon." The other giant said sniffing the air. "I don't smell nothing."

"Ha! You wouldn't after that punch in the nose I gave you earlier," Gongo laughed.

While the two giants continued to poke fun at each other, Ringo slipped away. He untied his horse and quickly rode back to the eastern pass. He found a quiet spot to bed down for the evening, and slept soundly. In the morning, he rose early, played his flute, fed his horse and continued down the mountain.

He traveled a few hours past strange looking circular terrain in the land of Oe. The ground was muddy and grey and nothing grew for miles. After a few hours more, he came to the land of Comdorah. The land was rich with flowers and springs. It was more beautiful than his father described. He crossed a familiar-looking grassy field before he came to a dark and misty pass. There did not seem to be any other way to go but through it. His horse began to stomp and neigh in protest, so Ringo climbed down and held the reins to calm her.

He had begun to walk the horse through when he heard a deep

growl. He grabbed his sword and looked around in an attempt to locate the origin of the growl. He looked from side to side but saw nothing. Another growl came from behind him. As he turned a dark and hairy creature jumped on him, knocking away his sword. Ringo managed to throw the creature off of him, but it landed on its feet. It crept toward him slowly. The beast reminded him of the panthors kept in the Mantoo zoo, but this creature was far more hairy and its teeth and head were much larger. Another creature as large as the first crept slowly out of the mist and approached from his left. He steadied himself and waited for them to move. His horse ran through the pass in a panic. A third beast moved toward him from the darkness in front of him, which caused Ringo to back up slowly. He saw his sword on the ground and leapt for it. He fought them for what seemed like an eternity. He found himself surrounded again and was determined to fight until the end. He managed to kill one of them, but the other two were on him without mercy. They would have torn him to shreds if not for the Mantoo meshing that his father insisted he wear. They sprang through the air with their mouths open, each taking aim for his neck. Ringo closed his eyes tightly as if to embrace his inevitable doom. After a few seconds, he opened his eyes to discover both creatures were frozen in mid air. Ringo was confused, and touched one of them to see if they would move. When it did not, he pushed against it harder.

"Careful." A voice above him called out. "You'll break the spell."

Ringo looked up and saw a small, elderly man standing on one of the rocks about eight feet above him. He was dressed it a brown cloak and matching brown pointed hat.

The man did his best to make his way to the ground. "And freeze powder is difficult to come by," he said, falling to the ground from the last rock.

"Troldomen?" Ringo said helping him up. "Troldomen it is you! Ringo said excited to see him. "I am more than glad to see you, but what are you doing here?" Ringo asked, still surprised to see him.

The tiny wizard dusted himself off.

"I am here at the request of your father."

"My Father? I am not aware of any such request. And where have you been for the last ten years? Have you been out here in the wilderness all this time? And I can't be seen with you. My father took a Vad, and one of conditions is that no citizen of Mantoo can assist me. And what did you do to these panthors?"

Troldomen picked up his walking stick and moved toward him. "My dear boy, when was the last time you saw me in Mantoo? You are correct; I have not been on this side of the great mountain for ten years. By law, I have not been a citizen for at least eight of them."

"Not on this side of the mountain? Where were you then?' he asked in disbelief.

Troldomen smiled and looked in the distance. "Dear boy that is a tale for another time, and these are not panthors. They are Mashuni Tikats; very dangerous. The spell will not last long on them. We must make haste if you are to complete your journey. Come young master, your destiny awaits you, and it will be dark soon," he said looking up at the sky. Troldomen gazed down the long path and without looking back at Ringo, began walking as fast as his stout legs could muster.

"Troldomen!" Ringo said in protest.

"Come along dear boy. There are creatures with bigger teeth than the Tikats in this part of the mountain.

"Bigger and more vicious than those things?" Ringo asked as he reluctantly followed.

"Yes. Much bigger, far greater numbers and they eat Tikats when no other food is available. They are called Hunden, and Hunden hunt at night, and they will be hungry. Unless you plan to feed them your Mantoo liver I suggest you make haste."

As they cleared the misty pass, Ringo looked around for his horse. He whistled loudly and the horse came out from behind a large rock. He mounted the horse and followed Troldomen. He was amazed that his horse had to trot to keep up with Troldomen's short legs.

As the night came, the pair found a large cave. Ringo built a fire inside to keep them warm, while Troldomen blocked the entire entrance with thorny bush. Ringo took off his gloves and approached the bush.

"How do we get out?" he asked.

"What's that you say?" Troldomen asked.

Ringo's curiosity got the best of him as he stared at the thorny bush. He touched one of the thorns and cut his thumb. He placed the bleeding thumb in his mouth, and then shook his hand wildly for a moment.

"I said you've blocked the entrance and so we cannot get out." Ringo said.

Troldomen took a deep breath. "It is far more important that nothing get in," he mumbled. "Young master, I am confident that once you get a glimpse of the Hunden, you will wish we found more thorny-bush to block the entrance with."

As they slept, something outside the cave began to stir. Something was watching them through the thorny bush and growled loud enough to wake Ringo. He jumped to his feet and moved toward his horse in the back of the cave. He grabbed his sword and silently walked toward the bush at the cave's entrance.

"Leave the beast be Ringo. It will not cross the bush." Troldomen said, still half asleep.

"How can you be sure? What manner of beast is this?" Ringo asked as he tried to get a good look at the creature pacing outside the cave entrance.

"It is one of the Hunden; the scout. He will alert the others of our presence."

"The others?"

"There are many of them; they do not hunt alone. But have no fear they will not cross the bush. Their leader, Stygg, was caught in such a bush once. He barely made it out alive. He is forever scarred and will not venture near another."

"Troldomen!" A raspy voice uttered from outside the cave.

Troldomen smiled and rose to his feet. He walked to the cave entrance a looked through the thorny bush.

"Ha. You would think we rehearsed it." Troldomen said with delight.

"Rehearsed indeed sorcerer." The creature said.

Troldomen sprinkled a powder on the fire, which intensified the flames and made it easier to see outside the cave.

Ringo stared in amazement. "He's talking. The dog is talking!" he quipped.

"I am no dog." Stygg fired back. "I am the hunter, the chaser, the bringer of death. I will crush your bones between my teeth and chew on your flesh before the sun rises."

"Be gone death-dealer" Troldomen shouted. "You will find nothing to satisfy your hunger here."

"Not so wizard. I smell the Mantoo pet. Give me the pet and I will spare your lives." Stygg offered with an oddly polite tone.

"You would spare my life? It was my mercy that has granted you breath. Breath you now seek to use to devour me and my companion."

"Liar!" Stygg shot back. "Were you being merciful when you threw me headlong into the thorns years ago?

"When you consider the fact that you have tried to eat me every day for the last ten years, a few scars on your face is merciful indeed."

"A few scars? This is not a few scars," he said pushing his face close to the bush. The light from the fire allowed Ringo to see the mangled face of the beast; the sight horrified him."

"I will show you the meaning of mercy Troldomen. Give me the Mantoo pet, and I will let you live."

"At what price? To slow our paces so we are easy prey tomorrow? I think not. My companion and I will outlast you here."

Stygg lifted his head and smelled the air in the cave. "Yes the other in the cave, Give him to me."

"I will do no such thing. Be gone! There is nothing for you here save death. Be gone!" Troldomen shouted.

"I smell him. My ancestors once tasted the flesh of those from Mantoo. It has been passed through many generations of my clan that the flavor was unsurpassed. And so, no, I will not leave. I will not relent until I have tasted it for myself. And now we have another to add to our table as well," Stygg said.

"You and your kind have had your fill of Mantoo flesh. I swore then, and I do so now, Hunden will never again know what is to have a Mantoo in your mouth. Now you have taken up all the time that my friend and I can provide. I say for the last time tonight… be gone."

"Friends, did you say? You have no friends. You wander the mountain aimlessly pretending to master the forbidden arts, while using your cunning to avoid my teeth. You grow old. Your flesh rots on your brittle bones even as we speak. Yes, old and bitter. I am afraid once I finally catch you, I will have to spit you out."

The Hunden laughed, but Troldomen was offended. In his anger, he took a pinch of powder from a pocket in his vest. He threw it on the ground just missing Stygg, and uttered something in a language Ringo never heard before. One of the thorny bushes outside of the cave began to grow and shake. It grew tall and wide and quickly took the shape of a bear. The Hunden would not normally fear the bears of this region, but this bear was very large and was made of thorny bush. One swipe from its massive paw could kill one of the Hunden with ease. The thorny bear let loose a horrible growl that scared the Hunden, and sent them fleeing up the trail. The bear gave chase and continued its pursuit until all of them disappeared in the distance.

"Well, I doubt strongly that we will see them anymore tonight. Get some sleep Ringo; we have many miles to travel in the morning."

"That was very impressive Troldomen. Where did you learn to do that?"

"What Sleep? I've been doing that for four hundred and fifty years."

"No, the trick. The bear. The bush turned into a bear; you froze the Tikats, how did you do those tricks?"

"Tricks? Young master, tricks are not real. Tricks are deception. I do magic, which of course is outlawed in Mantoo, but I may show you a thing or two one day. As long as you let me get some sleep."

"Yes of course." Ringo said fighting his enthusiasm. Ringo went back to his space on the floor next to the fire. "Troldomen, were you this interested in magic when you were my age?" he continued.

Troldomen lifted his head and sternly said "I was interested in sleep. And I did it well," he looked over at Ringo, rubbed his beard, and thought for a moment. "I suppose I was, young master. In my youth, magic was only found in the pages of our books. But, as I traveled the mountain, I found the truth about magic and learned of legendary magicians. They say a great magician named Boolderag defeated a dragon on his flying horse. Ha, a flying horse. What I would give for that spell?"

"Is that a complex spell?"

"It's difficult at best. You would have to have a lot of magic in you to change the physical make up of any creature. And more to allow for it to be a blessing and not a nuisance to the bearer I would say."

"What are my odds of becoming a great magician like you?"

Troldomen smiled. "I am no game smith. You will have to learn that you will have to leave your desire to gamble behind the gates of Mantoo. Moreover magic, as you are well aware, is forbidden in Mantoo. A person could use it to cheat."

"Who needs to gamble when you have such a gift like magic?

"You're saying you could give up gambling in exchange for magic?"

"Without a second thought. I've beaten every table and won every game there is. There are no more adventures in the gambling halls for me." Ringo said adjusting himself on the floor in an attempt to get comfortable.

"We may yet see. Two to one, those are the odds I'll grant you. If the choice is yours to make, we shall see how you make it."

"I'll take that bet."

"Yes. I knew you would."

"Rest well Troldomen." Ringo said lying by the fire.

Troldomen smiled and warmed his hands near the flames. "You rest well young one. Rest well."

"I have one request Troldomen." Ringo said sitting up.

Troldomen rolled his eyes and turned to face him.

"How long have you and my father planned this?" Ringo asked standing to his feet.

"Planned what? Troldomen asked.

"This. This ruse, this vad to make me more responsible?"

"Do you think that is what this is young master?"

"I don't know what this is. Talking wolves and giant cats, and bears made out of bushes. I've seen more in the days since I've left the gate than I've seen my whole life. I have no idea what I'm doing or why I'm doing it for that matter," he said leaning against the cave wall.

"Let me show you what I can then young master, so you have no doubt about the seriousness of your mission," Troldomen said picking up dirt from the floor of the cave. He reached into his pocket and pulled out a small blue bottle. He pulled the top off with his teeth and sprinkled the contents on top of the dirt in his other hand. Troldomen threw the bottle over his shoulder and rubbed his hand together. When he opened his hands in front of Ringo, the mixture took form and a small, glowing image began to take shape. A few seconds later, a tiny image of Aubaultmor appeared in Troldomen's cupped hands. "This is what we face young master. The embodiment of evil; Aubaultmor."

Ringo stared into the glowing form within Troldomen's hands. "He doesn't seem so scary. I imagined him differently from father's stories," he said.

"He appear quite small in my hand, but he is at least fifteen feet taller than any Mantoo. If you are unafraid, young one, you should be. The path to defeat him will not be easily reached. Some say he is older than the great mountain. Others say he was once an evil dragon that fell in love with a fair maid. The maiden was, of course, the great spirit of the mountain, the very essence of all life on the great mountain, and his love for her transformed him into the human form you see before you. But their love did not last as he turned her frail human form to ash with his kiss. In his anger, he cursed the mountain, and swore his revenge on anything that lives. He will not stop until he has destroyed every living creature on the mountain." Troldomen gave Ringo an odd gaze.

"What?" Ringo asked.

"You didn't believe him." Troldomen said rubbing his hands together so the image would disappear.

"Didn't believe who?" Ringo asked, pretending not to know what Troldomen meant.

"Your father. You thought this was some fool's errand and yet you went."

"Of course I went. After he told me that the elders did not believe him, how could I join their ranks? I saw how hurt he was by it when he thought no one believed him. I had to go. His days are short and..."

"His days are not short. You see now this was not some drunken tale or the whim of a king gone mad. You are the best solution to the worst possible problem."

"Am I Troldomen? How can I kill something like that?"

"Kill him? No. You can halt his progress, you can stop his advancement, but you cannot kill him. We were able to detain him for the next generation, but kill him? No, I do not believe he can be destroyed. We must gather all of the forces on the mountain to bind him once more."

"And you and my father have planned this exactly how long?"

"To say you father planned this would imply that he had knowledge of these events prior to initiating the Maisha Vad. This would violate the laws under the Vad and would forfeit the Vad and your father's life. So, we will speak of this no more."

Ringo thought about what Troldomen said for a moment, and then simply said "Agreed".

"Then why do I get the sneaking suspicion that your curiosities are far from satisfied young master?"

"Well I do have one more question."

"Yes….I thought you would."

"Why was it necessary for father to use a Vad to do this?"

Troldomen thought for a moment. He looked around as if to make sure no else would hear what he was about to say. "The last time we faced him, Aubaultmor, he showed the ability to bend some to his will. Some of the men from Alusta were put at odds with the men from Alkotten. We do not know why some are able to resist him, while others cannot, but he was able to turn the best of friends into the worst of rivals. Many died because we were ignorant to that power. I'm betting your father saved his vad knowing full well that Aubaultmor would mask his return. The prophecy scrolls said that in the days before his next coming, the good people would be at odds once again. And so the halls and parlors would be thick with jealousy and hatred for winners and losers alike. And the Kings would distrust and seek the destruction of the others. It stands to reason that no matter what solution Wyler made, the elders would be set against him. So the Vad, and the law, had to be kept. And Aubaultmor's hold would not yet be strong enough to stop a Mantoo from gambling or seeking to defy the oldest laws. Your father was wise to do this." He leaned over toward the fire and said "It was the only way. So now, on to the most pressing matter of the evening; Sleep!" he said finding his place on the ground near the fire.

"One more question please Troldomen"

"Yong master I am quite tired, we walked very far today."

"You said that you were here at the request of my father."

"Did I now?" he said looking surprised.

"You did."

"A bet I made with him a long time ago."

"And your loss resulted in exile?"

"Who said I lost? Good night young master!" Troldomen said turning his back to Ringo.

Ringo looked at Troldomen in an attempt to figure out his motives. After a few moments, he curled up next to the fire and looked around the cave. He playfully pulled on his left ear as he stared out beyond the thorny bush at the cave's entrance and laid his head on the blanket. "Good night Troldomen," he said softly.

5 RIVER CROSSING

In the morning, Ringo awoke to find that he was alone in the cave. He looked around for Troldomen, but saw only his horse. The cave entrance was clear and the sunlight shone brightly through the entrance. The smell of something cooking was enough to lead Ringo from the cave. He walked to his left as he exited the cave and saw Troldomen cooking.

"Bless the day young master. Come and eat. The eggs are fresh, and the fruit is ripe," Troldomen said happily.

"Bless the day Troldomen, thank you. You will no doubt spoil me if you continue to care for me in this manner."

"You are already spoiled, but you carry the crown of Mantoo on your head. Your meals should be prepared for you. It is the least I can do to assist you on you quest."

"The least you can do? We have not been together a full day, and you've saved me from certain death twice. Why do you assist me Troldomen? If you've not been to Mantoo in ten years, how do you even know of my quest?"

"So we begin a new day as we left the old one, with questions. You ask too many questions on an empty stomach, young one. Eat. There will be plenty of time to talk while we walk. Until that time though, I wish to know your plan for the day."

Ringo gave him a puzzled look. "My plan? I'm not certain I understand." Ringo answered.

"Am I to understand that there is no plan then?" Troldomen fired.

"I have a plan…that is there is a plan, you see," Ringo started.

"It is only through careful planning that one can hope to rule the day. Without a plan to rule the day, the day shall most assuredly rule you. And so young master, which shall it be?"

Ringo smiled and politely said "I plan to eat my fill, and then sit with my uncle and plan out the day. How is that for a plan?"

"It's a start." Troldomen said as he began to clean up the pans. "It is a start."

When they had finished eating and packed up their belongings, Ringo sat by a nearby pond and played his flute. Troldomen sat quietly in meditation for a few minutes, and then fed the horse ground oats. They continued east down the mountain and kept walking for the next ten hours.

As the daylight began to fade Ringo looked toward some dark clouds to the north and paused for a moment.

"Missing home by now I'd wager," Troldomen said very sure of himself.

Without taking his eyes off of the clouds Ringo smiled and said "A little bit I guess." He walked the horse over to a brook and let her drink, while he prepared the feed bag.

"It's peculiar, but I find myself missing the things I didn't think were important," Ringo said.

"Like the smell of fresh bread baking in the morning, or purple hibiscus after a summer rain," Troldomen interjected.

Ringo looked away and softly said "yes."

"The way the sun would fall on the west side of the castle as the day gave way to night," Troldomen continued. "Or better still the smell of...."

"New perfume and old books," Ringo interrupted.

Troldomen looked puzzled for a moment. "New perfume and old books?" he questioned. Troldomen quickly caught himself. "Well... I should say young master...whatever is her name?" he asked slyly.

Ringo smiled as he placed the feed bag in position on his horse. "Ayana," he said gracefully.

"Why you are quite smitten if you are to sing her name every time you call it."

"Smitten?"

"Is she as smart as she is pretty?"

Ringo smiled and looked at the ground.

"I would dare say she is then," Troldomen added with a big smile.

The next few days were somewhat uneventful. Ringo took a moment to look at the thirty-foot mushrooms in Dowabler field. He was amazed with the floating flowers in Bartilbear bend, and her marveled at the millions of butterflies in Eurwundr forest.

As they walked past Clofedifr's rift it was obvious to Troldomen that Ringo was lost deep in thought. He hardly spoke as they walked and seemed to be replaying the events of the last few days in his mind. Troldomen pretended not to notice, as he preferred the quiet and did not like being questioned.

Ringo looked over at Troldomen periodically in attempt to measure his mood. When he figured out that Troldomen's scowl was merely a ruse to keep his distance, Ringo decided to speak.

"I'm confused about something Troldomen," Ringo began.

"Yes, I've come to expect that lately," Troldomen snapped.

"That's hardly funny, but if you are intent to make sport of me..."

"Oh don't be so sensitive young master. I have not had the pleasure of any company for some time now, let alone a Mantoo. Of course I intend to make a bit of sport of it, but now that I have, you have my full attention. Please ask your question."

Ringo looked away for a moment.

"Please young master. I promise. No more jokes," Troldomen begged.

"Very well then," Ringo said hesitantly. "It seems that…."

"Wait." Troldomen said cutting him off. "Is this to be another Aubaultmor question?"

Ringo paused for a moment before softly saying "yes".

"He does not know about you."

"Who?"

"Aubaultmor. He does not know you exist. We clearly have the element of surprise," Troldomen said confidently.

Ringo gave him a very puzzled look and notice that Troldomen had placed his thumb firmly in his belt. This was a sign of contentment, as if Troldomen had concluded their conversation. Ringo became increasingly annoyed.

"What does that have to do with anything?" he asked angrily.

Troldomen removed his thumb from his belt and took a deep, slow breath.

"Aubaultmor corrupts all he touches. He has the power to reach out to all that desire to do evil. He can infect the hearts and minds of those that have left themselves open to such recklessness, chaos, evil, and…"

"Wait!" Ringo said cutting him off. "The truth now. No answering my question with a question. No riddles, no sport; this is my life and the life of every Mantoo we are talking about. I want…no…. I deserve to know everything."

Troldomen weighed the seriousness of the moment and gave a quick nod.

"Did you place a spell on me, Wesley and Dionne to hide us from Aubaultmor?" Ringo asked.

Troldomen hesitated before answering, but nodded slowly and softly said "Yes".

"Who else knows?" Ringo asked

"No one knows. Your father does not know if that's what you mean."

"How could he not know?"

"No one besides your father, Brutus and Meccah knew I brought magic back to Mantoo. I used it to hide the passage to the gate. It was magic that kept Mantoo safe from those that would call themselves her enemies. And magic that kept the royal family, my family…safe from the evil of Aubaultmor!" Troldomen realized his tone was angry and swallowed hard. He took another deep breath and rubbed his beard. "Your father would not approve if he knew Ringo. He would have me to keep the law and prevent all magic within the gate."

"And you took it upon yourself to defy his law."

"He suspected as much. Your father is no fool, but Mantoo laws only apply to Mantoo citizens."

Ringo took a few more steps and stopped. He turned to face Troldomen but looked to the ground first. "My Uncle is no fool either. And he knew that what he was doing to protect his family would come at a great sacrifice," he said gently.

Troldomen smiled and looked down at the ground as well. "Your grandfather once lashed your father and me for not completing our chores. We were just lads, younger than you, but just as adventurous. He told us that we were to seek to do what must be done before we seek out the thing we desire. Do what you must, before you do what you like and your road will be paved with accomplishment and success. I still have the whelps from that lashing. It was a good lesson; one that all Wantoo men have learned to follow."

Ringo nodded and smiled.

"Mine was not the only sacrifice." Troldomen said matter-of-factly.

"I am not my father's sacrifice."

"No you are not, but then… I was not talking about you. Your father believes in your ability to claim victory, but he would gladly change places with you if he could. Were this just fifty years ago, he would have, but I think that he realized something a while ago."

"And what was that?" Ringo said adjusting the bridle on the horse.

"First, that he could not stop the coming storm; none of us could. But second, and more importantly, you are all that he is and more. And if anyone could turn the tide as he did when last we last faced Aubaultmor, it would be you. It's his love and confidence in you that drives him."

"So you are saying that he is not simply doing what must be done Troldomen?"

"Would you do any less to save everyone you loved? Do you think he does not love you because he sent you to face certain death?"

"I think he sent me to complete an impossible task."

"I know for certain that you are correct."

"What?" he said surprised by Troldomen's words

"I also know for certain, that he would not have sent anyone else to see it done."

Ringo looked to the sky and tried to hide his face as he wiped a tear from his eye. He took a deep breath and coughed lightly to clear his throat. "Then it will be done Troldomen, no matter the cost. I will do what I must."

Troldomen looked at him for a moment and smiled. He watched as Ringo began to walk the horse down the thin passage and then lit his pipe. He took a puff and softly said "Indeed" before following. Neither of them said another word that evening.

On the morning of the fourth day, they came to a waterfall that let out into rapids. Troldomen scanned the rushing river looking for a safe place to pass. He approached the narrowest area and peered across to the other side.

"We should cross here." He said.

Troldomen picked up five stones and sprinkled dust from his back pocket on them. He threw the stones into the water and watched them grow into a stone path. He jumped onto the first stone and looked back toward Ringo.

"Hurry along young master," he shouted as he hopped across the other rocks to the other side.

Ringo brought the horse to edge of the water directly across from where Troldomen stood. He shook the reins and the horse proceeded into the water.

"Could you not use larger stones?" Ringo asked as he attempted to move the horse on the path.

"Your horse is too heavy for that spell, but she should be tall enough to pass while walking on along the bottom. Hurry now!"

Ringo led the horse into the water. When they got half way into the river, Ringo tossed the satchel holding the maps and scrolls to the edge near Troldomen. Troldomen picked up the bag, and draped it across his shoulder. Ringo quickly realized how deep the water had become. As the water rose up the neck of the horse, it began to panic. Ringo did his best to calm the animal, but nothing seemed to work.

"Steady. Steady." Troldomen shouted from the river's edge.

Suddenly a large fin swam past them. Ringo sat up straight in the saddle and stared at it. The fear that gripped him was almost paralyzing. The fin disappeared a few feet from them, but emerged behind them. Ringo turned in the saddle to face it, but again it went under and out of sight. He slapped the reins hard, and dug his heels into horse's sides, trying to force the horse to move forward, but the current suddenly picked up and became strong. Ringo studied the water and saw that tremendous numbers of little fish were swimming in the same direction around him. He could only guess that somehow their speed and numbers were affecting the current. He looked at Troldomen.

"It's the fish. They're doing something to the water," he yelled.

"Keep moving!" Troldomen commanded, but in an instant, Ringo and his horse were swept away by the current. Troldomen ran along the edge shouting instructions. As the current drove Ringo away from the horse, he tried desperately to reach the reins. He managed to make his way to a rock near the edge of the river, just ten feet from Troldomen. Troldomen moved close to them and looked down river for a way to help. Troldomen called to the horse, which at that moment seemed happy to see him. Ringo swam in order to get to the shore of the river and gasped for breath as he rolled on his back. As he turned over to get his bearing, the large fin appeared once more in the water and was moving quickly toward his horse. Ringo sprang to his feet and ran along the edge screaming at the horse.

"Ahdora!" Ringo called.

Troldomen reached out his hands to grab the reins. Ringo watched the fin rapidly closing in and yelled as loud as he could.

"Come on Ahdora. Come to me!" Ringo yelled.

Troldomen hooked the curved end of his walking stick around a small tree near the edge and leaned over the river as far as he could. The tips of his fingers touched the reins as the horse came closer. Without warning, a large river shark lifted half of its body out of the water and took the horse into its mouth and continued to swim downstream.

"No!" Ringo screamed as he fell to his knees. He watched as the fish disappeared below the water. His scream seemed to echo against the surrounding valley. Troldomen helped Ringo to his feet and moved him away from the edge. He sat Ringo against a tree and looked around nervously.

"I loved that Horse." Ringo said sadly. "Hold the reins he told me, hold the reins. Now look! And my supplies…How do we eat?" He despaired. Ringo was obviously shaken, but noticed Troldomen's nervous pacing.

"Unless that thing can somehow walk on land, I think we are safe Troldomen. Dash! That was my favorite horse. Well, thank goodness my sword was strapped to me instead of the horse and you have the scrolls. Humph. It's not even my sword, its Wesley's. I hate this stupid Vad!" He yelled.

"Please stop yelling." Troldomen pleaded. "We are far from safe young master. Once we crossed the rapid stream, we entered into Farrador land."

"Well… Ringo started, seemingly unimpressed by the name. "What is a Farrador?"

Troldomen nervously looked around. "Many ages ago there was an uprising in Alusta. A small faction within their army wanted to take power, but they were outnumbered and cast out by the king's honor guard. With nowhere to go, they made their way up the mountain. They live here, and hunt everything that moves. They are known to eat whatever they catch in a hunt. They are skilled hunters and swordsmen. They move across land and rock as quickly as cats. The two of us will be no match for them. As they were once Alustans I have no doubt they heard us, and will head this way. We must press on."

Troldomen helped Ringo to his feet. The two began to walk east as quickly as their legs could take them. Ringo was still upset about his horse, but was more concerned about the Farrador.

"You say, they will eat us if the catch us?" He asked.

"Yes, as I said, they will eat whatever they catch in a hunt."

"Then I guess the better question is.... are we being hunted?"

Troldomen looked around as he walked and tried to be as quiet as he could. He practically whispered when he said, "I would wager that we are."

6 FARRADOR

The Farrador camp was active. Some of the women were cooking outdoors, while others were washing clothes in the nearby lake. They were muscular like their Alustan brethren, but not as dark-skinned. They were scantily dressed in animal skins and materials that were made from natural fibers like wool and cotton whose colors were dull and faded. Their curly hair and tough skin were almost the same shade of dark brown. The footings they wore came up to their ankles and were sewn together with thin strips of leather. The children were playing various games, and the young men were wrestling as the young women cheered them on. The older males, were teaching a few of the younger males to fight and hunt. They wrestled each other and shot arrows into targets that were shaped like rams. It was truly a day like most others until a soft noise carried by the wind was heard in the midst of their laughter and talking. The sound of Ringo's scream echoing through the valley had made its way to them.

Their leader, Isantor, was the largest male in the group. He wore a necklace of Hunden teeth around his neck, and carried a Pearl-handled bone knife strapped to his thigh. He was watching the young men wrestle when the sound reached his ear. He issued a command, and all of the males ran toward the river. Their muscular frames gave them the ability to jump, flip and run great distances effortlessly. As in all of the hunts, the young males followed the elders to learn the skills needed to survive the rough land. None of them noticed that one of the young males, a skinny awkward boy named Gallra, tried to follow, but was having trouble keeping up. The other young males usually teased him because he was clumsy and frail and very different from the rest of them. As with all of hunts that he could remember, the other males were too fast for Gallra to keep up with.

Their speed was too great, and they extended the distance from him with every step taken. They were generally content to leave him to fend for himself, but one of the young males stopped and called out to him.

"Gallra come on," he yelled.

"I'm trying Fetter." Gallra yelled back.

Fetter, called to him again, but Gallra was not physically strong enough to keep pace with the group and fell farther behind.

"Fetter!' Gallra called.

"They will leave you again. Move faster." Fetter urged.

Fetter tried to keep an eye on Gallra, but he also started falling behind as a result. He was losing pace with the group, but stopped to look for Gallra once again. Suddenly, Fetter felt a strong hand on his shoulder. He was startled and turned quickly to find himself facing Isantor's second in command, the Farrador Captain Onkeel. Onkeel looked at Gallra in the distance struggling through a rocky pass, and let out a loud sigh.

"I know he is your cousin Fetter, and you care for him, but he is weak. In the wilderness…in this wilderness, the weak become food for something stronger than themselves. As much as it may pain you young one, you cannot allow him to make you weak."

"I am not weak Onkeel." Fetter fired.

"You are weak with emotion like a girl, and he…..he is more a girl than your sister."

"What are you saying?"

"I am saying that you cannot allow your love for your cousin to stop you from fulfilling your duties to our people. It affects the entire clan; all of us," he said, pointing to the rest of the warriors who had stopped running and were watching from a distance. Fetter sighed in frustration after seeing them.

"Gallra will make his way back to camp like he always does Fetter." Onkeel assured him.

Fetter turned and ran with Onkeel toward the other warriors. He covered his ears as he ran as fast as he could to escape the calls he heard from Gallra in the distance.

Gallra decided that this time he would not give up. He turned to the west toward Liten falls. He ran up to the edge and crossed the narrow stream to the other side. He moved a few vines and bushes and uncovered the small raft that he had hidden there days ago. He threw it in the water and jumped on. He held on as the raft tossed from side to side in the narrow stream. Gallra used a rudder -like device on the back of the raft to help him steady the raft and negotiate through the current. The slow-moving waterway quickly met with a rapidly moving river. Gallra maneuvered the small craft through a set of rocks and managed to position himself in the center of the river. He was pleased with himself until he saw that he was about to go over Liten falls. He braced himself, but that did not stop him from screaming all the way down. He landed safely in the water below and climbed back on his raft. The pace of the water quickened again without warning and Gallra was once again swept away on his tiny raft. He did his best to remain on the raft, but he was thrown into the air with great force when it hit a large rock. He landed high in a tree on the east side of the wild river. Gallra began making his way down, branch by branch, when the sound of voices approaching caused him to freeze in his place. He tried quietly to see who it was, but could not see through the thick leaves. Gallra moved through the tree to get a better look, but lost his footing and fell to the ground on his face.

When he lifted his face out of the dirt, Gallra found himself in the middle of the Farrador warriors.

"Gallra!" Fetter called running to him. "How did you get here before us?"

Isantor looked at Gallra, and pushed Fetter out of the way. He bent over to get close to Gallra.

"What did you see up there weakling?" Isantor asked forcefully.

Gallra stuttered when he said, "I..I..I did not see anything."

Isantor scowled. He muttered "Useless" as he walked a few feet away and took a deep breath through his nostrils trying to pick up a scent. He turned his head slowly from left to right as he breathed in. He looked east and smiled as he picked up a faint smell in the air.

"Continue along the river," he commanded. As all of the warriors began to move, Fetter extended his hand to Gallra and helped him to his feet.

"How did you get here before us? You must have flown down the mountain."

Gallra smiled and happily threw his arm around his cousin and patted him on the back. Casting a quick glance at the remnants of his shattered raft, Gallra laughed and said "I did".

As the warriors ran east, Onkeel looked up into the tree and then toward the river. He looked up river for a moment and wondered how Gallra arrived at the tree before they had. He spotted remnants of Gallra's wooden raft stuck against the large rock near the river's edge and watched as the raging water pulled it free. Onkeel watched the broken wooded fragments float down river and smiled before running to catch up to the other warriors.

7 FIRE AND WONDER

Troldomen and Ringo were running on the side of the wild river when Ringo stopped and leaned against a tree to rest. Troldomen urged him on, but he was too tired.

"A moment Troldomen."

"We could be killed in a moment young master. We need to press on. We are not too far from the border."

"What border?"

"Did your father not provide you with a map?"

"Yes." Ringo said, with a very puzzled look on his face."

"I will walk, but we need to discuss something Troldomen."

"As long as we walk, we can discuss whatever you like young master."

Ringo eased himself off of the tree and began walking with Troldomen."

"You have a lot of knowledge that someone truly ignorant of my quest would not possess. Yet as far as you say, it has been ten years since you've graced the grasses of Mantoo with your feet."

"I know a great many things young one," Troldomen said looking around.

"As do I. I know when someone is avoiding a question."

"A question? You've yet to ask one."

"You have intricate knowledge of this Maisha-Vad. How am I to trust you if you do not share the truth about how you came to have such knowledge."

"Maybe you should not trust me."

"Why do you answer my questions by raising new questions?"

"Can answers not also be in the form of a question?"

"You know a whole lot more than you say."

"As should we all young master."

"Why do you keep doing that?"

"What is it that I am doing?"

Suddenly, an arrow shot past them. They turned around to see the Farrador warriors a few hundred yards behind them, and closing fast. They ran as fast as they could, but the speed of the Farrador was incredible, and they were quickly catching up. Troldomen pushed Ringo and himself into the wild river. The current swept them both downstream quicker than the Farrador warriors could run. When they could no longer see their pursuers, Troldomen grabbed onto Ringo's collar and used his cane to grab a tree branch that hung over the river.

After making their way on land close to the river's edge, Troldomen directed Ringo to climb into the tree. Ringo climbed high enough to get a clear view of their surroundings. Seeing no sign of their pursuers, Ringo quickly made his way down.

"Troldomen, was there no other means of escape besides this retched river?" Ringo exclaimed.

"It seemed like the best idea at the time."

"That was the Farrador you mentioned of earlier?"

"A small band of them, yes."

"Why didn't they jump in after us?"

"I don't suppose they had a way stop. This river lets out to the Grand falls, and the jagged rocks on the mountain wait below. They did well not to follow us that way," Troldomen said confidently.

"I still don't understand. If you and I Jumped in.."

"I believe they thought we were eager to kill ourselves rather than face them. They may be looking for our bodies along the edge somewhere, which may have bought us some time.

"Be that as it may, they will figure it out sooner than later, and they are fast runners. We need horses."

"Aye, but horses do not venture this far down the mountain."

Ringo placed his hands on his knees and leaned forward, trying to catch his breath.

"I do not understand. I shouldn't be breathing this hard. I swim all of the time, I ...I run."

"It has nothing to do with your ability to run or swim great distances young master. The air grows thicker as we approach Alusta. It will take some getting used to."

"Will it slow down the Farrador?

"I am afraid not."

They walked away from the river until they came across a small forest. There were plenty of fruit trees and berries to choose from, and Ringo helped himself to odd looking fruit. "This is delicious," he said biting into it once more.

"It's called Winterop. It's very sweet and filling. Most of the local birds crave it. Come, we must press on," Troldomen said looking behind them.

They soon came upon a grassy field where Ringo marveled at the strange, tall birds he saw grazing there.

"What manner of bird is this Troldomen?"

"Keep your distance young master. This bird is not for stewing or baking. If you're not careful, it might have you for dinner. It is called the Osteridge. Quick as a horse, and as mean as a snake. Makes for a fairly good fritter I'm told. Although you would have to travel back to Mantoo for the rice oil and the..."

"Troldomen wait." Ringo said cutting him off.

"I know, I'm babbling again. We older Mantoo do that from time to time."

"No, not that. Did you just say as quick as a horse?"

Ringo and Troldomen took a few vines and tied them together to make a lasso after gathering a few winterop from the nearby trees. Troldomen tied a winterop to the end of the rope and threw it near one of the large birds. The Osteridge looked at the fruit and attempted to bite it, but Ringo pulled the rope. It took a few steps toward the winterop, and Ringo pulled the rope a few feet again. They repeated this until the Osteridge walked under the tree and into a noose that Troldomen was holding. The bird pulled hard, and yanked Troldomen out of the tree. He fell onto the birds back and screamed as the bird ran across the field. Ringo laughed and took another Winterop from the pile. He tied it to a vine and tossed the winterop next to one of the birds. The bird looked down at the Winterop for a moment, and then ignored it. Ringo pulled the vine back and studied the Winterop. He threw it out again, but the birds ignored it. He yelled out to Troldomen.

"This thing is not working."

Troldomen was able to sprinkle a powder on the beak of the bird he was riding. The powder somehow tamed the bird, and he moved it next to Ringo. He went into his top left vest pocket and placed a bit of the pink dust in Ringo's hand.

"Walk over to the black one over there and sprinkle a little of this on her tail feathers."

"What?" Didn't you say these things were dangerous?"

"Look to the far hill." Troldomen said, handing Ringo his spy glass.

Ringo fixed his eyes in the distance and saw the Farrador running toward them. He focused on the leader, Onkeel, and studied his rugged face.

Ringo crept up behind the bird as quietly as he could and sprinkled the dust on the bird's tail feathers as instructed. The bird spun around and head butted Ringo to the floor. She lunged and pecked at his leg, but Ringo rolled out of the way. The bird followed him and began to peck again, but shook her head as the spell began to take effect. The bird stopped moving for a moment. She looked down at Ringo and sat on the ground.

"Let's go!" Troldomen shouted. "Get on; they are coming."

Ringo jumped to his feet and got on the bird's back. She stood up and ran carrying Ringo as if he weighed nothing. Suddenly, arrows began to fly past them as the Farrador pressed their attack. Troldomen led the way, and Ringo's bird followed. He looked behind them and saw that the distance between them and the Farrador was widening quickly. He let out a joyful yell as the birds ran.

"This is amazing!" He yelled as the birds made their way through the field. The grass got taller as they moved away from the trees, but the birds kept running at top speed. The joyful yell turned into one of terror as the birds jumped off the edge of the cliff, which was hidden by the tall grass. The birds spread their wings and glided gracefully down the side of the mountain. Ringo looked out toward the setting sun and saw nothing but ocean. The birds landed at the lowest, grassy point that Ringo could see, and immediately sat on the ground. Ringo and Troldomen dismounted and watched as the birds stood up and flew up the side of the mountain.

Troldomen and Ringo turned to walk away from the mountain side facing them, but immediately found themselves face to face with ten Alustan warriors. They were tall and muscular like the Farrador, but were darker-skinned. Ringo studied the helmets that stopped just above their eyebrows the dark-colored armor that covered their torso, forearms and lower legs. Ringo immediately thought that it looked too thin to protect them. The armor was simple, but beautifully embroidered.

Troldomen held up his hands in submission and seeing him, Ringo quickly followed. The warriors looked at Ringo and bowed their heads, which startled him momentarily.

"Your Highness," one of them began. "I am Dakahn, captain of the Alustan honor guard. We are here to escort you to Alusta. Our King, Meccah awaits your arrival."

Ringo studied Dakahn's face. He took note to how much Dakahn looked like the Farrador tracker despite his clothing, darker skin and straighter hair.

"Forgive me. I thought you were Farrador warriors. We've been pursued for some time now. Ringo said.

"They will not pursue you here. You are safe." Dakahn said confidently.

"How does Meccah know of my coming? And how do you know who I am?" Ringo asked.

"We've known about your coming for three nights. We could hardly sleep with all the noise … "You are already spoiled, but you carry the crown of Mantoo on your head. Your meals should be prepared for you," Dakahn mimicked.

"How is it that you heard that? Ringo asked.

"That is how we know who you are. Dakahn answered.

"I can't believe you heard that." Ringo said again.

"Our hearing is unsurpassed."

"I did not expect them to resemble the Farrador so closely. "Ringo whispered to Troldomen as they walked.

"They can hear you young master." Troldomen said in a plan voice.

The path seemed to be descending as they walked. The area became hotter, and more humid, and the sun soon disappeared, leaving them in near darkness. There were glowing pools of fire water all around them, which provided a little light as they walked. The heat did not seem to bother the Alustans, but it was draining to Ringo. Troldomen reached into his pouch and took out a tiny bottle. He handed it to Ringo.

"Place just one drop on your tongue. Just one." Troldomen instructed. Ringo did as he was told and immediately felt cool and refreshed despite to growing heat.

"Thank you Troldomen."

"You are most welcome young master."

"Do you have anything to help my eyes adjust to this darkness?"

"No, I do not, but you will not need it."

They turned a corner and Ringo saw an amazing city. The city was lit using the magma in the form of signs and lines that ran along the structures which allowed the flow of the magma to pass along the walls in steady streams. There were homes and businesses carved into the side of the mountain that seemed to go on forever. The streets were flowing with fire water, but horseless carriages that the citizens were riding in seemed to float above it without falling in.

"This is spectacular." Ringo said. "How is it that the fire water does not fall or run down the walls?"

Dakahn smiled. "We have found many uses for the fire water in Alusta. It lights our homes, and parlors. It provides us the means to move about freely in our city."

They stepped onto a small landing at the edge of the walkway. Ringo looked down and studied the fire water. A dimly lit carriage made its way to them, and they all piled in. The carriage was made of a shiny rock-like substance that reflected the light from the fire water pools around it very well. It was shaped like a large Mantoo coach, but was easily twice as wide. It was cool to the touch, and its interior was lined with a soft black material that felt plush in Ringo's hand.

"To the Palace!" Dakahn told the driver.

The driver touched a control rod that was in front of him causing the carriage to move forward with great speed.

"These carriages, how is it that they ride above the fire water? They fly like a bird."

Dakahn smiled. He seemed amused by Ringo's ignorance. "The fire water gives off heat which helps to lift the vehicle off of the surface," he said.

"How does heat lift something so heavy? Ringo asked.

Ringo looked at two of the honor guards across from him whispering and laughing. He was bursting with questions and was amazed at the things he saw, but he remembered what his father told him about asking questions of the Alustan people, and remained quiet the rest of the way to the palace. When they arrived, Troldomen pulled Ringo aside.

"Young master before you enter the palace and meet King Meccah there are a few things you must know. He loves music and he loves to be flattered. He loves his daughter Dinatru more than anything in the world. He is a very logical and practical king despite the lavishness that you will see. You will be in the dark most of the time, but trust not your eyes to guide you. You have other instruments at your disposal that must be used to barter for what you desire. You must devise a symphony of trust and respect as you speak. You know what is at stake, so speak from the heart. The best musicians play with their hearts."

"Meccah likes music?"

Troldomen looked frustrated. "Well, you may have to offer up a song and dance.

"I have another question Troldomen."

"Yes?" Troldomen said leaning in to hear it.

"How do they get the chariots to fly above the fire water?"

Troldomen huffed and walked away. Ringo shrugged his shoulders and followed him. "Well I can't very well ask Meccah now can I?" he asked equally frustrated.

At that very moment, deep within the core of the Great Mountain, hidden away for hundreds of years, was a large blue crystal. It was more than twenty-five feet tall and at least twelve feet wide at its base. There was a large, dark and menacing figure that appeared to be frozen inside the crystal. His armor was black and thick. The headdress was adorned with two large horns in the front and spiked about the top. The twenty-foot creature within the crystal looked as stiff as the rocks that surrounded it. Without warning the index finger of the armored figure began to move, which began to crack its crystal prison. Within moments, the crystal was shattered and dust and smoke filled the surrounding cave. When the smoke settled it was clear that Aubaultmor was free, and nothing would be the same ever again.

8 EVIL INTENTIONS

Princess Dionne and Prince Wesley were walking the stone path in the forest on the western end of Mantoo's castle. The trees and flowers along the path were neatly trimmed and were set in place according to color. Every Hundred yards along the path, the color of the foliage would change slightly. The blue foliage gave way to purple, which gave way to violet, which gave way to pink. The Pink became red, and red became orange, which became increasingly lighter until it gave way to yellow, which eventually gave way to white. The colors were designed to be soothing to anyone that walked through that section of the woods.

Although the walk through Soothing Wood was mandated by their father, neither Wesley nor Dionne would describe their mood as pleasant.

"I can scarcely remember a time that the three of us were not in the castle." Dionne said, touching a blue orchid.

"The honor guard drills. You were just a baby then." Wesley said touching a blue rose on the other side of the path.

"I saw something in the hidden room a month ago," she said changing the subject.

"You know father would stand on his head if he knew you were playing about in there."

"Well he came out one day acting strangely. You should have seen him; he was nervous and looking around to make sure no one saw him."

"What's so strange about that?"

"A King doesn't need to sneak around in his own castle."

"So you decided you would have a peak at what made him so nervous."

"I did. He is my father after all."

"Stop trying to justify your misdeeds and tell me what it was."

"It was a scroll."

"Really? In a room full of maps and scrolls? Well, I can see how that would send me quivering," he said sarcastically.

"Honestly, Wesley Wantoo I can never have a serious conversation with you about anything," she snapped.

Wesley laughed as she walked to the other edge of the path and turned her back to him. "All right I'm just having a bit of fun. You are so sensitive these days," he said.

"Why aren't you scared? I mean, aren't you afraid that he won't return?"

"Father left many times, and he returned."

"Weren't you afraid for him?"

Wesley walked to her and placed his hand on her shoulder. "Mother was there in those days. She had a way of making things better. But it was Father that actual put things in perspective for me."

"What did he do?"

"He taught me a poem."

"A poem?"

Wesley gestured with his chin, and they both continued walking along the path. He cleared his throat and began the poem.

"Though my heart be troubled by the unknown,
My enemies rise, their number grown
my friends are gone, and I'm alone
I will know no fear
The battle rages, warriors die
Kingdoms fall and widows cry
They come in droves with sword and lie
I will know no fear
The crops fail and the buildings burn
Disaster looms at every turn
Pain and death is payment earned
I will know no fear
The tide will turn before days end
Vengeance mine as borders bend
Pride restored as bodies mend
for I have not known fear
I will not shed a tear
and I will know no fear"

Dionne gave him a look that told him she was somewhat terrified and disgusted.

"You say Father taught you that?" She said maintaining the look.

"Yes. Was it helpful?" he asked innocently.

Far ahead of them on the trail, Swoggle, Dugan Shipnor, Devonshire, and lady Arna were walking and whispering.

"I don't believe any of you. Wyler is your oldest friend." Arna said.

"Friendship has nothing to do with this Arna. Wyler is not fit to be king anymore," Swoggle said.

"His quest to see Ringo take the throne is proof that he no longer has the judgment needed to maintain his lordship over Mantoo." Dugan added.

"Is it his judgment you now question, after all of this time? After Wyler used to scrolls to save us time and time again?" Arna protested.

"How do we know the scrolls are not some trickery set up by Wyler to maintain his standing?" Swoggle asked.

Devonshire walked closer to her. "Arna, of all of us, you have been granted the most favor," he started. "You were sister-in-law to the king, and as such, were given the lands of your husband to govern after his passing. Such a kind gesture from so noble a king, but.."

"But what?" She asked.

"When was the last time you heard him mention his brother? He has two more children that will be of age soon. It is customary for the king to appoint his family members to govern the best, most profitable land. As they grow, they will each require lands to govern, and you are no longer related. How long do you think he will continue to show favor to the wife of his dead brother?"

Arna looked away and thought silently for few moments. "How dare you mention my husband here, in this of all places?" she said angrily.

"It is not my intention to offend his memory Arna. He was ever a good friend to me, but that does not change things. He left and did not return through the gate. His nephew will follow in his place."

"If you are so confident, then why not wait the forty days Devonsire?" She quipped. "When Wyler loses the Vad, he loses his life and the throne. With Ringo dead and his siblings too young under the law, we could elect you king."

Devonsire became angry "I have waited long enough. I was cheated out of my throne. My blood line..".

"Is his blood line as well Devonsire. Wyler is your cousin after all," She said interrupting him."

"Yes he is. And let us look at how he treats his relatives. His brother, his wife, they left through the gate and the mountain claimed them. So now he sends his son, and surely the mountain will claim him. Wyler has something up his sleeve, and I do not intend to wait forty days for him to unveil it. He is too cunning. He will find some way to win, he always does. And we will ever rest at his doorstep like pets awaiting scraps at the whim of the master. I was not bred for such a fate. We were not bred for such a fate. We must act to secure our own destiny. I could never do this alone, but together we stand a real chance of success."

"What you propose is treason Devonsire. The laws around the Vad are clear. Once the rules are in place no one can break them. The sentence is death and I for one wish to go on living," she snapped.

"Death if we're caught for certain, but Wyler's wager is no less dangerous, and given the recklessness of the prince, no different an outcome. Wyler is blinded by his love for his children. Should we sit idly while others decide our fate?" Devonsire whispered.

"This is a dangerous game you play. You are gambling with all of our lives."

"This is the one time I will beat Wyler…at his own game no less. I will have the proof I need soon, and when I take the throne it will be legal. Wyler and his children will not get the opportunity to disappoint us."

"Wyler has never let us down before." she said softly.

"This is clearly not the same Wyler we all know and respect. He is mad with power and ambition for his children. Be honest with me Arna as you are the boys Aunt; would you send him to this task knowing the odds and what is at stake? What does your heart say to you?"

"It tells me that Wyler knows more than he is telling us. There is something more happening than he wants us to know." She whispered.

Devonshire gave her a short smile. "I believe you shall soon trust your heart Arna, just as the rest of us have come to do in this matter. Five hundred years is far too short a time to walk the grasses and the hills of Mantoo. We are each near the end of that walk, and with so little time left, we should plan accordingly."

She nodded, but gave a curious look. "Accordingly? What are you planning Devonsire?"

"I am planning to live the rest of my days in comfort surrounded by my friends and if possible my family," he said kissing her hand. "We have each been dealt a harsh blow Arna. The four of us have lost our spouses far too early in our lives. But we don't have to suffer needlessly."

"There is a lot of truth in what you say Devonshire, but we are not family, so what is it that you are proposing?" She asked. "Say it plainly Devonshire," She demanded.

"Help me become King Arna. Help me to take back my rightful place on the throne and you….you shall be Queen."

9 ALUSTA

The palace in Alusta was carved from fine stone. It was surprisingly cool despite the lava chandeliers and large round orbs placed on each column to light the halls and rooms. Ringo was amazed at the Alusta's ability to harness the power of the fire water for light and energy. He thought a society as intelligent as this, must have a fantastic weapons capable of defeating Aubaultmor. The trick would be how to get them to hand it over willingly without telling them what it's for. As Troldomen and Ringo entered the dimly-lit throne room, they could hear a faint whisper in the dark. Troldomen did not speak, but pointed to the throne. Ringo nodded and continued to walk.

"Stop." A deep voice commanded from the throne. "You look a great deal like your father young Mantoo. Where is Wyler? I long to see him."

It was so dark around the throne, that Ringo could only see a portion of Meccah's body. He took note to the beautiful scepter in his right hand.

"My father is too old to make the journey great Meccah. He sends his highest regards."

"He is alive then, despite the sickness?"

"Sickness?" Ringo asked. He was surprised, and the information caught him off guard, but he quickly composed himself. "Yes great Meccah. My father yet lives."

"Then why do you wear the Mantoo crown I wonder?"

"Great Meccah as you are well aware, no common Mantoo can address the king of Alusta. Only a king of a foreign land may seek the council of another king. It is..."

"It is the law I made with your father, and Brutus of Alkotten young one; the law of the mountain. You are well taught," Meccah said interrupting him.

A door to Ringo's right opened casting light into the room for a moment. Ringo caught a glimpse of a beautiful girl about his age walking into the room. She stood next to the throne and handed Meccah a small note. He smiled as he read it. Ringo exchanged a glance with the girl, and respectfully lowered his head.

"Princess," he said acknowledging her.

Meccah stood up and walked into the light. He was tall and muscular. He wore the traditional Alustan robe and his clothes were adorned in diamonds from top to bottom. His crown was long and shiny. It has four points; the points on the side of his head, around the ears, were much smaller than the two in the front and back of his head. It too was covered with diamonds. Ringo thought that Meccah's clothes alone were worth more than all the riches in Mantoo, but still did his best to look unimpressed.

"How did you know this was my daughter?" Meccah asked.

"The beauty of Princess Dinatru is legend in Mantoo."

Meccah lifted his left hand, and the lights in the room were brightened so all could see.

"She could have been a chamber maid, yet you were so sure."

Ringo paused and looked back at Troldomen for a second, then turned and said,

"She looks like you."

Meccah was flattered. "Ha!" He let out joyfully. "Well that is truly a compliment, but I hardly think you traveled all of this way to gaze upon the legendary beauty of my daughter. There are many dangers on the mountain. I am sure Troldomen has led you here in the safest ways known to all the mountain folk, but it is dangerous trek none the less. So tell me my young Mantoo King, to what do I owe the pleasure of your company? By the way, I can hear your heart beating. It will tell me if you lie."

"I seek your indulgence kind King Meccah."

"Indeed you do. I hardly believe you came all this way to pass compliments. Make your request plain."

"I am on a quest of enlightenment and a mission of peace. As the new king of Mantoo, I must be wise enough in the ways of the mountain to rule. The only thing that threatens to interrupt the course of my education is the threat of war between the Alusta and the Alkotten."

"And so you seek an assurance of peace?"

"In a manner of speaking, yes."

"What makes you believe the peace on the mountain is in jeopardy of being broken?"

"The treaty was written for two hundred years of peace and is due to expire soon. My sources tell me there have been Alustan scouts spotted above the plains of Mantoo."

"We have many scouts on the mountain young king, mapping the mountain and surveying our borders, but none are sent for mischief. I can assure you that if there is war, it will not be because of any action taken by Alusta."

"I'm afraid that's not enough."

"Have a care Mantoo. The word of a king on this mountain should be enough for anyone to hold as truth no matter where you reside."

"What I meant was Mantoo lies between Alusta and Alkotten. I need more than assurance that yours will not being the first arrows exchanged between you and Alkotten. I need you to get along."

"Arrows?" Meccah snorted. "Alusta has far greater weapons than arrows. Brutus knows this and is afraid of confrontation. It is our great weapons that have secured the peace on the mountain. Peace that has lasted for over a hundred years."

"Yes wise Meccah, but the absence of war by itself, is not evidence of peace."

"I am denied your logic."

"If there were peace, real peace, would you need to create a weapon to prepare for war?"

"You would prefer Alusta were defenseless against its enemies?"

"No my lord, but you can never hope to have peace with anyone you refer to as an enemy. Alusta would have nothing to fear from its friends."

Meccah laughed. "You are indeed well taught. How do you propose Alusta aid you in your quest?"

"Come with me to meet with King Brutus. Extend the treaty and guarantee peace for another two hundred years."

Meccah laughed at the irony as he returned to his seat on the throne. "Like your father, I too am far beyond my years for such a journey."

"I think to show Brutus that you are serious, you could send someone close to you to represent you in a meeting to extend the treaty of peace."

"Dakahn could..." Meccah began.

"No your highness." Ringo paused to swallow hard as Meccah gave him a piercing glare. "What I meant was, while Dakahn is certainly capable, Brutus may think that you sent him to scout Alkotten for weaknesses in its defenses. The representative must be close enough to you that Brutus sees your sincerity."

"As your father has done? My son then."

"You have a son?"

"And what a son he is" Meccah said proudly. A tall figure stepped from the darkness and stood in front of Ringo. He was as muscular as Meccah, but not nearly half his age. He seemed to wear a scowl on his face and Ringo found him to be very intimidating. "Troldomen, Ringo, this is my son, the prince of Alusta, Warrendr."

They politely nodded their heads in respect.

"Did you say War-render-er?" Ringo asked. "As in he who renders war? With all due respect King Meccah, this is to be a peace treaty negotiation. The name alone may interrupt the proceedings."

"You have yet to convince me to aid you in your quest young Mantoo. And as such..."

"Meccah," Ringo interrupted. "You are indeed the wisest king on the mountain."

"That goes without saying," Meccah added; forgiving the interruption because of the compliment.

"Then you know it is in the blood of every Mantoo to wager."

"You want to wager with me?"

"Just a simple wager really, with simpler terms to boot. I win; you help. If I lose, I leave empty handed."

"Under those terms I gain nothing when I win Mantoo."

"Hmmm. Well that will never do. What would you like…If you were to win?"

"I have a crystal in my possession that I would like for you to bring to Alkotten."

"Ah, a gift then. I would bring this without…" Ringo began but noticed the slight movement of Troldomen's finger waving him off. "Errr…without hesitation if you were to win your highness," Ringo finished.

"Well done. We have agreed. What is your wager?" Meccah asked.

"A riddle sire. You answer correctly, you win."

"A riddle?"

"Yes, just a riddle. If you solve it, then you win."

"Fine. Begin." Meccah said shifting his position on the throne to get comfortable.

"My father and Troldomen have traveled the Great Mountain for years, and have found something unique. I heard you too have traveled the Great Mountain at great length. So tell me, where can you find roads without carriages, forests without trees and cities without houses?"

Without giving it much thought, Meccah gestured with his right hand and pompously said "The dead Zone."

Ringo lowered his head and did his best not to smile. "I'm sorry your majesty," he began. "You can find those things on a map."

"A map?" Meccah asked. He seemed surprised and somewhat embarrassed.

"I take no pride in winning your majesty. I simply seek your aid and cannot complete my mission without it". Ringo handed Meccah the map from the satchel.

 Meccah was content with Ringo's humble attitude. He smiled slightly. "You are indeed well taught young Mantoo. You represent your people well. So now… who would you suggest represent me?"

"The Princess sire. Dinatru."

Although the hearing of the Alusta is sensitive enough to hear the wings of a fly from almost two miles away, it did not stop Meccah from yelling "WHAT?" so loud that every Alustan in the kingdom had to cover their ears.

The next day, Meccah was sitting on his throne when Warrendr and three of the Alusta Royal guards entered the room, approached the throne from the front, and bowed. Meccah stood up and gave a quick nod and the doors were shut behind them, leaving just the four of them in the room.

"Remember your task above all else," Meccah demanded, as he began pacing in front of the throne with his hand clasped behind his back.

"Yes Father," Warrendr said, still bowing.

"Let no harm come to the Princess, and let nothing stand in your way. Make them show you the hidden passage to Mantoo and retrieve the maps."

"Won't Mantoo be on the map father?" Warrendr asked.

"No, Wyler is no fool. The Mantoo passage is hidden from all eyes outside of the gate. It only becomes visible on the map when you are in Mantoo. Once you are in Mantoo, you must retrieve the map and mark the point on the map where it is located. When you leave Mantoo with the map, the markings you would have made will guide us back there. Are you clear on your objectives?"

"Yes my Lord," they all said together.

Meccah turned away from them and began to breathe heavily. He glanced over his shoulder and said "Do not fail me!" before exiting through a door behind the throne.

10 GALLRA'S SECRET

Gallra approached a clearing to the east of the Farrador camp. He was looking around as he picked his teeth. He turned around completely as if looking for someone, but let out a deep sigh when he realized he was alone. He picked up a rock and threw it at the large boulder that was in front of him. Suddenly, he was hit with a blow from behind that knocked him to the floor. Gallra scrambled to his feet and turned to face his attacker. His left foot slipped on a leaf while trying to stand, and he immediately rolled his body in front of the large boulder.

Fetter laughed as he extended his hand to assist his cousin.

"You have to be on your guard at all times; I keep telling you" Fetter said sternly as he helped Gallra to his feet.

"I know, I know." Gallra said, frustrated with himself. "You didn't have to hit me so hard."

"I shouldn't have been able to hit you at all. You were picking your teeth so loud that I was able to sneak up on you."

Gallra smiled and punched Fetter in the arm. "Next time I'll have the fish and leave the mutton to the women."

"You're right; it was a bit chewy today. I think Onkeel made it," he said jokingly. "So are you ready?"

"On a full stomach?" Gallra protested.

"Next time have the fish." Fetter snapped.

Gallra ran to the closest tree and jumped to the low branch. He flipped into the tree and then somersaulted to the ground. He ran to the giant rock and did a reverse flip off of it and went straight into a cartwheel. He stopped in front of Fetter, who looked completely unimpressed. Without saying a word, Fetter ran from his position and jumped into the tree. He landed on the low branch and back-flipped onto the giant rock.

"I can't do that!" Gallra yelled up to him.

"I can't do that what?" Fetter asked.

"I can't do that ....yet." Gallra replied.

Fetter jumped down and landed next to Gallra. "Look Gallra you have great instincts. When I knocked you down and you slipped, you did something really..."

"Clumsy." Gallra interrupted.

"Smart," Fetter said correcting him. "You rolled next to the rock to protect your back while facing your attacker. That was really smart, and in a real fight, that move would probably save your life. Now, I'm going to show you one more move; let's see if you can get it."

Fetter ran to the boulder and threw himself toward it. He kicked off of the rock into a double front flip before landing perfectly on his feet. He gestured to Gallra who immediately took off toward the rock. Like Fetter, he threw himself toward the rock, but when he kicked off, managed to flip sideways.

"What was that?" Fetter laughed

"I don't know it was just how it came out."

"I didn't think our bodies could bend that way. Come one, you do it like this," Fetter said showing him the flip once more.

Gallra kept trying, but each time, the flip still came out the same way.

"I'm beginning to think that I'll never get this." Gallra said softly.

"Come on, we've been doing this since we were kids." Fetter said, trying to reassure him.

"You've been doing this since we were kids. I was never as good as the rest of you," he said sitting on the ground.

"That's no excuse to stop trying," Fetter said sitting next to him. "I'll tell you what. Since it's the first time we've ever seen that flip, we have to name it after you. We'll call it the crazy flip."

"How is that named after me?" Gallra asked.

"Well…you have to be a little crazy to try it." Fetter joked.

Gallra stood up and walked a few feet away. He picked up a small broken branch and looked over at Fetter.

"Watch this," He said removing the band from his arm. He quickly fashioned a slingshot from the objects and held it out proudly.

"What's that?" Fetter asked reaching out for it. He studied it for a moment and handed back to Gallra.

"It's a slinger for rocks. See the coconuts in that tree?" Gallra said pointing.

Fetter looked in the tree with the curiosity of a child. "Yes," he said.

"Go to the tree," Gallra ordered.

Once Fetter was under the tree, Gallra motioned him to his left.

"Hold your hands out," Gallra said, taking a smooth rock from out of the dirt. He placed the rock into the slingshot and fired a single shot into the tree. The coconut he hit fell directly into Fetter's waiting hands."

"How did you do that?" Fetter asked. "That could be used to knock the eye out of Hunden guard," he said excitedly.

"I have a much larger one hidden in the forest. We figure we could wrap coconuts in thorny-bush and sling them from great distances at the Hunden," Gallra proudly proclaimed.

"Can I see it?" Fetter asked.

Before Gallra could answer, Onkeel entered the clearing. Gallra placed his slingshot behind his back to hide it.

"What are you two doing out here?" Onkeel asked.

"Gathering coconuts," Fetter quickly answered.

"It's getting dark, and we're going to close the gate. Get back to camp," Onkeel ordered.

"Hey Onkeel do you know what Gallra can do?" Fetter began.

"I can climb the coconut tree without a rope," Gallra interrupted.

As Onkeel walked to the coconut tree, Gallra laid the slingshot behind a bush quietly. He gestured to Fetter so that he knew to keep quiet about the slingshot.

Onkeel stood under the coconut tree and looked at the two cousins. He jumped into the air and grabbed a coconut out of the tree and landed easily on the ground. He tossed the coconut to Gallra as he walked by him and said "We don't need ropes."

In Mantoo, Wyler sat on the throne and look at the window at a robin that landed on the Winterop tree in the royal garden. He thought about what a good omen this must be to have the bird that represents peace in Mantoo perched in his favorite tree. The royal caller entered the room and bowed before him.

"I thought I asked not to be disturbed?" Wyler said, still studying the robin.

"My lord the elders are here."

"So? What of it? Wyler barked, turning toward him. "Am I not still Lord of these lands?" He said in and angry tone.

"Begging your pardon, highness." The caller said lifting his head to display bruises on his face. "But they are being quite persistent."

"Let them in."

The royal caller opened the door, and four of the elders stormed in. Devonsire of Lumdoren spoke first.

"Bless the day Wyler," he said in a serious tone.

"Bless the day to you all." Wyler returned.

"We have no desire to disrupt you in the middle of the Maisha-Vad for as you know the rules forbid it. We are interested in the Haurookena scroll and what it tells you now that Ringo is on his quest."

Sitting back in the throne, Wyler looked to the ceiling.

"Ah, so you would care to know if things are already in place to alter the destiny of all that dwell on the great mountain. Then you are also trying to see if the wager is going your way, which is a violation of the …"

"Wyler Wantoo!" Lady Arna interjected. "This Maisha-Vad is not just for your life, but for every life on the Great Mountain. We have a right to know. Moreover, Ringo is like a son to me. You do not suffer alone. I know you have a need to know. A need that is stronger than ours, because despite all that has transpired between the council over the last few days, it is your son that risks his life to save us all; lest any of us forgets." She said hitting Devonsire on the shoulder.

Wyler wiped a tear. "My friends, I thank you for remembering our friendship in a time when we are all most bound by our duties. Yes, Lady Arna I do desire to know if the future has been made better by the decision from this court. But for the first time in too many years to count, I am gripped by an emotion I am not prepared to confront."

"We are all fearful Wyler. Some of us just manage it better than others. What we fear most is the unknown. I believe you can remedy that," Arna said.

Wyler took the scroll from its pillow next to the throne and carefully opened it. He placed it on the marble table and rubbed its center. As before, a moving picture began to take shape before their eyes. They all watched as the blue comet approach the great mountain from the east. But this time, it passed harmlessly over the mountain. They all cheered and hugged each other. But Swoggle drew his eyes back to the scroll, which revealed the same blasts and explosions that they witnessed earlier.

"Look!" He cried out.

As the eruptions and blasts continued, the silhouette of a rather large arm came into view. Then the form could barely be made out amidst the dust and fire.

"What manner of demon is this? We do not have the means to defeat a creature such as this!" Swoggle said in despair.

"Aubaultmor" Wyler whispered beyond their hearing.

"Is this the dragon of legend?" Devonsire began. "It spits fire, and throws fire at will. This beast is beyond any weapon we could form Wyler. Ringo is…."

"Ringo will find a way." Wyler interrupted.

"What will we do Wyler? Lady Arna asked.

"We will not panic. If word were to get out, there would be panic across the entire kingdom. Lawlessness and anarchy would be our end. No, that cannot happen. If we are to meet our end at the hands of this beast, it will be done with honor. We are Mantoo, and while we are a great many things, cowards are not one of them. We will keep the law."

"Absolutely not Wyler. Our very destruction it at hand!" Dugan Shipnor cried out."

"We will keep the law," Wyler repeated.

"It is just as I've said. He may be seeking the destruction of Mantoo itself!" Devonsire Shouted.

Wyler pulled on a rope hanging next to the throne. "I said we will not panic, and I said we will keep the law. What I have not said is something you fail to realize. My son wears the crown, but until he returns I am still Lord of these lands."

As Wyler said that, a group of guards entered the throne room and surrounded the other elders. Dugan Shipnor looked around nervously. Devonsire wore a grim scowl on his face. Wyler walked up to him and looked him in the eye.

"I am still the law in Mantoo, not the elder council. If I have to remind you of this, as much as it would pain me to do so, I will. Since you above all others desire action Devonsire, you will choose the next course of action taken in this very room. Do we obey the law, or must the King address the civil unrest?"

Devonsire cleared his throat and looked around at the guards. He took a deep breath and nodded before trying to speak.

"Wyler, quite often you lead through servitude, and those around you eventually forget that your patience and your kindness are your greatest strengths. I behaved in a manner not befitting an elder of this council, and for that I am sorry. I meant no disrespect. We will keep the law."

Wyler gestured with his hand and the entire room cleared. As they exited, each elder bowed as they left the room. Wyler nodded and walked to the courtyard. He looked to the sky and wiped a tear. "Blessed spirit, protect him," he whispered.

In the palace garden Dionne was sitting quietly reading a book. Her hand maidens were standing a few feet away awaiting her commands. One of the royal callers approached her from the rear entrance holding an envelope in his hand. He bowed as he handed it to her.

"The gentlemantoo that handed me that letter asked me to tell you that he did as you instructed milady. Will that be all Princess?" the caller asked.

"Yes, and thank you Marcio," she said as he turned.

Dionne paused to watch him walk toward the garden's main entrance before she opened the envelope, but stopped once more when she noticed the maidens watching her.

"That will be all today girls," she said politely. As the girls walked toward the main entrance she quickly unfolded the letter and began reading it. She was overcome with anger as she read it and quickly gathered her books and stormed into the castle.

11 ASCENSION

Early the next morning, Ringo, Troldomen, Warrendr, Dinatru and three members of the Royal Guard began their ascension up the mountain on the Alustan air riders. The air riders were small and looked like metal tea cups, but they were very effective. Each one of them had their own air rider, which Ringo found easy to maneuver, despite having had just one lesson. Although traveling this way was saving a lot of time, Ringo was bothered by the presence of the Alusta Royal guards. Warrendr's presence troubled Ringo most because he, above all others, seemed to be watching him at all times.

Whenever they stopped to rest, the Princess seemed to forget that the guards were there to protect her. Instead, she used them to do her bidding, serve her food and bring her water.

Their travels on the first day up the mountain were without incident. At sunset, the guards secured the air riders and set up tent-like sleeping quarters for Dinatru. The guards lay circling the tent while she slept. Not able to sleep, Ringo and Troldomen went to a nearby stream to collect water in the very early hours of the morning.

"They don't smile much. I've certainly seen Meccah more jovial, but that one is a puzzle," Troldomen whispered while looking at Warrendr.

"It's been my experience that when characters like that smile, they are up to something crafty. It's usually before they cheat you in the parlor," Ringo said nodding his head. "It's how you tell what they're planning," he added.

"well, I'm a bit lost to your plan young master." Troldomen said quietly.

"All will be revealed soon Troldomen. Tell me, why is it neither you, nor my father ever told me he was ill? He looked fine to me, when last I saw him.

Troldomen glanced over his shoulder. "If he is ill, it's the first I heard. It could have been a ploy of Meccah's to gain information. Fear not young master; all will be revealed soon."

As Troldomen walked toward the camp, the princess walked past him to the stream.

"Can I get you anything Princess?" Ringo asked as she approached.

"You are a gracious host King Ringo, but my guards will tend to my needs."

"Ringo," he said correcting her.

"What?" she asked puzzled.

"King Ringo seems so formal. I'm not sure I'm ready to have

everyone refer to me that way."

Dinatru continued to give Ringo a very puzzled look. "I'm not sure I understand," She said.

"I would consider it a favor if you simply called me Ringo."

She sat on a rock at the streams edge and touched the water with her fingertips and playfully made little swirls. "My father said that you were well taught. Did your father not teach you to accept the crown, and all that comes with it?"

"Does that include treating your guards like servants?"

"When you are royalty, everyone else in the kingdom exists to serve you."

"Mantoo is not like that. We rely of the elders to assist with the matters of state."

"So you have many kings?"

"No just the one. The king has final say, but the wisdom of the elders allows for other points of view. The council is filled with elders from each province throughout Mantoo, so the wisest representative from each area may be heard. This way the King can make a decision that takes in to account all the people he governs."

"And would the king not do that without a council?"

"I'm sure he would try." Ringo said smiling.

"Your people are very strange king Ringo."

"Why do you say that?"

"Well for one thing, I've only seen you wear your crown in the presence of my father."

"Am I any less a king because I choose not adorn my head with metal and jewels?"

"Where I am from, the crown is worn with pride as a symbol of our heritage."

"We have pride, but more in the role and the importance of our duty."

"Duty?"

"To our people."

"Where I am from, you exist to serve the crown. It would seem that in Mantoo your King exists to serve the people."

"Humph. I must say, I've never actually thought about it that way."

"How did you think about it?"

Ringo scratched his head, and looked bewildered. "It's funny I guess I never really have."

"Then I guess your quest of enlightenment has not been very fruitful." she said walking back toward the camp.

"Perhaps not until just now," he said following her.

A few hours later, the group continued on their air riders up the mountain. Ringo and the princess remained close and talked most of the way. At just over half way on their journey, the air riders began to sputter. They continued upwards until they came to the very next inlet and parked them near the edge of the mountain as Warrendr directed. After the camp was set up and all of the supplies were removed, Warrendr gave a nod, and the guards pushed the air riders over the edge. He gave another nod and the guards quickly set about catching wild horses. Troldomen and Warrendr made camp while Ringo and Dinatru continued their conversation.

Ringo turned to Warrendr, and then looked to the area where the Riders were parked. "What happened to the riders?" he asked as politely as he could.

"They must have underestimated the amount of fuel needed to make the trip the entire way. We are short on provision as well. We are half the way up by now, and should be near Mantoo. Is it possible to get more provisions there?" Warrendr smiled.

His smile caught Ringo by surprise, but Ringo managed a slight smile in return and gave a single nod in agreement. He quickly turned his attention to Dinatru and smiled at her too.

"Your guard is almost done with your tent. I believe the other two went to gather horses. I'm not sure horses could go more than a day or two higher before it gets too cold. We really could have used those riders another day," he said.

"The great spirit will provide. Your journey is already been blessed, has it not?" She replied.

Ringo was caught by surprise by her words. He smiled and nodded in agreement. "You are nothing like they say in Mantoo," he said to her, still smiling.

"Whatever does that mean?"

"You know, you hear a lot of things. I heard your people were taller."

"Is that all?" She asked, sounding unconvinced.

"Well your skin is very dark, that much was true, and you all seem to have a lot of… muscles," he said looking at her from head to toe.

"That's not true," She giggled.

"No?"

"No some of us are …"

"Dinatru!" Warrendr called.

She forced a smile and looked away.

"I guess every culture has its little secrets," Ringo smiled.

She walked back to her tent quietly. One of the guards opened the curtain for her to walk through and closed it behind her.

When they woke in the morning, Ringo noted that there was a horse for each of them. The horses were saddled and loaded with all of the supplies. They quickly ate an egg breakfast and continued up the mountain on the horses.

Ringo pulled out the map and studied it as they passed Notting plains. The forest ahead of them was not on the map. Taking note to his actions, Warrendr looked at him and asked, "Is this a map of the mountain?"

Ringo did not answer, but instead looked at it again. Troldomen moved his horse over to him and looked at the map Ringo was holding.

"Where did the horses come from?" Ringo asked.

"They caught them in the night," Troldomen answered. Troldomen looked at Ringo who appeared confused as he looked around. "What's wrong?" He asked.

"The Forest…It's not on the map," Ringo said, still looking around.

"Humph. That could only mean that it was not here when we made the map."

"How old is the map?"

Troldomen ignored the question and kept looking at the forest.

"Troldomen. How old is the map?" Ringo asked again.

"Oh about two, maybe two hundred and fifty years."

"Well, I guess you could grow a forest or two in that time." Ringo quipped.

"What would you have us to do?" Yahkar the guard asked.

Ringo looked at the Princess and smiled. "We are under the watchful eyes and ears of the Alusta honor guard. No harm will come to us. We go through. Going around may add days to our journey."

"Are we going for provisions?" Warrendr asked with a smile.

Ringo took notice to his smile again, and simply nodded as he had before. They entered the forest and made their way to the tall trees a few miles in. The guards suddenly stopped to gather in a circle around Warrendr and began to whisper. Troldomen moved his horse next to Ringo and leaned toward him.

"What's that about?" Troldomen whispered.

Before Ringo could answer Warrendr came out of the circle and moved toward them.

"We have been followed since we entered the forest," he said.

"Hunden? Tikats?" Ringo asked.

"Much larger. Much more cunning. It knows how to hunt. It is staying down wind. It only moves when we do."

"So we are being hunted? Where is the hunter now? Is it the Farrador?"

"Behind you about one thousand steps. I can hear it breathing. Each of the things you mentioned hunt in packs. There is only one creature out there, and it is ...large." Warrendr said with a concerned tone.

"Then let's keep moving. The pass to Elwindor should be beyond these trees. We need to be on higher ground if we have to engage it." Ringo said bravely.

Their pace was hurried now. Troldomen looked surprised. "You mean to take us to the caves of Elwindor?" He asked.

Ringo did not answer. He was too busy taking note to the drastic change in temperature.

"What just happened? Why is it so cold all of a sudden? According to the map, we are not close enough to Alkotten for this bitter cold." Ringo said confidently.

"The fire water that warms most of the Great Mountain does not run on this side of it. The rain can become snow or ice very quickly here." Troldomen answered. "Ringo, the caves are dangerous, we must turn around." Troldomen continued.

"We cannot. Some manner of beast is behind us. We must press on." Warrendr said.

"Then we are doomed. Death waits for us in either direction. It haunts our steps behind us and also lays in waiting before us." Troldomen despaired.

"What do you mean Troldomen?" Ringo asked.

"Your father never told you about what took place in the caves of Elwindor?"

"No." Ringo said, looking up at the snow.

The wind began to howl, and suddenly snow seemed to come at them from every direction. The forest stopped at the base of a large rock wall on the mountainside. The air was too cold and thin for the horses, and each of them began to panic at the smell of something foul in the air. At Warrendr's command the guards quickly took the supplies off of the horses and set them free, leaving the group on foot. One by one they climbed up the thin, icy ledge and up to a cave as the horses fled east. Troldomen did not want to enter, but did so reluctantly when he heard a loud roar come from the forest. They built a fire with scraps of wood that were in and around the cave entrance. Dinatru sat by the fire and warmed her hands.

"I would think the Alustan skin would be sensitive to cold being around that intense heat all of your lives." Ringo said.

Our skin is thick and can withstand temperatures of all kinds." Dinatru stated proudly. "You being Mantoo are not so fortunate."

"No," he said wrapping a blanket around his shoulders. "Mantoos' need extra skin to manage the colder temperatures."

She stared at him curiously for a moment, and then looked to the forest. "What do we do now? Without the riders or the horses, must we walk the rest of the way?" She asked.

Ringo looked out at the forest and saw the tops of the trees moving as the creature came closer to them. "Do your guards have weapons?" He asked.

"Yes." Warrendr answered. "We have weapons. We are prepared to fight."

Troldomen walked to the entrance and looked through the raging snow to the forest. In a soft voice he said, "We may have no choice, but to fight Warrendr," he looked around the cave and said, "We now have no place left to run."

12 LONGING TO BELONG

At the Farrador camp, everyone was gathered around a large fire listening to the hunting story Onkeel was telling. He was interrupted by Isantor, who interjected his own version of the events every few seconds. There was a lot of laughter as he told the tale of the day's events. Away from everyone else, Fetter and Gallra were sitting on the ground, and were telling the same tales to a few of the young females. One of the young females smiled at Gallra as Fetter told his story. Gallra did not know how to react to this attention, since it had not happened before. He managed to form a very clumsy smile in return. From a distance Dunau, one of the strongest of the young males saw what was going on and decided that he had seen enough. He walked up to Gallra and stood in front of him.

"How did you get there first "stummy?" he asked him. "How come no one saw you climb into that tree stummy?"

"Stop calling me that." Gallra shot back.

"Oh, so stummy finally keeps up on a hunt for the first time, and now he's big enough to challenge me?

"Leave him alone Dunau!" Fetter said sternly.

"Are you going to fight your cousin's battles for the rest of his life Fetter? Answer me stummy. I saw how far back you were. You did not pass us, and there is only one way down that side of the mountain. How did you do it? You are built like a bird, did you fly?"

The girls laughed at Dunau's joke, but it enraged Gallra. He lunged at Dunau, who quickly threw him off and wrestled him to the ground. Fetter stood up and said, "That's enough Dunau."

Dunau held him down another second before letting Gallra up. Gallra was embarrassed and ran toward the lake to get away from the camp. Fetter ran after him, but did not see him as he approached the lake.

He walked around for a few seconds and looked in every direction. Fetter knew the lake was dangerous at night, and making too much noise could attract a nearby predator, but he had to take the chance. He loudly whispered "Gallra," and looked around. Before he could do it a second time, a hand reached out from the darkness and covered his mouth and then pulled him behind one of the giant trees.

He was surprised, but stayed still when he realized that it was Gallra.

"Shhh," Gallra commanded. He pointed to the lake, where the Hunden were sneaking toward the Farrador camp.

"They're going to attack the camp. We need to warn everyone."

Fetter whispered.

Gallra took a few steps back and pulled a vine. When he did, the ground beneath them moved and lifted them into the tree.

"How did you do that?" Fetter whispered excitedly.

"Shush," Gallra reminded him.

They looked down and saw that one of the Hunden was sniffing around the base of the tree. They hid behind the thick branches in the tree and were not seen. As the Hunden scout rejoined the pack, Gallra climbed higher.

"Where are you going?" We have to warn the others." Fetter protested.

"We will. I just don't want to get killed in the process," Gallra whispered.

He tapped on the tree in a particular spot and a door opened leading to a room inside the tree. Fetter was surprised, but he followed him in. When the door closed behind them, it was completely black. Gallra lit a lamp on the table in the middle of the room and Fetter looked around in amazement. Gallra had carved out a room in the tree and used it to store things. There were objects hanging on all four walls. Some looked like weapons, and other objects looked like nothing Fetter had ever seen before.

"Where did you get this stuff?"

"I made it all."

"You made this stuff?" "How? Why?" Fetter said staring at it in wonder.

"I don't know why. I just can, so I do it. We can talk about it later. Right now we have to warn the others."

Gallra took a shiny circle from its hanging place on the wall and walked outside. He pulled out a small telescope and looked through it. He saw Isantor and held up the mirror. It reflected the moons light so brightly that Isantor noticed right away. "We are under attack!" He yelled. "Sound the horn."

As the horn sounded the warriors grabbed their weapons and ran toward the light. The women and children fled to the safety of the tall rocks that surrounded most of the camp. The sound of screams and war cries filled the air as the Hunden attacked.

"Bring me meat," Stygg commanded.

The warriors shot arrows and threw spear in the dark. A loud yelp let them know that one of the Hunden paid for the attack with its life. But a cry of a different kind followed. One of the Farrador warriors was taken, dragged away screaming in the darkness. The warriors tried to save him, but the Hunden were too fast. They fled into the night and carried him away.

The camp grew quiet as the Hunden ran off in the distance. Fetter and Gallra were running back into the camp, when Gallra tripped over the body of the dead Hunden. Fetter helped him to his feet, and then picked up the small mirror Gallra dropped. One of the Farrador warriors almost threw a spear at them, but was stopped by Onkeel.

"Where were you two? Dunau yelled. They took my brother while you two hid like cowards."

"No." Isantor said softly. He looked at the object in Fetter's hand. "We have lost two warriors tonight, for Lotoka the scout must also have been taken if they were able to get this close to us. But Fetter was able to warn me with this," he said taking the mirror from Fetter and holding up for all to see. "He cast light in my face with this, and because of that warning, we were able to bear arms and to fight. More would have died, women and children, if the warning had not come. He took up the watch post when all else failed and has saved us from destruction. For this, he should be honored. Dunau, your brother fought bravely, and died a good death."

"He died because we did not have all of the warriors fighting! Gallra was hiding. He ran off. He must have known an attack was coming!" Dunau lashed out.

"He died because he was a warrior!" Isantor fired back. "And it is the wish of every warrior to die in battle. Your mother and your sisters are alive because of it. Do not cheapen his death in your grief. Honor him with your deeds."

Dunau ran to his hut, while the others watched. Seizing the opportunity, Fetter raised his hands and tried to speak. "I have something to say. Gallra…."

"There will be plenty for all to say later." Isantor interrupted. "For now, we must secure the camp in case they return. In the morning, we make war with those that would bring war to us. The Hunden will pay for this attack with their lives."

As the warriors divided to take their posts, Fetter pulled Gallra to the side. "Why didn't you say anything?" he asked.

"You tried to say something, and look how far you got. It's okay. No one would believe that I had anything to do with saving the camp anyway. Plus, Isantor said you would be honored. They'll probably make you a warrior Fetter. You've been waiting for that all of your life, but it means nothing to me."

"Then why do you try so hard? I see how tough it is for you not being as strong as the rest of us, but you never give up. If it means nothing, then why do you keep trying?"

"You don't know?"

"Well I do. I know. It's the way of our people. The warrior spirit flows within you."

"Good answer, but that's not it."

"Then what?"

"To belong Fetter. I just want to be like everyone else. I just want to belong."

"Then this is your chance. Once we tell them that you were the one that warned them Isantor will..."

"You still don't understand do you?" Gallra said cutting him off.

"What? What don't I understand?"

"It's not enough for me to want to belong Fetter. They don't want me Fetter. Do you understand now? They just don't want me to belong"

13 TRAPPED

While looking out from the cave's entrance at the cave's entrance, two of the Alustan guards spotted something moving in the snow. The fierce winds and blinding snow made it very difficult for them to see it plainly. The wind was causing the snow to fly into their eyes, and whatever it was kept moving opposite the wind, which made it impossible to get a fix on it. Warrendr moved slowly to the edge of the cave entrance. Troldomen moved to his right to get a better look.

"Something still watches us from inside the storm. I cannot be certain of its size, but it is big." Troldomen whispered back toward the others in the cave.

Warrendr closed his eyes and tilted his head to listen to whatever was moving outside of the cave. "It is weighs 15 rocks if it weighs a stone. It bears large feet and hands, massive teeth, but it stands upright. It has a great deal of hair, the color of the snow, and must be as tall as three Alustan soldiers," he said calmly.

Troldomen looked at him. "You can tell that with your eyes closed?"

"I can hear the wind and snow hit against him. I can hear his feet hit the snow-covered ground. I can hear his heart beat in his chest, his claws hit against each other, and…"

"And What? Ringo asked.

Troldomen and Warrendr moved back into the cave to talk with Ringo.

Warrendr looked back toward the entrance. "He hears us" He began. "He knows how many of us there are, and he is cautious despite his size. This means he is intelligent. He is really close now, his heart is calm; he is planning."

"Planning what? Dinatru asked.

Before anyone could answer, a flurry of snowballs entered the cave. Everyone hit the floor except for Troldomen, who quickly chanted a few words and watched as the snowballs exploded as if the hit some invisible shield in front of him. Once the bombardment of snowballs ceased, a load roar echoed through the cave from outside.

"Well. It must be big to let out such a roar like that." Ringo said brushing himself off. He turned and noticed the Alustans were covering their ears with their hands and were grimacing in pain. The load roar caused the mountain to rumble; an avalanche began. As the snow began to cover the entrance, Ringo ushered everyone back deep inside the cave. A large hairy arm entered the cave and attempted to grab Ringo, but Warrendr jumped on him, forcing him to the ground. The creature missed its target and quickly withdrew its arm from the cave as the snow blocked the entrance. The beast let out another roar, which was drowned out by the avalanche. After a moment, the large fire was the only light in the cave. The Alustans were comfortable in the dark, and stood close to the fire. Troldomen pushed his stick into the wall of snow blocking the entrance, and tried to move it around. "It's no use," he said. "He is blocked out, and we are blocked in."

"We need to press on." Ringo said. "We cannot remain here."

"There is no need to." Dinatru interjected. "There is a passage between these rocks. I hear the sound of water. It may lead us out."

"Then let's go." Ringo urged.

Troldomen rubbed his hands by the fire and placed them on his face. "Young master, the caves of Elwindor are legendary. None that enter have ever been seen again."

"They say that about Mantoo." Ringo fired back.

"Yes they do, but knowing the dangers on the mountain, your father borrowed it to keep people from leaving Mantoo. He and I made plenty of trips away from home. Where do you think the stories about the Alustans and the Alkotten came from? You think someone made up all of those things? And the map, who do you think made the map?"

"Father told me once about the warning on the gate being something he made up. And the map, why are the caves not on the map?" Ringo asked.

"To stop anyone from entering them, young master. Shortly after your sister was born we set out to explore the mountain, to have yet another adventure. The odds were 50 to 1 that we would not return. And it goes without saying that we had to take a bet like that, you see. There were four of us on the journey that time. This was the first time your mother accompanied us on an expedition to chart the Great Mountain. You and your siblings were left in the care of your aunt Arna. On the ninth day, we came across the caves discovered by Elwindor of Gratham. He was a great explorer in his own right. The snow began to fall and we needed a place to camp for the night. Your Grandfather, on your mother's side, insisted on going into the caves for shelter. He knew old Elwindor and went along in the hopes of having something named after him too. We begged them not to go; Elwindor himself disappeared exploring those caves. Your mother and Grandfather went in to get out of the cold. Wyler and I built a fire and a shelter with large sticks. We were all settled in for the night when we heard the screaming. We ran fast. We were young then, like you, but we were not fast enough. Whatever took them left their clothes a bloody mess. Your father said he could hear your mother's screams in his sleep for years. When we got back, your father placed the sign on the great gate, and began to say that no one who ever left Mantoo was ever seen or heard from again. For my part, I removed the location of these caves from the maps so that no one using them would ever come here again."

Ringo was saddened by the story. "This explains a lot Troldomen. A lot indeed, but it does not change our reality. The caves appear to be our only option. Even if we could dig our way out of here, we would have to contend with whatever buried us in here. And who is to say that the beast isn't responsible for the perils within the caves. If that is so, then we need not worry; he is blocked out as you said."

"Indeed young master. Indeed."

"You still hesitate, are there other perils in the caves besides the beast that has trapped us?"

"I am not certain young Master, but I would wager that we will find out."

"Another thing Troldomen; is this beast responsible for killing my mother?

Troldomen paused and looked to the blocked entrance. "I do not know."

"Did that thing kill my mother?" Ringo shouted.

"I do not know!" Troldomen shouted over him. "That was a long time ago. This creature could be related in some way; it could be the same one, I have no idea Ringo. But we must press on. You…we cannot face it on its terms. We do what we must before we…"

"Do not quote my father here…in this place…in this instance! I know my duty. I will see it done. And that thing will know my blade before the end," Ringo said storming through the gap in the rear of the cave.

Troldomen looked at the snow covered cave entrance and could hear scratching as the creature outside was trying to dig through the snow. He looked to the rear of the cave and sighed. "Well, he's passionate now Wyler… and passion begets results," he said as he entered the gap. "Passion begets results," he repeated.

14 STYGG

In the darkness that surrounded the Hunden den, Stygg was eating the last remnants of his meal. The moment that he walked away, the rest of the Hunden quickly jumped on the carcass. He went to the river and put his head in to drink and was taken by surprise by a voice from the bush near him. "Two kills are hardly enough to meet the terms of our agreement Stygg."

"I am a slow starter. The Farrador will be expecting us to again tonight, but in addition to killing two of their men, we took all of their meat. They will have to hunt in the morning, or risk starvation, and the Hunden will press the attack at first light."

"That is a good plan, but I do not want you attacking the hunting party." The voice said.

"Why? If we kill the hunters, the rest are easy prey."

"They will have weapons, however crude, but weapons none the less. Moreover, before you kill Isantor, I want him to suffer. I want you to kill his brood. He has a wife and young child." Said the voice from the bush.

"Yes." Stygg said in delight. "The women and the children will be alone. There will be tender, fresh meat; the kind that the Hunden have not enjoyed since the great war."

"Yes Stygg. Killing them will bring him much pain. Then, when he is stricken with grief, you put him out of his misery."
Stygg chuckled. "You are far more devious and blood thirsty than any Hunden." He said.

"Coming from you, I consider that a compliment."

"I have a question. This is a dangerous mission and many Hunden may be killed; I would like to know why you want the Farrador destroyed."

"That is no one's concern but mine. You are being paid well to simply accomplish the task….without question."

"I am certain you have your reasons."

"I do, but they are mine, and mine alone."

"I still expect prompt payment."

"Yes, of course. You will have more meat than you could eat in a hundred years."

"Ha! That would be wonderful if it were possible."

"It is possible Stygg." Do this for me and I will show you the secret way into Mantoo. You will have all the meat you could ever eat there."

"Did you say Mantoo?" Stygg asked as his mouth began to water.

"Yes." The voice said.

"Very well. I will do this as you have instructed, but I desire something in return; something that I must have, as payment, as soon as it is possible."

"What is that?"

"Troldomen and his new companion. They bested me a few nights ago. Troldomen has bested me for the last ten years. He must die by my teeth."

The bush moved and Meccah stepped out from behind it. He smiled and nodded. "Do not worry Stygg; I have already set a plan in motion for just that thing."

Stygg looked at him with a great deal of concern.

"After all of these years Meccah, why now? Why is it that only now do you seek to help us? Stygg asked.

Meccah folded his arms and flashed him a very confident look. "My timing in my concern. You leave the planning to me, and you and your companions bring your teeth. I will fill your bellies with my enemies before the cycle of the stars in done."

Stygg watched him leave. He waited until he disappeared from sight and turned to find himself surrounded by the other Hunden. "What are our orders?" The Hunden captain asked.

'It is curious, don't you think? That strange look in his eyes," Stygg began. "Yes I have heard about it before," he said as he began pacing. "Our elders told a tale of a great giant among the two-legged ones. He was dark and cunning, like us perhaps. The dark one had a way to control some of them, and when he did, there was a strange look in their eyes. I believe I just saw it for myself," Stygg said looking in the direction that Meccah exited.

"Old black tail used to tell us stories as pups," The captain started. "He said that when the dark one walked the mountain, he brought war. And he said that the Hunden fought alongside him. He also said that..."

"I have heard the stories," Stygg said cutting him off. "If the dark one returns, we will fight with him until we find his weakness. And when we find that weakness, we show him our teeth. The days are gone when we serve the needs of others. In this case, we will pretend to do so until we no longer need to."

"We have heard whispers of his return Stygg. Meccah may be under the spell of the dark one."

"He may be working directly for him for all we know, so we will continue to hold court here near the dead zone. Our voices will not travel far here, and the Alusta will not hear our plans," Stygg said confidently.

"Speaking of plans, has anything changed?"

Stygg smiled and said, "There is no other evidence of the dark ones return, so we will keep to the plan.. The Hunden will feast on every

Farrador on the mountain, and once we gain the path to Mantoo, we will sit back and let Alusta declare war on Alkotten. We will feast on the bodies they leave behind in their petty war until there is none left. We will grow strong, and multiply in number, while they grow weak from battle and plague. Then, when each side is at their weakest, we attack. After that, we enter Mantoo, which will be unprotected and we will feast some more. We will fight their war, but none of the two-legs will win the day. When all is done, the Hunden…Stygg will rule this mountain."

15 THE CRYSTAL CAVE

Ringo held his torch out in front of him as far as he could. He struggled to see in the darkness that was all around them. After an hour, they began to notice bright crystals scattered throughout the cave that dimming lit their path. The sound of running water was all around them, and he wondered for a moment if he would lead them to an opening behind a waterfall. He did his best to find the path that would lead them up higher into the caves. They stopped to rest for a moment, and Warrendr scouted the path ahead. One of the three guards walked up to him and looked around to make sure it was safe to speak. "What of the plan?" He asked in a whisper. Warrendr looked around also before speaking.

"Once we are rid of this beast, we will take the map and when we have the path to Mantoo we will dispose of these two."

"Why can't we just take their map?"

"If these caves were not on the map, their secret path to Mantoo will not be there either. My father says that Wyler is no fool. When we are near the center of the great Mountain, we will trick them into taking us to Mantoo for supplies. Then we do what my father sent us to do."

"And what would that be Warrendr?" Dinatru said walking toward them.

"Sister, you should not listen to the conversations of others, it is not polite."

"Remove yourself." She commanded the guard. While he left, she walked within a foot of Warrendr. "You speak to me of what is not polite, when you sneak off to conspire against members of our party? If father knew…"

"It is father's will I do. This is not a plan I devised."

"You lie," she whispered.

"Do I?" He said walking around her. "Father has been planning such a thing for years. He only lacked the opportunity."

"Father has…. not been himself lately. He spends more and more time alone. He has been brooding and somewhat ill-tempered of late. It's as if he is taken with sickness."

"Father is fine and above all else, as regent, his will is beyond the questioning of any spoiled little girl."

"It was father that taught this little girl that true intelligence questions everything without prejudice. So my dear brother, be careful you do not play the role of fool while you seek marks for obedience."

"Have a care sister. You may be father's favorite, but you are far from mine."

"Have you considered what will happen to you if you harm a single hair upon my head?"

"Remember this whelp. Father will not live forever, one day I will be king. You would do well to worry about what will happen to you then."

"I pray I will never see the day."

"It is far more likely that you will not see the day after," he whispered angrily.

The intensity of their conversation made them both deaf to Ringo's approach. Ringo coughed to alert them to his presence. "We must press on," he said politely interrupting them. Without saying a word, both the princess and prince joined the others. Ringo was concerned, and walked alongside Dinatru. "Is everything alright?" He asked.

"My brother is ambitious, and sometimes a bit of a bully. Nothing I cannot handle."

"Well, that's comforting," he smiled.

"Do siblings not fight in Mantoo?" she asked.

"With great frequency I assure you, but not to the death."

"Oh. Exactly how much did you hear?"

"Only his threat to kill you."

"I'm embarrassed."

"You don't need to be. My little brother is always wishing me dead." Ringo stared at the blue comb in her hair. "We speak of your long hair and the blue fire comb that holds it perfectly in place. These were images told to us by my father. It is pleasing to know he did not exaggerate."

She laughed and said, "Then we have more in common than I thought…. Ringo."

"May I?" He asked extending his hand. She took the comb from her hair and handed it to him. "This is marvelous," he said studying it.

"I cannot remember a time when I did not have it. I'm told it belonged to my mother."

"Where is she?"

"She died having me, I grew up without her," She said sadly.

"We really do have much in common Princess", he said handing the comb back to her. He watched as she put the comb back in her hair.

"You remind me of my sister," he said smiling.

"How so?" She said eagerly.

"She is the consummate princess. She loves to give orders, spoiled by her father the king, and likes to get her way in all matters."

Dinatru smiled. "I like her already. Being the children that our fathers appointed to this task I was wondering in what other ways are you and I alike?"

A roar in the distance caused them to focus once again on their task.

"Well, for a start, we both want to make it out of here alive." Ringo said looking in the direction of the roar.

"You two may not have that in common with the rest of us if you continue to dawdle." Troldomen said. "Keep pace with the group. We must stay together," he insisted.

They walked for a few more hours and decided to settle in for the night. They found a thin, deep space to crawl into. It was dry and too small for the creature to fit in, which gave them a level of comfort they had not felt since entering the cave. Ringo looked at the strange crystals on the walls and touched them softly. "These look very much like the crystals in your father's throne room and on his scepter." Ringo noted.

Warrendr looked them over and nodded. "They were gifts from Alkotten."

One of the guards picked up a small piece from the floor and walked away to show the others. Ringo sat against the large crystal formation embedded in the wall closed his eyes. He began to hear voices coming from the wall and opened his eyes. He placed his ear on the wall and looked at the guards. He realized that the voices he was hearing from the wall were those of the guards.

Troldomen looked at him and said "It is an echo. The guards speak and you hear it bouncing off of the walls."

"Oh." Ringo said settling into spot against the wall. He placed his left hand to his left ear and gently rubbed it before falling asleep.

A few hours later Ringo awoke and looked around. He touched the crystal on the wall closest to him, and then stood to touch a few higher up.

"They are not diamonds. We call them O'craru, the heart of the mountain," Dinatru said without opening her eyes.

"O'craru." Ringo repeated while touching the crystal once more.

He sliced out a small portion of the crystal with his knife and picked up one of the small pieces from the floor. He placed one of the small fragments next to Troldomen, who was snoring, and placed the other piece next to his ear. Ringo walked to where the guards were and gestured to them, making them believe he had to relieve himself. When he was far enough away, he placed the crystal next to his ear, and could hear Troldomen snoring as if he was next to him. He returned to Troldomen and removed the smaller piece from near his nose smiled as he placed both of the crystal pieces in his pocket.

A few more hours into their rest, one of the guards awoke and listened to a strange digging sound that he heard in the distance. He woke one of the other guards, and they made their way to the edge of the crevice. Warrendr stuck half of his body out, and looked at the guards. They gave out a few hand signals and waited. Warrendr listened to the digging for a moment and gave them a nod to continue. They walked away from the crevice and disappeared into the darkness. Warrendr woke the others and placed his index finger over his mouth to let them know to be quiet.

Without warning, a long white object slowly broke the darkness and passed over the fire a few feet from them. It was a large bone that the creature was pushing into the cave to flush them out. They quietly moved to the sides of the crevice and scaled the walls to higher points in their hideout. From the outside the creature tried to look into the crevice as he moved the bone in and out. He knocked the fire over and sprinkled the amber ashes throughout the crevice. Soon, the creature became frustrated and let out a loud roar, and jammed the bone into the crevice repeatedly. The end of the bone broke off and became sharp and pointed. The creature pressed his attack. He let out another roar, but this one was different from all of the others; it was more like a scream, Ringo thought. Two Alustan guards shot a fire dart into the creature, catching him in the back. The creature tried to pull it out, but could not reach it, and began running off into the darkness and howling in pain.

"Hurry!" Ringo yelled. "We must follow it."

"Are you mad?" Dinatru cried.

"The creature's back is burning"

"He is not on fire."

"He is burning with pain. Run! It knows the way out," Ringo demanded.

"Good thinking! This means he will lead us out." Troldomen added as he ran past them.

The group ran to follow the creature as quickly as they could. After what seemed like an eternity, they came to a large opening and looked out into the snow-covered surroundings. A roar in the distance let them know the creature was far enough away for them to move. They quickly exited and climbed carefully up the icy mountain to a ledge twenty feet above the large opening. It was not long before they heard the footsteps of the large beast approaching, and laid flat against the ground. Each of them held their breath and tried to remain absolutely still. They waited patiently as it entered the cave, and then continued to move up the mountain without saying a word.

Ringo pulled out the map when he noticed a strange marking carved into a large boulder to his left.

"It would appear that we continued north even as we entered the caves," he said.

"How far north?" Troldomen asked.

"Very," he said putting the map away.

After traveling a few hours on the snow covered pass known as

Alkottinius, the group came to the snowy flatlands. They stayed close to the mountainside and continued to make their way up along the trail through the deep snow. The wind hitting shallow openings along the mountain wall made the flatlands a very noisy place to be. As they walked, Ringo looked at the princess and smiled. "It's surprisingly warm despite all of the ice!" He yelled.

The princess leaned in to hear. "What? She asked.

Ringo gave her a surprised look.

"The noise makes it difficult to hear. Maybe it's the effect of the cold. We all seem to be losing our gifts." She said looking at the guards.

Ringo turned and saw their difficulty in moving through the snow. Although it did not seem to bother them at first, the cold was beginning to take its toll on the Alustans. Ringo went into his pocket and handed her the piece of the crystal core the carved from the cave, and moved his hand next to his ear. Following his cue, she held the crystal next to her ear. In the distance, he saw Warrendr coming toward them. Ringo quickly placed the crystal in his pocket. Troldomen moved next to Ringo and looked at Warrendr.

"In our haste, we have left the provisions behind. Would it be better to go into Mantoo before we move on to Alkotten? Warrendr asked.

"I don't think so." Ringo answered.

"Why not?" Warrendr replied in an angry tone.

"Because we are here." Ringo said pointing to a large ice castle in the distance.

"I Thought Alkotten was at the top of the Great Mountain. Warrendr said looking at the distant castle in amazement.

"I guess I neglected to mention that we passed Mantoo on the air riders' days ago," Ringo answered. "Moreover our trek through the cave seems to have shortened our trip considerably," he continued. "It would seem that old Elwindor found the path he was looking for after all. We will consider stopping in Mantoo on the way back."

As they walked, Troldomen grumbled. "The castle looked far too close for us to walk this far, are we seeing an illusion?"

"I don't think so." Ringo said rubbing his eyes. "The deep snow slows our speed."

"I would hardly call this speed." Troldomen mumbled.

They walked a few minutes more and came to a large gap. They looked from side to side, but saw no way to cross across to reach the castle.

"I have heard the leaping ability of an Alustan guard is without equal." Ringo said.

"Do not believe all you hear Mantoo, even we cannot leap this distance." Warrendr answered.

"We may all have to fly." Troldomen added looking in the other direction. They all turned to see what he was looking at and saw what surely must be giant, hairy creature that was hunting them in the cave, slowly approaching them.

"What are our odds?" Ringo asked.

"I would say none right now, young master."

"I'll take that bet," Ringo said nervously. Ringo looked up and saw a tiny streak of light and fire pass high overhead. He smiled for a moment wondering if they had somehow changed the future after all.

"Look," he said pointing to the shooting star. "Is it too much to hope that by our reaching here, we have somehow changed our destiny Troldomen?"

"Anything is possible I suppose, but I think we need to focus on what's in our immediate future young master. It would seem we have a shared destiny with the beast that haunts our steps."

"Indeed in does," Ringo replied.

A chill went up his spine, as he faced the hairy beast. In a fleeting thought he wondered if he had gotten this far only to fail.

16 AUBAULTMOR

In Mantoo, Wyler sat in the courtyard looking at a life-sized statue of Ringo. He began to weep at the thought of never seeing his son again. A hand touched his shoulder from behind him. Wyler looked up to see that it was Wesley.

In the parlor, Dionne was waiting anxiously with a rolled scroll. Within moments, a short, old Mantoo in a dark cloak approached her. She handed him the scroll and bent down to whisper to him.

"Remember, absolutely no one must know where this came from." She said softly.

He nodded without saying a word and left as quietly as he entered. She quickly made her way to the throne room and turned her attention to the scroll Wyler had left on his throne. When she heard her father's voice in the distance, she placed the scroll back in its case and moved close to the door to listen. She opened it slightly so that she could hear her father and Wesley.

"I miss him too father, but I don't think Ringo has met his end," Wesley said. "Do not despair. Although you are without a doubt, the wisest and kindest in all of Mantoo, it could be argued that he is the bravest and the most cunning. And there is a lot one could say about those qualities," he continued.

Wyler cleared his throat and did his best to compose himself. "My son, I know you seek to comfort me with your words, and on any other day and for any other reason, I would be. But today is not a day like any other."

"Why Father"?

"I Fear I have truly sent your brother to his doom."

"Father…"

"What do the Mantoo citizens say about my luck?"

"Your luck?"

"Do not think that I do not hear the mumblings from the parlors of the less fortunate. We Mantoo gamble to pass our time. We have always done it. In doing so, we have failed to advance our halls with discoveries in science like Alusta or Alkotten. But I have done my best to give the people what they wanted. We Wantoos' above all others in Mantoo are very lucky. We win when no other Mantoo can. Many years ago, they thought to banish us all together. So what do they say about a kindly old king, that never loses?"

"They say you are too lucky. No one has such luck without ….."

"Without what? Cheating?

"Cheating…sometimes, but mostly magic. They say you have been granted such fortune through a spell. That you met a witch that granted you luck for the rest of your days; Luck that has passed to your children."

"That is what they say, is it?"

"Do not listen to them father. They do not …"

"They are not far from the truth Wesley."

"What? Father you don't mean… I …I don't understand."

"A long time ago, when I was just about your age, I went on a great adventure. Troldomen and I came across a cave that did bear the most dreadful warning. We ignored the warning and found, among other things, a scroll of great power, for it foretold the future. In our zeal to take all we could from the cave, we moved a large mystic stone, and accidentally unleashed a great evil on the great mountain. It was formless at first. It moved about like smoke before it took form, and resembled a great horned beast with glowing eyes. The spirit was dark, and cold; we could feel the darkness surround us as it grew. It called itself Aubaultmor, and it somehow looked into our souls and knew all there was to know about us. We were affected too, because we somehow knew of its plan to devour the very souls of all who dwelled on the mountain. But with this exchange of knowledge, we also knew how he came to be defeated and trapped within the cave. While it remained in the cave gaining its strength, we sought out Meccah from Alusta, and Brutus of Alkotten and combined minerals that are only found in each of our regions. They were formed into an orb and were placed into the fires of Alusta. The orb remained so hot that it glowed white until it was cooled in the ice of Alkotten. When it cooled it formed blackness darker than Aubaultmor himself. Troldomen and I were able to get close enough to him to cast the ancient spell found on one of the scrolls from the cave and we trapped his spirit within the orb. There was only room within the orb for his evil, so the orb expelled all else into those closest to it."

"You and Troldomen." Wesley said.

"Yes and when it was finished the orb shined a bright blue. His thirst for revenge caused Aubaultmor's heart to grow darker, and with each day the orb grew larger. We feared one day it would not be enough to contain his evil so we used another spell to bind his spirit inside the heart of the Great Mountain. The writing on the elder scroll changed and foretold of a time that Aubaultmor would walk again, two hundred years later, at a time when a blue comet passed over the Great Mountain from among the stars. The trapped Aubaultmor could not take his gifts into the core of the mountain; they would be left to his conquerors. Such is the ways things have always been. At first, we did not know what gifts were left to us. We only knew that there was a new power that each of us felt within our hands. As I said Aubaultmor kept all of his evil and gave us all else. I suppose Brutus was given whatever skill for science Aubaultmor possessed. Troldomen came to have the magic that was within him, and I received whatever good fortune was due him. It is a fortune that I have been able to pass to my children, who are considered the best gamblers on the mountain at such a young age."

"If fortune is on our side, then I don't understand why you despair father."

"The scrolls tell us that the blue comet arrives soon, and it marks Aubaultmor's return. I have done a great many things to prepare over the years, but I am not sure that I have done enough."

"So you thought Aubaultmor would return to the mountain and seek revenge on you, Troldomen, Brutus, and Meccah?"

"There is another prophecy that I fear; one I have not mentioned to anyone," Wyler said sadly.

Dionne pushed her ear as far out of the doorway as she could without being caught eavesdropping. She was expecting Wyler to say something, but the next thing he said caught her by surprise.

Wyler rubbed his beard and looked to the sky. "I fear the orb we cast Aubaultmor into is broken. I don't pretend to know how long, but I fear his essence has leaked to both Alusta and Alkotten. To what end, I do not know, but I fear he has worked to defeat us before we started. I do not know the extent of his efforts, but for all of our efforts, we are not prepared."

"Aubaultmor!" Wesley said excitedly. "The demon that haunted our dreams as children? You used to tell us the tales of how you banished him to the outer realm, but if ever he returned we could destroy him with a magic Mantoo muffin."

Wyler smiled. "Yes Aubaultmor. I told all of you that story when you were young."

"So, the stories were real?" Dionne said coming from behind the door where she was listening. "If that is so, was the method of killing him also real? Did you really have to trick him into eating a magic muffin?"

"No, Aubaultmor does not eat. He opens his mouth only to breathe fire and ash." Wyler answered.

"Then how will we kill him with it?" Wesley asked in a tone of desperation.

"I have a better question father." Dionne interrupted. "Father, I read a scroll this morning and…"

Before she could finish, a loud rumbling filled the air. The sky grew dark and day turned to night in an instant. Wyler looked to the sky and saw the blue comet passing overhead. Wesley could hardly believe what he was seeing.

"Is it him father? Is it Aubaultmor?" Dionne said rushing into his arms.

"I fear it is. It is the sign of his coming. This is far too soon. How is this possible? Blessed spirit be with us."

"Ringo will find a way to beat him father, as you have. He is his father's son; he will find a way." Wesley said confidently.

"You have great faith in your brother." Wyler said watching the comet fall out of sight.

"You do also father or you would not have sent him." Dionne added.

Wyler smiled. "Yes I do have faith in him. I have gambled heavily upon him."

Deep within the core of the mountain, the large armored figure stiffly walked through the caverns away from his prison. As he made his way through the inner caverns of the Great Mountain toward freedom, Aubaultmor extended his arm to touch the nearby wall. As he dragged his hand along the wall, a large amount of dense rock turned to dust at his touch. He continued to look straight ahead as he labored forward. He kept touching the cave walls as he moved. The dust produced from the walls he touched, fell to the floor and covered his steps as he walked. His strength grew with each step, and Aubaultmor made fist with his other hand as he walked into the darkness.

17 ALKOTTEN

The air around Ringo was thick with fright. The huge, hairy creature continued its slow and steady trek toward them. Ringo leaned over to Troldomen gave him a small bump. "Would that spell you did on the Tikats work on something this big? He cannot be any more ferocious than they were."

"He is a big as ten Tikats!"

"Then use ten times the spell."

Before anyone could move, Warrendr shot a fire dart at the creature, but with speed that defied his size, the beast knocked it to the ground. The dart quickly melted the snow where it landed and made a large puddle of water. The beast stepped into the puddle on his way to Warrendr, but was stuck as the puddle quickly froze over. He roared loudly, which caused the Alustans to cover their ears in pain.

Ringo looked at the foot of the beast frozen in the puddle and grabbed Troldomen by the arm. "Hold him off," he yelled to the guards. They stopped close to the edge of the gap in the mountain. He bent over and looked Troldomen in the eye.

"Do you have a spell to make wind?"

"I have several, but what would you need them up here for? Don't you feel this breeze?" he said with as much sarcasm a he could muster.

"Focus! Do you have a spell for fire?"

"Yes, but it's too hot to manage once it gets started." Troldomen replied.

Ringo turned around and saw the princess. "Dinatru I need your help," he yelled.

She cast a worried glance at the large creature making its way toward them and ran over to Ringo. "Warrendr and the guards are managing the beast right now princess; I need you to help me for a moment. Can you do that?" he asked calmly.

Ringo quickly turned to Troldomen. "Can she hold the fire?" he asked.

Troldomen nodded. "Her skin is used to it, but the sudden change in temperature…is harmful to them."

"How would you know that?" Dinatru asked.

"Princess I cannot do something that will put you in harm's way," Ringo protested.

"If I do nothing, we will all be in harm's way," she replied. He looked at her and waited for some form of assurance. When she nodded, Ringo looked to Troldomen with confidence. "Give her the spell." Ringo yelled.

Troldomen shielded the bottle from the harsh winds and poured a small amount of dust into her hand while he whispered the spell in her ear. The three of them looked at Warrendr and the guards who were trying to keep the creature at bay by shooting more fire darts. Their swiftness was the only thing keeping them from the creature's claws. Ringo was impressed, but knew that they could not keep up the pace forever. The creature punched at the ice boot it received earlier and smashed it to pieces. Now it could move faster, which made the situation all the more desperate. Ringo turned back toward the castle. He nodded to Troldomen then looked at Dinatru.

"Alright Princess it's up to you. When Troldomen blows the snow into the gap, you follow behind it with the fire. Do you remember the spell?"

She managed to flash them a very nervous smile and nodded her head.

Ringo looked at Troldomen. "What are our odds?"

"They grow thinner each moment." Troldomen snapped.

Ringo yelled "Go!" Troldomen chanted a few words and the wind began to blow the snow from all around him in a strange pattern across the large gap. Dinatru quickly chanted the words Troldomen taught her, and the dust in her hand began to sparkle and burst into flames. She chanted the words again, and the fire began to shoot from her hand across the crevice. She pointed the end of the flame in the direction of the snow with a slow wave of her hand. When she was finished, she clenched her fist and the flame was gone. She stared at her hand and was amazed that she could hold such a fire and not receive a single burn. She looked up when Ringo yelled, "You did it." and saw that a bridge made of ice had formed over the gap.

Ringo screamed "Let's go!" and the three of them quickly crossed to the other side. Warrendr quickly followed them to the middle of the bridge and turned around to see where his guards were. When he saw that all three were running behind him, Warrendr ran to the other side with Ringo, Troldomen and Dinatru. He turned around in time to see the creature snatch one on the guards in its massive claws. The creature closed its grip and squeezed with its long thumb nail into the belly of the guard. The creature's nail pierced his body with relative ease, which caused the other two guards to gasp with fear. Warrendr looked on in disbelief as the monster placed the guard in its mouth and began to chew. It quickly noticed the other two guards on the bridge and lunged itself in the air after them. They were almost to the other side, when the creature's heavy body came crashing down on the bridge. The ice bridge shattered beneath them, sending the guards and the beast into the gap.

The creature fell hundreds of feet below the bridge before it managed to grab onto a jagged cliff. Although it was able to stop its fall, the two remaining guards fell all the way to the bottom, and into a flowing river. The bodies of the guards continued to be pushed downstream by the river until it turned into a waterfall. Their bodies went over the falls and into the Alustan Sea, where at least fifty other falls delivered water into the ocean.

Ringo looked over the side, but could not see the beast or the guards from his vantage point.

"They are gone," Warrendr said calmly. "We must press on," he continued.

Ringo gently lifted Dinatru's hands and looked at them. He smiled when he saw that she was unharmed by the fire. Warrendr quickly swatted Ringo's hands away from his sister's and stood between them.

"I am making certain she was not hurt," Ringo said sternly.

"No one touches the Princess without the consent of the King," Warrendr fired.

As they turned and began walking away, Ringo watched them for a moment and rubbed his arm in the place Warrendr hit. He looked at Troldomen as he began walking and whispered "Then I guess no one will ever touch the Princess."

Warrendr politely said "I heard that," without turning around.

Ringo walked alongside Troldomen and said "I bet you did," to which Dinatru playfully said "We heard that too."

The four surviving members of Ringo's party made their way to the ice castle, which was the largest single structure any of them had ever seen. Everything from the columns to the steps was sculpted from ice. The front portion of the castle rested against the mountain's north-east side. They looked at the gigantic doors at the castle entrance in awe.

"I would wager that this goes deep within the mountain." Ringo said in awe of the structure.

"Yes it does," Troldomen said confidently. "What you see before you is the façade. The majority of Alkotten is built within the mountain. So you see Warrendr, the idea of building this on the very top was never an option."

Warrendr nodded his head in agreement and continued to marvel at the size of the castle. They followed Troldomen to the main door and gazed in amazement at the fifty-foot doorway. Dinatru noticed that one of the designs in the door was actually a small gong made out of ice. She hit the gong with a small ice mallet that was attached to it by a chain also made from ice. The sound rang out like two fine crystal glasses, and as soon as the ringing stopped, the gigantic doors opened.

Ringo and Warrendr walked through first. The room was completely empty, but each of them noticed another large crystal door at other end. They walked over to the door and stood in front of it for a moment. Ringo studied the fine carvings and craftsmanship around the door and extended his hand to touch the crystal. Before any of them could say a word, the door opened, and a tall, thin male dressed entirely in white stood in the doorway and looked them over. His hair and face were as white as snow. His pupils were a very pale blue. He stared at Warrendr and Dinatru for a moment, but did not move.

"We come seeking council with King Brutus of Alkotten." Ringo said.

"Two Mantoos and two Alustans are here. Where are the other three Alustans? The tall figure asked still starring at Warrendr and Dinatru. Warrendr began to speak, but Ringo cut him off. "I wear the crown of Mantoo, and the law of the mountain guarantees me council with Brutus." Ringo snapped.

This caught the Alkottenian's attention, and he turned his gaze on Ringo.

"King Brutus." The tall Alkottenian said correcting him. "And does the young Mantoo king have a name?"

Ringo looked at Dinatru and smiled. He turned his host and proudly said, "I am King Ringo Wantoo, son of Wyler, and Lord of Mantoo and all of its provinces."

The Alkottenian looked impressed. "Well met milord. Does anyone else wear a crown?" He asked of the group.

"We are Prince and Princess of Alusta," Warrendr said proudly.

"But you are neither king nor queen of Alusta," the Alkottenian quipped.

When nothing else was said, he turned back to Ringo and said, "You alone may see King Brutus."

Troldomen interjected and said, "Do you have any place safer for us to wait? There was a rather large and hairy creature that pursued us without pause."

"It killed three of my best men!" Warrendr said angrily.

"Aye. It would have killed the lot of us if he wasn't so heavy." Troldomen added.

"Are you not from Alusta? The land of liquid fire, the land of endless night, the land of steaming, sweltering molten lakes, and ash?"

"I am of Alusta." Warrendr said proudly.

"Then the Hoynarr was doing exactly what it was created to do."

"And what would that be?" Dinatru said. She was obviously offended and did not mind showing it.

"It protects us Princess Dinatru?"

"So you do know who I am, but who are you? And what do you

mean by "it was created?" To protect you from what?" She asked firmly.

"You ask a lot of questions for a visiting princess," he said sharply.

"I only need one answered." She snapped.

"And you shall have it," he fired.

Suddenly the floor began to sink, then turned and slid into a completely different room under the ice. Walls rose up around them, and they found themselves in a room made entirely of crystal and Ice. The floor was covered in a thin mist, and everything, including the furniture in the room seemed to be made from ice or crystal. There were guards surrounding the throne that looked exactly like their host. In the center of the room was an empty Crystal throne that was more beautiful than anything Ringo had ever seen. The Alkottenian left their side and walked across the room to the throne. He placed the crown on the table next to it on his head, and took up his scepter and sat down on the throne.

"I like answering my own door," He smiled. "If you're all done looking surprised, I can officially bid you welcome. Welcome to Alkotten one and all; my name is Brutus."

18 THE HUNDEN

Gallra was asleep in his tree and began to dream. He dreamed of a time long ago when the Farrador walked the mountain, before there was a village, and a place they could call home. In his dream, Gallra saw the Farrador walking in single file moving across rough terrain in the snow. He saw his father at the front of the line talking to the other males, while he, just a youngling, was in a warm pack on his mother's back. He saw the Farrador bravely moving across a thin, icy ledge on the side of the great mountain. He could hear them begin to screen in horror as they looked up toward the ice above them. His heart raced in his sleep as he saw the snow and ice crash down on top them. He began to sweat in his sleep as he dreamed that some were swept completely off the side of the ledge and fell off of the mountain. He saw darkness as he and his parents were buried under snow and remembered of the cold and the darkness. He saw Onkeel pick him up, remove the snow from his eyes, and then pass him to another. He saw the warriors' frantically digging in the snow to find survivors. He saw his parents lying motionless in the snow and ice. He saw everyone turn their heads to Isantor. He saw himself as a youngling crying out to his motionless mother, who did not answer.

Gallra woke from the dream breathing heavy and covered in sweat. He made his way to his feet and walked over to a large wooden bowl of water that was on a small wooden table against the wall. He splashed some of the water on his face and grabbed his scope as he walked out of the tree house and on to a large branch. He took a deep breath and looked through the scope toward the rising sun. The looked at the village and noticed that the Farrador were unusually active at this early hour. Hardly anyone in the camp slept at all. Looking through the scope, Gallra saw Onkeel walk up to Isantor after leaving the hut used to store the smoked meat. Onkeel shook his head from left to right, gesturing the negative. Isantor gave a small nod acknowledging that the meat supply was low, and with winter so close, they had no choice but to hunt. They could hardly wage a war, or survive, for that matter, without food.

Isantor left with a hunting party of ten warriors. He left Onkeel and Woodah in charge of securing the camp. Fetter and most of the young men went with the hunting party, but Dunau, Yuandro and Dyken, stayed behind. They watched as Dunau sharpened his spear. He had a very faraway look in his eyes, which frightened them a bit.

Yuandro could no longer sit in silence. "The tip of that spear is sharp enough to cut through the mountain Dunau. Why do you keep at it?" he asked.

Dunau ignored the question, but smiled when he felt the tip of the spear. He maintained the faraway look as he spoke.

"When the Sun came days ago, my brother and I were part of a great hunt. Though we did not catch our quarry, we came back with fowl large enough to feed the entire camp. Before the sun could rise again today, he was taken; eaten by those dogs like some rabbit or mouse. He was a great warrior and did not deserve to die in the jaws of those dogs. I will have my revenge on the dogs that took him, and the pitiful mouse that caused all of this."

"Dunau," Yuandro pleaded.

"I don't care what Isantor said, Yuandro! It makes no sense to hunt right now. If we declare war on the Hunden, we can use them for meat to get us through the winter. We are Farrador, we eat what we kill. We could get revenge and fill the storeroom in one blow."

A voice from the entrance of the hut said, "When you hunger for revenge there is no meal that will fill your belly young one." Onkeel said from the entranceway

"What do you want Onkeel?" Dunau fired.

"I want to know that every female and youngling left in my care will be safe. I want the storeroom filled enough to take us through the winter because our survival depends on it. I want every young warrior on his post doing what our leader expects of us. I want to take the pain that you are feeling away from you, but I cannot. And since I cannot, I want you to use the anger inside you to avenge your brother when the moment is at hand. But you cannot create that moment, it will come to you. You must be ready when it comes. If you try to create the moment you deliver yourself into the hands of the enemy, and risk all of our lives as well. You sharpen your spear and that is good, because your enemy will have teeth just as sharp. But he sharpens his mind, and will be cunning. He is hoping that in your despair, you act out of rage, and become mindless. And when that happens, you will become food for your enemy."

"Do you think I plan to become food for those dogs?" He asked angrily.

"Either they will be food for us, or us for them, but that will not depend on who has sharper teeth, or the sharper spear. It will depend on who has the sharper mind." Onkeel shouted.

"I sharpen my spear to be as prepared as I can for war with these dogs, and I by my brother's spirit I swear…I will kill Stygg before the new moon rises," Dunau declared with confidence.

"Stygg? Stygg! You will be lucky to kill a Hunden pup."

"Luck will have nothing to do with it. It is only by skill that I…"

"That you avoid getting yourself killed. The Hunden are not mindless elk or birds. Only the greatest warriors can…"

"And who is the greatest warrior among us Onkeel? Is it not Isantor? And yet, he only killed two Hunden, when they attacked."

"Isantor was killing Hunden before you were born. I once saw him kill six Hunden in a single battle." Onkeel said proudly.

"Six Hunden?" Dyken asked, obviously impressed by the number.

"That was before Stygg became their leader." Dunau snapped. "No one has killed more than three in battle since Stygg took leadership of the pack; not even Isantor. I will kill seven when next we meet; more than any Farrador before me. Even Stygg himself will fall to my spear."

"Dunau the wrong kind of confidence can get you killed in battle." Onkeel said, while turning to depart.

"The Hunden attacked us when every warrior was here, including Isantor. Did they have the wrong kind of confidence Onkeel?" Dunau lashed out.

Gallra was still in his tree looking through his scope. He stopped to rub his eyes for a brief moment. He was tired because he had been up all night secretly building things around the camp. He looked at the guards surveying the land from their posts on the hills that surrounded the camp. When he did not see anything exciting, he went into the tree-house and took a boomerang from the wall. He placed it into his waistband and went back outside. He looked through the scope once more and saw the warriors moving down the mountain a few miles from the camp. He looked at the area surrounding the camp, and saw movement in the bushes on the start of the hunting trail. He adjusted his scope for a better look and saw the bushes shake a bit more. He decided that it was the wind, and turned to look at the guard posts again. When he focused on the far post and noticed the guard was missing. He quickly looked to another and found it empty as well. He began to breathe heavily and looked to the third post. He turned just in time to see the silhouette of a guard get snapped up into the jaws of one of the Hunden. Gallra quickly turned his scope on the bushes he saw moving earlier. A dozen Hunden broke from behind the bushes and quietly ran toward the Farrador camp. Gallra took a crossbow from its place on one of the branches and placed the scope on a holder made into the bow. He took careful aim through the scope and fired a single shot. The arrow cut a rope a few feet in front of the Hunden. The rope was holding back a large tree limb. When it was cut free, the large limb swung down and knocked three of the Hunden into the air.

The other charging Hunden noticed, but continued their charge. Gallra fired another shot. The arrow hit a stick that was holding a rock wedged into the mountain, which triggered a rockslide that fell on top of five of the Hunden. The sound of the rockslide caused the Farrador warriors at the camp to rush the camp entrance. Gallra took a horn from his waistband and blew into it. A few miles away, the hunting party heard the horn, and stopped in their tracks.

Fetter looked back toward the camp. "That's Gallra! The camp is under attack," he yelled.

Every member of the hunting party ran toward the camp as fast as their feet would carry them.

In the distance, Stygg watched the tree that Gallra was in from the moment he heard the horn. One of the scouts ran up to him and bowed.

"There are traps that they must have set in the night." The scout said panting out of breath.

Stygg looked at him and snarled. "I thought I gave orders to eliminate all of their scouts," he said.

"I thought we did." The scout answered.

"Fool, you missed one, and now he has alerted the others. Their hunting party is miles away by now, so keep to the plan; press the attack. I will take care of this one myself."

Still perched in the tree, Gallra shot another arrow, which cut a rope near the entrance of the camp. When the rope was severed, it sent the thorny bushes placed on each side of the camp entrance hurling toward the oncoming Hunden. The Hunden in the front the line saw the bushes coming and leaped out of the way, but the ones behind them were struck forcefully with the bushes and cried out in pain.

Hearing the horn also, the entire camp went on alert. Onkeel and a hand full of young warriors ran to the entrance armed with spear, bows, and large wooden shields. Dunau and his party joined them.

"Now I will have my revenge" Dunau said looking at Onkeel.

They readied themselves as the Hunden approached. Gallra watched from his perch and ran back into the tree house. He grabbed three boomerangs, two wooden and one metal, and then ran out to the limb. Suddenly the tree shook violently enough to knock him to the ground. He scrambled to his feet and felt a cold chill run through him when he heard the deep unmistakable laughter that he had heard it the night before. He pressed his body up against the tree and watched as Stygg came out of the darkness provided by the bushes near the tree.

"I have seen you before. There is hardly any meat on your bones and yet look at what you accomplished so early in the morning. Of all the Farrador, who would think that you could have killed so many Hunden? Skinny two-leg, I could kill you with one bite. And to amuse myself…I think I will."

19 THE DEAD ZONE

There was a large cave entrance on the north end of the Great Mountain near the barren lands. There were no trees or life on that part of the mountain. The ground was hard and dense, and the sun never seemed to shine there. The Alusta called it the dead zone because not even the fire water that warmed the mountain ran through it.

An ancient dialect that had not been spoken in several hundred years came from the inside of the cave. The voice was deep and menacing, and every word seemed to shake the mountain around it. The soil began to crumble as Aubaultmor passed his hand over it and continued to speak the ancient spell. The dead zone seemed to respond to his voice. The rocks, dirt and ash move toward him and formed a circle around him. The mixture began to swirl around him until he was fully engulfed. A glowing light shined from within the swirling mixture and became brighter and brighter. But as suddenly as it began, the dust storm ended. Aubaultmor stood tall as the dust quickly settled to the ground around him. His black armor gleamed as if the dust storm he created had polished it. He clenched his fist and took his first breath of fresh air. When he breathed out, flames burst from his mouth. He closed his mouth and smiled. He raised his hands and shot fire balls into the side of the mountain from his palms. Aubaultmor roared in delight and continued to blast away at the mountain. He looked at his palms, which continued to smolder after he stopped blasting the mountainside, and clenched his fist as he looked upwards. Aubaultmor stepped toward the mountain side and, grabbing a ledge, began to climb. As he ascended from the dead zone he looked upwards and said only one word in the Great Mountain's common tongue, "Mantoo."

In Mantoo, Dionne, Wyler and Wesley ran into the courtyard after the minor earthquake stopped. Wyler closed his eyes looked toward the sky.

"He is here," he said.

Clouds began to fill the sky and the air grew cold.

"Do not despair father." Wesley assured him. "Ringo is quite resourceful."

Wesley ran back into the castle and took his father's feather pen up from the desk. He dipped the pen in ink and wrote something on a piece of parchment. Wesley ran outside and gave out a loud and steady whistle.

"What are you doing?" Wyler asked.

Wesley held his arm out and looked to the sky. "I am sending a message."

The falcon dropped out of the sky and landed on his arm. He tied the message to the bird's leg and looked the bird in the eye.

"Tara, find Ringo," he said.

"You are breaking the Maisha-Vad. You cannot help your brother." Wyler screamed as the bird flew into the air and quickly disappeared.

"Father, I am fully aware that under the terms of the Maisha-Vad, I cannot help him on his quest. I am simply paying my debt for a lost wager."

"What was the wager?" Wyler asked.

"When we lost mother you cried for three days. I said you cried enough for a lifetime and had no more tears. Ringo said you would cry at least once more. Even through the funeral of family and friends throughout the years, you did not cry. I thought I would win."

"So you wrote him to tell him he won your wager?"

"No, I am paying the debt."

"I did not see you give the bird any gold."

"Gold was not the prize."

"No gold? Then what was it?"

"Ringo has won my secret recipe for Mantoo muffin."

Wyler thought for a moment and then smiled. "Mantoo Muffin? Ah yes, Mantoo Muffin…quite delectable on a long journey," he nodded. "I pray the bird knows the way."

Wesley watched Tara disappear and grinned proudly. "In the meantime Father, we have a war to wage. With Ringo gone, I guess that makes me captain. It's about time too, all that training for all these years and not one battle," he said wiping the sweat from his head?

"Wesley, what's wrong with you? You're sweating profusely." Dionne asked as they moved back into the castle.

"This is no game my son. Our enemy wishes to destroy every Mantoo to the last, beginning with me." Wyler said, ignoring Dionne's comments.

"He was beaten before; surely he can be beaten again. The only question is how will we find him father?"

"Find him?" Wyler snickered. "I do not think we will have to look very hard. I suppose that a part of him, however small, is within me. He will be nothing more than darkness and evil incarnate, but I have all that was luck in him once, and he should know where to find it. No, we do not have to find him my son, he will find me."

Dionne placed her hand on Wesley's head. He quickly pushed it away. "Stop it!" he ordered.

"You're burning up with fever. What have you been doing?" She asked.

"Nothing. I had a small lunch and then I came to see father."

"What did you eat?"

"Soup," he said shaking his head in an attempt to clear the fuzziness.

Wyler placed both hands on his cheeks and looked into his eyes. "Dionne go down the hall and tell the crier to come here," he said calmly. As she ran out of the room Wyler moved Wesley a chair that was close by. "Be still Wesley. We must tend to this illness."

"I feel fine," he said as the sickness began to take hold of him.

The Royal Crier quickly returned with Dionne and bowed.

"No time for that now." Wyler ordered. "Find my doctor and bring him here with all haste. Then go to the blue garden. There is a flower there that has seven petals on each stem; bring three."

The Crier left quickly, and Dionne looked at her brother fearfully. Wyler took note to her look and nodded. "This is no time to be afraid my dear. There is much to do."

"Then what would you have me to do father?" She said bravely.

"We must fight. We fight or we will surely die. You are third in line within the house of Wantoo. In the absence of both of your brothers, you are the Captain of the guard. Fulfill your duty. Muster the Army."

20 DEVONSIRE'S DEAL

In a small gambling parlor just north of the Mortorton border with Bublem sat four elders. The parlor was dark and loud, but it was the kind of place where people minded their own business. The tables were made of an old wood that had lost its color long ago, but retained what seemed to be the smell of every drop of ale throughout the ages. The windows had heavy drapes on them to keep out the light, but at the corner table where the elders sat, a bit of light seeped through. Lady Arna took a sip from her cup and looked across the table at Devonsire, Swoggle and Dugan Shipnor. She waited until the server placed all of the food from her tray on the table and walked away before saying anything to the other elders.

"I do not understand why in the midst of the impending destruction we elect this course of action?" Lady Arna asked.

Swoggle took a sip of ale. He wiped his mouth with his right hand and extended his left. Devonsire placed a gold coin in the open hand.

"What?" Arna asked insulted by the gesture.

"Swoggle said you would be the first to question whether what we were doing was right. I lost."

"The nerve." She said looking at the door. "Oh she's here. Move over Swoggle so she has someplace to sit."

"Lady Tulip," The four greeted her in turn as the large woman smiled and sat down. Without saying a word, she immediately began picking at the food on the table.

Lady Tulip was the eldest daughter of the August Elderbee, Mantoo's most famous judge and law-writer. Since she was little, the old judge had spoiled her with colorfully loud dresses and food. Despite her age, she continued to wear dresses that had the most colorful, floral patterns and the biggest hats in Mantoo. She also carried a very large purse, which was almost always stuffed with food.

"Do you have it?" Arna asked of Lady Tulip.

Lady Tulip was the type of person that liked knowing everyone's business. She would often hold long conversations and eat simultaneously, which disturbed those not used to her mannerisms. She nodded her head to acknowledge Arna, but took a moment to swallow the piece of cake that she placed in her mouth. Before Lady Arna could repeat her question, Tulip said, "I do."

She slid a rolled scroll across the table to Lady Arna and let out a large belch.

"Of course this cannot be my usual fee. If it is as important as you say, my fee will be double."

"Why that's robbery." Dugan said, wiping the ale from his beard.

"Call it what you will, it is still my price." Lady Tulip snapped.

Lady Arna unrolled the scroll and studied it. She looked at the others who were waiting impatiently for her response. She gave a single nod, and Dugan passed two gold coins to Swoggle and Devonsire.

"By the way…why is this so important? It is just looks like a tree with words on some of the leaves." Lady Tulip asked slyly.

"Oh my Lady, it is far more than that." Swoggle replied.

"Then what is it exactly?" She asked. When no one answered, lady Tulip looked around the table and popped another piece of cake into her mouth.

"It is exactly worth double the price." Lady Arna said firmly while rolling it up so no one else could see it.

Lady Tulip stood up and smiled. "Well I take my leave of you then. I trust you will know what to do with this rather valuable piece of information?"

Dugan lifted his hand to order another round of drinks. "Don't leave just yet lass, stay and celebrate with us," he said. Lady Arna sat down and pulled out her folded fan, and began to wave it in front of her face.

"I could use a cool drink and more cake of course. So, whatever are we celebrating?" Lady Tulip asked.

They were quiet until the barkeep brought over five pints of ale on a large tray. He placed the tray on the table and exchanged the full glasses on the tray for the empty ones at the table before returning to the bar.

Dugan leaned over to lady Tulip and whispered, "We are celebrating a changing of the guard," he had a bag of blue flowers sitting under the table.

"What guard?" She whispered back placing a peanut in her mouth.

Lady Arna looked around the room to make sure no one was listening.

"It would seem that the Mantoo is about to get a new Captain and very soon… a new King" Swoggle whispered.

"What are you talking about dearie? There isn't but one King around these parts." Lady Tulip snapped.

"You are mistaken my dear, you are in the presence of royalty." Arna said.

Lady Tulip looked amused "Royalty? My dear, who are you referring to?" she asked.

Before lady Arna could speak Dugan gestured to Devonsire on his right and said, "Devonsire; the true king of Mantoo."

21 THE ICY THRONE

Brutus sat back in the icy throne and smiled unpleasantly at his guests. "I have seen this plot before" He said slyly. His voice seemed to fill the royal chamber as he spoke. "I am aware of how it plays itself out. You see the royal children, while little more than a distraction, are not the peacemakers they claim to be. Isn't that right princess? They are here to find the hidden pass to Mantoo, and to discover the nature of the new weapon I have crafted. Am I not correct Prince Warrendr?

"You seem to know more about the intentions of each peacemaker than I do King Brutus." Ringo said looking at the princess. "How is this possible?"

"How is what possible? How all of you could come this far with less than noble intentions and not have killed each other by now? Brutus said playfully. "You are certainly learning a lot on your quest for enlightenment. Your father must be proud Ringo," he continued.

"King Ringo." Ringo said correcting him. Ringo noticed that Brutus shifted his position and scowled at being corrected. He didn't like it at all.

Troldomen paid special attention to Brutus and his mannerisms while he spoke. He sensed something was wrong, but did not want to alert the others until his suspicions could be validated.

"King Brutus you know much, of this I am certain. You may very well be the wisest man on the mountain. Will you not share a bit of your wisdom with those who come seeking it?" Ringo asked politely.

"And what of your mission of peace? It would not be wise for me to grant each of you the knowledge you seek. Warrendr seeks knowledge of my weapons and strength. He also seeks something from you. He seeks the pass to Mantoo as well. I would not provide him with either of these things, lest I seduce my so-called allies into becoming my enemies."

"Is such a thing possible? Dinatru asked.

"Alusta history has a way of repeating itself, does it not Troldomen?" Brutus asked.

"What does he mean by that sorcerer?" Warrendr asked.

All eyes turned to Troldomen, who had been very quiet up until this point.

"You've hardly spoken a word since we arrived in Alkotten." Dinatru added.

"And what would the wizard tell you Princess? Tales of betrayal and deceit? Would he tell you that your father rewrote Alusta history? Would he tell you all he knows I wonder," Brutus devilishly snickered.

Again all eyes were upon Troldomen, and now he had no choice but to speak. "That is more than enough!" Troldomen said sternly.

"Very well wizard." Brutus nodded. "I shall let you tell them."

"King Brutus, with all due respect, there is more going on here than I can lay a hand on at the moment. Firstly, I do not think their father sent them here for a lesson on…"

"Their father sent them here to kill me!" Brutus shouted. "To restart a war that ended over a hundred years ago."

"My father would never do such a thing." Dinatru lashed out. "He is good and proud. He sent us here to extend the peace."

"No." Troldomen said dropping his head. "He did not. Your brother and his men were given instruction by your father. They were given a war-stone and told when they were close enough, to set it ablaze. The explosion would kill the one carrying the stone, but each was willing to sacrifice for what they thought was the greater good."

"How did you come to this knowledge?" Warrendr asked.

Brutus laughed coldly. "Alustans' are not the only ones on the mountain that hear everything young prince. Were those not the words spoken in Alusta nearly a week ago?" Brutus said holding a very smug look on his face.

Ringo looked at Brutus who seemed to be enjoying a victory that was not apparent to everyone else.

"Answer my question!" Warrendr shouted. "No one has the ears of Alusta save the Alustans. How is it you know these things?"

Brutus made the slightest gesture with his hand and a guard pulled a rope on the left wall of the throne room. A panel in the wall slid open, and a tall figure moved across the mist covered floor on top of a thick sheet of ice. The figure was dark and muscular and looked to be from Alusta. He held his head down, while his arms where pinned to his sides. Dinatru tried to look at his face, but his long hair was course and matted, which hid his features from them. He had many scars on his body, which given the toughness of Alustan skin, was as incredible feat.

"Who is this?" Warrendr asked Brutus. You have taken one of our citizens' captive to spy on us? This is enough to be considered an act of war."

"Oh were it so, great Warrendr. This Alustan is here of his own free will," Brutus answered.

"You used an Alustan to listen to us? To be your spy?"

"You assume too much young prince. And you are overstating the gifts of your kin. While Alustans can hear great distances, I've yet to meet one that could use only his ears to hear beyond your borders,"

Brutus said confidently. "They use Kama-stones strategically placed throughout the mountain to hear things that their ears cannot tell them," He continued.

"O'craru crystals?" Ringo asked.

Dinatru nodded and turned back to Warrendr.

"Is this how you claim to know so much of my father's intentions?

"Then you admit to the plot to kill me?" Brutus fired.

"I admit nothing." Warrendr fired back angrily. He turned to the Alustan. "Speak your name," he demanded.

"The prisoner slowly lifted his head, and rolled his eyes toward Dinatru and said, "Forste."

Warrendr moved the hair from Forste' face. "What have they done to you?" he whispered.

"We have made certain ….modifications to him." Brutus said wryly.

"Modifications? How did you pierce his skin? This is sorcery."

"It is not sorcery Prince Warrendr. This is science. I have improved his hearing and increased his strength. Unlike the rest of his kind, he can hear Meccah sneeze on his throne." Brutus said grinning.

"We too have science King Brutus, yet we use it to better the lives of our people. Dinatru said as she walked over to Forste and studied him. "I know you." She said. "This male was a criminal in Alusta. He was banished when I was but a child, but I remember. It was the time of the great hunger. You were stealing food from the palace pantry to feed your children you said. You were a guard there. Father would not have his own children going hungry, so his punishment was swift and severe. He banished you."

"In the presence of my own children." Forste said.

"I do not recall any other children there, just Warrendr and me. We were both so small, but so great is the memory of an Alustan, that we can remember such things." Dinatru said looking at Ringo.

"Do you remember your mother young one?" Forste asked.

"No, she died as I was born."

"What of you, great Warrendr?"

Warrendr looked around not knowing what to say. "Simple things really. Just images. Why do you ask these things?"

"My wife died at the birth of my daughter. In the time of the great hunger I had to feed my younglings, who were already so small and frail. My son was so handsome, and my daughter; bright and beautiful. I placed a blue fire comb in her hair that day. When Meccah held court, he banished me not only from the home I loved, but from my children. There were no other children in court save my own."

Dinatru pulled the blue fire comb from her hair and stared at it. "Where did you get a blue fire comb to place in your daughter hair?

Mine is the only one I've ever seen?"

Troldomen stepped forward and appealed to Brutus. "King Brutus please, you must end this."

"Must I? It is far too late for that now Troldomen. We have all faced lies for far too long. It is time the truth be told. Do you not agree?"

Troldomen rubbed his beard. He cleared his throat and began speaking.

"Before the peace, there was a great war. All that lived on the mountain fought for control of the three lands. Many souls were lost in those days and from them, a great evil was formed. The evil was defeated by the combined might of all those on the mountain. In the wake of our victory, new minerals and precious rocks were found on the mountain. One of the Alusta royal guards found a blue stone that seemed to harbor a blue flame around it. He quickly took it to the Alustan Utvinder, who crafted it into a comb for his young daughter's hair. This is the tale I heard."

Dinatru was filled with conflicting emotions. "If I am following this correctly, then you were that guard. If that is so, then how did I come to have the comb?"

"Perhaps your father gave it to you after he allowed my children to starve to death." Forste said in despair.

"My father would never do that!" Dinatru lashed out.

Brutus took that moment to interject a few words of his own. "The Meccah I know would do such a thing Princess, but in this case I believe you are correct. Those children did not starve to death did they Forste?"

"No they did not," he answered softly. "They live. They were not taken with starvation; my children are alive." Forste said happily.

"If his children are alive, then how did I come to have this comb? Is there another comb such as this on the mountain?" Dinatru asked again.

"There is only one such comb on the entire mountain Princess." Troldomen said. "And there has only ever been one bearer. It was crafted for a beautiful Alustan girl that would scarcely remember a single day without it."

Dinatru's hands began to shake. "No, that can't be true, she began. "What you're saying is that this...this is..."

"Your real father." Brutus laughed.

22 THE UTVINDER

Outside the Farrador camp, Gallra and Stygg were walking in circles around each other.

"You are called Stygg?" Gallra asked.

"What of it? You desire to know the name of Hunden that will feast on you before you die?"

Gallra stood up straight. "I have killed many Hunden this morning. I desire to know the name of the biggest one I'll kill today."

Stygg leaped at him, enraged by his words. Gallra pulled on a vine hanging overhead and was thrust into the air. Stygg hit the tree truck with his head and was dazed. As Gallra gently landed on the ground, another Hunden came out of the bushes and tried to attack him from behind. Gallra reached into his pouch and threw round nuts on the floor and moved out of the way as the Hunden guard slid right into Stygg. Gallra ran toward the camp, while Stygg and the other Hunden struggled to their feet.

They ran after Gallra as quickly as they could. As Gallra reached the camp, the sunrise provided the light he needed. Gallra turned back toward Stygg and threw his wooden boomerang. It passed over their heads as they charged. "He missed." Stygg yelled. "Kill him!" Gallra turned back toward the camp and ran to his left. The Hunden guard chased him, but was hit from behind by the returning boomerang. When he did not get up, Stygg ran over to him picked the boomerang up in his teeth. He easily snapped it into pieces and snarled. He ran after Gallra, who was now just outside the camp entrance.

Onkeel was doing his best to hold off the Hunden at the entrance. Oku, the Hundens' youngest warrior attacked, but was met with Dunau 's spear. Dunau killed six Hunden before Ronka, Stygg's oldest son charged. He grabbed the spear from Dunau 's hand and broke it with a single bite.

Dunau pulled out his knife and walked toward Ronka. As Ronka charged, Dunau rolled out of the way and grabbed the half of his broken spear that was left on the ground. He lifted the spear as Ronka jumped at him. Dunau felt the spear pierce flesh and he smiled even as the large beast came down on top of him. He was pinned to the ground and tried to move Ronka off of his chest but could not. Onkeel and Dyken ran over to him and tried to lift Ronka. No one understood why it was so difficult, but they counted to three and lifted together. When they moved Ronka, the answer became apparent. The other half of the broken spear had pierced Dunau 's stomach. Onkeel got on the ground and lifted Dunau 's head. He placed his hand on the wound, but he knew it was too deep.

"You have killed many Hunden today Dunau." Onkeel whispered.

"I killed seven," he whispered. "More than any Farrador before me," he said in a weak voice.

"Your brother's spirit watches you. I know he is proud. I am very proud"

"Yes, he is watching me," he said looking in the distance. "I see him," he whispered with his last breath. The light faded from Dunau's eyes as Onkeel held him.

The fighting between the small band of Farrador and Hunden was still fierce, but Gallra had to focus on Stygg, or he would be killed easily. Gallra ran to the camp entrance then turned and threw his metal boomerang over Stygg's head. Stygg growled and stopped running. He looked at the boomerang in the air and smiled.

"Foolish pup! Do you think me some senseless animal? I am Stygg; Master of the Hunden."

Gallra turned toward him and said, "I am Gallra, master of Farrador weapons, dog!"

Stygg growled and said, "You are nothing without your weapons Gallra. Once I take your weapon, I will feed on your heart."

Gallra smiled. "I just threw my favorite weapon. If you can take it, you would have taken my heart."

Stygg turned to see where the boomerang was. It made its turn and was headed right for him. He jumped toward it and opened his mouth. The metal boomerang was sharpened on both sides, and kept passing through his throat and neck as he bit down. He fell to the ground in front of Gallra, who wasted no time in blowing into his horn. The fighting stopped for a moment and Gallra lifted Stygg's head into the air.

"Hear me Hunden! He yelled. "I know you understand me! Your master is dead! If the rest of you value your lives, you will leave now, and never return. The next Hunden I see, I will kill!"

The remaining Hunden stopped their fight to look at Stygg. Once they saw their leaders head, they fled in fear. Isantor and the hunting party came swiftly off the trail in time to see them leave. Isantor studied Gallra holding up Stygg's head by one of his ears.

"What happened here?" He asked.

Onkeel was still holding Dunau when he said, "Gallra. He has saved us all."

"Many Hunden are dead". Isantor said looking around. "How is this possible?"

Fetter stepped forward and stood next to Gallra. He picked up the boomerang and showed Isantor. "Gallra has crafted many weapons," he said.

Isantor looked at the boomerang and was astounded. He studied the Stygg's lifeless body and whispered "Utvinder".

Onkeel smiled and nodded.

"What's that?" Fetter asked.

"Many seasons ago we were expelled from our home. Some of us were able to craft objects such as this to help us defeat our enemies and to do many great things. They were called Utvinder. They could shape things and make objects out of the simplest items like wood and rock. Many generations must pass before they are born. I have never seen one, for the king of our old land kept them hidden. My eyes never gazed upon one until now. Utvinder; the chosen one." Onkeel said looking at Gallra.

Isantor studied Gallra and looked around once more. He nodded his head and once again whispered "Utvinder".

23 DIONNE'S VAD

The Mantoo army was lined up in battle formation in the center of Kuningas field. They were silently waiting for the enemy they knew was coming. The soldiers stood at attention and watched the far eastern edge of the mountain that they were directed to study. In the back of the line, Wyler and Dionne sat on their horses between the Mantoo flags.

"I do not understand it," He started. "How is it possible that the blue flower is missing from all the gardens across our lands?"

"Something is afoot father." Dionne said looking around. "There are other forces at work against us. Do you remember the hand game father?"

Wyler smiled and nodded. "I recall being quite bad at it."

"You would hide something in your left hand, but twirl the right in front of me. All the while distracting me from what was truly in the left even as you described the contents."

"You never lost as I recall my dear."

"That game is being played with us once more." She said looking across the field. "It would seem our true opponents are about to reveal themselves."

She moved her horse next to Wyler's as the four chief members of the elder council and a game-smith walked across the field and approached them.

"We need to talk Wyler." Swoggle said firmly.

Wyler ignored them for a moment. "I am clearly in the middle of something."

He said as politely as he could.

"That is why we need to talk now before you plunge Mantoo headlong into the next Great War. Part of your Maisha-Vad included the extension of peace. Why have you called us to battle? Has Ringo failed?"

Wyler ignored him and kept scanning the horizon. Lady Arna nudged Swoggle, which made him remember the real reason for being there.

"Wyler we have come across a document that will put an end to this nonsense," he continued. "You cannot declare war."

"I have not declared war, war is being declared against Mantoo." Wyler said.

"Then Ringo has failed." Lady Arna said. "Oh Wyler I am sorry."

"Ringo's victory or failure is not yet evident. This war..."

"This war is over before it has begun!" Devonsire yelled.

"What are you going on about? We are all in grave danger." Wyler insisted.

Devonsire handed him the scroll. Wyler read it over as Dionne climbed off of her horse.

"Father we do not have time for this." Dionne said nervously.

Wyler looked at Devonsire and the game-smith that accompanied the elders and let out a little laugh.

"So, your brother had a standing bet with you regarding the throne of Mantoo. A bet that would ensure if he lost the one he had with me, your family would somehow keep the crown. And where have these documents been for the last few hundred years that I've worn the crown?"

"They were lost, which halted any claim to the throne I had." Devonsire explained. "Wyler I am sorry, but...they are legal," he whispered while looking at the nodding Smith.

"No. Do not be sorry. I said I would keep our laws and so I shall. A wager is a wager." Wyler said trying not to sound upset. Dionne watched as his father removed the crown and handed it to Devonsire. "Father No." she exclaimed. "What of Ringo and your Maisha-Vad?" Wyler ignored the question and continued.

"But Devonsire, as the new king you must realize war is at your doorstep and your enemy will not wager or bargain with you."

Devonsire looked confident as he placed the crown on his head. "I have met Brutus and Meccah, but I have no worry here. I can establish peace where all others failed."

The other elders looked proud, which angered Dionne even more. And the exchange of coins that was taking place between a few of them incensed her. She looked at Devonsire's horse and noticed a blue flower sticking out of a leather satchel draped over his horse's saddle.

Wyler tried to warn Devonsire once more. "So your majesty, you believe you face Alusta and Alkotten on this field of battle?" Wyler asked.

"Be silent!" ordered the new king. "You had your chance to lead us Wyler, and for your part did well, but your latter days have been wrought with madness. A sudden Maisha-Vad, the instigation of war, you have lost your mind. And now I will fix the peace you have so recklessly broken."

Wyler tried one more time to warn him, but Devonsire would not hear it. "Do not make me have to remove you Wyler. I had hoped you would be more humble than this."

Dionne looked to the far side of the field and saw a dusty wind approaching. She watched it turn sharply as if it were alive. "These fools will lead us all to our death." She said under her breath. She moved toward the elders to get a better look at the leather bag on Devonshire's saddle. When she saw for certain that it did have a blue stem sticking out of the top of it, she walked to Wyler and leaned toward him.

"Father…… Aubaultmor, were the stories true?" she asked tensely.

"What?" Wyler asked in disbelief of her timing.

"Aubaultmor! Were there any exaggerations, or were the bedtime stories as true as you made them? I believed them. I know Wesley and Ringo didn't, but I did."

Wyler shook his head sadly as he noticed the approaching dust storm. "They were my attempt to prepare each of you if this day should ever come my dear. They are true," he said softly. "But this is hardly the time…"

Dionne turned to Devonsire and wasted no time in yelling "Maisha-Vad!"

"No!" Wyler said softly as he grabbed her.

"That is a life bet you are asking for my dear. Are you even old enough for such a Vad little one?" Devonsire quipped.

"I know what it is, and I was old enough on my last birthday," she fired back.

"I have no desire to see Wyler lose all of his children young one."

"Youth blinds you to a great many things my lord, but hardly to the things that you desire most. My father taught me that, and he taught me to bet on the things and the ones you love the most."

"And what is it that you desire child?"

"The leather pouch on your saddle for one thing, but it will not be the only thing," she said feistily.

Devonsire looked annoyed with her, but managed a tight smile. "It would seem that you are wise beyond your age. What is your wager young Wantoo?" Devonsire said through his smile.

"Your enemy will soon be upon you and you intend to negotiate peace. I wager that not only will you and two other elders of your choosing not be able to negotiate peace, but your negotiations will not even last a full two minutes."

Still remaining confident, Devonsire yelled "Done!" without hesitation. He continued to smile and bowed. "Your terms young one?" he said playfully.

"Should you win and in addition to my life, you gain all my personal winnings which are second only to my father and Ringo in all of Mantoo. Should you lose, you forfeit all claims future and past to the crown and restore my father as king."

"Done." Devonsire said rubbing his hands.

"Counter terms?" Dionne asked looking past him to the oncoming dust storm.

"Two minutes? Once the negotiations exceed two minutes, you would have lost. Terms my dear? There are none needed." Devonsire laughed. "This will be the shortest Maisha-Vad in Mantoo history. The clock does not begin until one of the negotiating party begins to speak. The moment it passes two minutes, your life and your fortune are mine."

"Know this King" she snapped. "If Ringo where here to see your betrayal of our father and knew that while Wesley lay sick you hid the cure from us all, you would not have two minutes to pray for what is coming."

Devonsire smiled and threw the leather bag of blue petals to the crier. "I said that I had no desire to see Wyler lose all of his children. See that the doctor gives that to the former Prince," he said turning away from them.

Wyler looked at Devonsire and asked angrily, "What have you done?"

"Something had to be done," Devonsire said returning the intensity.

Wyler slapped the reigns of his horse and quickly rode his horse alongside the crier leaving the elders looking toward the approaching dust storm.

"Be certain the doctor tends to him right off. He will recover quickly once he's had a dose of the flower extract," He said before returning to Dionne's side.

The game smith completed documenting everything and gave a nod to Dionne and Devonsire. Devonsire adjusted the crown on his head and proudly moved his horse in front of the Mantoo army with Dugan Shipnor and Swoggle. When he reached the center of the long line of troops, they rode their horses about one hundred yards in front of the army and waited. Wyler and Dionne moved in front of the army line, but remained a safe distance behind the elders.

"Do you know what you've done child?" he asked painfully.

"I know what I've done. But I cannot allow what you thought would happen today. I am my mother's child," she said softly. "May the great spirit forgive me." Dionne's mind drifted to the day she read one of the scrolls in the palace. She was haunted by its tale of what was to come. When she heard of the elder's plot to unseat her father, she crafted the document they were searching for; it was a smith- recording of a wager between Devonsire and his brother. She did her best to make it look official and old, by writing it on very old parchment. When the moment was right, she had it passed from hand to hand until it found its way to Lady Tulip. This was the document Wyler now held in his hand. He looked at the handwriting with a sense of familiarity, and then looked to her once again as a feeling of disbelief washed over him. Wyler asked her once again "What have you done?" but his question went unanswered.

Devonsire looked back at Wyler and noticed the storm coming fast on his left and stared in its direction.

"What's that?" Swoggle asked trying to get a better look.

"You are losing your sight in your old age Swoggle. It's just a dust storm." Devonsire answered. "It should die out long before it reaches us."

"Where is this enemy Wyler spoke of? Dugan asked.

Before anyone could answer, the dust storm picked up speed, and suddenly swirled and spun in front of them. They backed up a few feet as the dust began to fall away and Aubaultmor took form. The elders struggled to move the frightened horses back, while marveling at his twenty-foot frame. Smoke and ash flew from the dark places underneath his armor. He turned his head toward them once he noticed them standing to his right. As he exhaled, a plume of smoke and ash flew from his nostrils and landed on top of them. He tilted his head and in a thunderous voice that shook the surrounding lands Aubaultmor demanded, "MANTOO?"

Devonsire composed himself and looked back at the army behind him. He cleared his throat and looked up at Aubaultmor. "This is indeed the edge of the Mantoo lands my dear giant friend. If it pleases you, what is your business with Mantoo?" He managed to say loudly.

Without moving his head, Aubaultmor's eyes began to glow with fire. "I will only hold council with the Mantoo king," he bellowed. Once again, his voice shook the ground as he spoke. Aubaultmor clenched his fist as he looked across the field at the Mantoo army.

Feeling a bit more confident, Devonsire cleared his throat and looked up at Aubaultmor. "I am the king of the Mantoo. I am certain there is a great many things to discuss between us milord, such as your name. May I inquire as to the name of the powerful being before me?"

Aubaultmor stared at Devonsire, "To the Mantoo king am I called death," and with that, a stream of fire came from his mouth and reduced the three elders to ashes. The crown that was on Devonsire's head flew through the air and landed a few feet from the Mantoo front line, where it rolled in front of Wyler. Dionne quickly dismounted, picked it up and handed back to her father, who instinctively placed it on his head.

"Dionne, after all the stories, you knew Aubaultmor would kill them." Wyler said sadly.

"They did not know what they were dealing with father. Their greed would have destroyed us all. Better he kill them than destroy all of Mantoo with them. Things are as they should be father, and the prophecy has been fulfilled."

"The prophecy? You've read the scrolls?"

"I read them a hundred times. I know that the seventh Prophecy was revealed to you. I know that the prophecy was that the Mantoo King would die facing Aubaultmor. I know that you set Ringo on this quest thinking you would die here today, and I know you felt that there was no other way. Well the Mantoo King did die facing Aubaultmor today. And now that the prophecy has been fulfilled, you are lord until Ringo finishes the Vad. Things are as they should be." She turned to face Aubaultmor and shouted "Ready!" and the entire army readied their weapons.

"Hold." Wyler said as he rode his horse out a few paces. "A father has never been more proud of his daughter than I am right now, and you are without doubt your mother's child," he whispered to her. Wyler turned toward Aubaultmor.

"Aubaultmor, I was told when you returned; a great battle of armies would take place. I have mustered the Mantoo army. Where is yours? The prophecies demand it!" he yelled.

Almost instantly, Aubaultmor was surrounded by swirling dust and ash. His body was reduced to a height twelve feet, and an army of soldiers formed from the dust, ash and rock in front of him. Aubaultmor waved his hand and creatures such as Tikats, and Crocodons poured onto the field from the east. He confidently looked across the field at Wyler and nodded.

Wyler returned the nod with an equal measure of confidence and then glanced at Dionne. "So it begins," he said looking at both armies. He moved his horse over to a flag bearer and extended his arm. The Flag bearer handed him a red flag, and Wyler raised it high. "Attack," he cried loudly. And with that, both armies rushed toward each other in battle.

.

24 MECCAH'S WAR

In Alusta, Meccah paced in his chambers. A knock at his door caught him off guard and gave him pause. "I gave orders not to be disturbed," he said to the guard entering.

"Sire we have a…problem." The guard said bowing.

Meccah walked out to the castle entrance and saw Dakahn approach with one of the King's fishers.

"Sire," he started. "This is one of your fishers. He reports seeing the bodies of two of the royal guards come off of the north shore where the falls carried them into the sea."

Meccah was angry. "Where are the bodies?" He roared.

The fisher gestured to a cart a few feet from them. Meccah walked over to the carriage and pulled off the covering.

"These are the guards that were protecting my daughter," he looked at their wounds. "What did this?"

Dakahn looked closely. "The rocks on the base of the mountain," he said.

"No. Not even those could pierce our skin. This is something else…some kind of…. animal. They stink of it."

"What kind of animal? Hunden? No, these are not teeth. Our scouts have never come across anything capable of this." Dakahn said looking over the wounds closely.

"The Hunden would never risk their own destruction. They know to eat one of us means death to them all. Their teeth are sharp enough, but these are not teeth. These are claws; very big claws. They tore to the bone with one swipe. There is no animal capable of this. The smell, the claws, this is nothing natural. This is the work of the Alkotten science. They have made something, or bred something for the purpose of destroying Alustans. It can rips our flesh, and kills with ease." Meccah turned to face Dakahn. "Brutus is behind this."

"Why would he? Brutus would not risk war with Alusta."

"Why not? I risked war with Alkotten. He knows."

"He knows what?"

Meccah was visibly shaken "He has them. He has my children. He may subject them to this beast, or use them as a trap for me."

"Sire?" Dakahn said trying to calm him. He began to question Meccah's sanity as he watched him pace back and forth. "Sire?" He said, louder the second time. "What would you have me do? I could gather the honor guard and find them."

"No! Muster all of the Alusta guard. Brutus has kidnapped the

Prince and Princess and in so doing has declared war upon us. Gather every weapon and every available male. Clear the storehouses and the armory. We go to Alkotten. We go to retrieve my children. We go to WAR!"

25 MEAD AND MADNESS

Troldomen, Ringo and Brutus were alone in the throne room drinking Alkotten mead from tall mugs.

"You knew this all along?" Ringo asked Troldomen.

"Mecca has many children; there is no way to tell for certain. As the story goes, when Forste was cast out, Mecca's wives naturally took them in. Forste's children would have been far too young to remember anything other than what they were told of that day.

"And each time Mecca banished a mother or a father, his wives took in the children left behind?" Ringo asked after taking a drink.

"Mecca has no idea how many of them are his and how many are not. Dinatru and Warrendr found favor where so many others did not. Favor above his other children. In truth, Mecca does not remember, and before today neither did the Prince and Princess."

Ringo turned to Brutus. "Warrendr and Dinatru; where were they sent?" he demanded.

"To find that which they have lost." Brutus answered wryly.

"Really? How can anyone in this room be so certain that this is correct? This does not feel right somehow," Ringo said, finishing his drink.

"Why? You knew nothing and cared nothing for these Alustans before the start of your journey, and now you are sympathetic to their plight. Had Warrendr gained access to Mantoo, you would be dead now. It is obvious your intent is to set your anger upon the caller, but it is misdirected, for I have had no hand in the events that caused anyone of you pain as of yet," Brutus quipped.

"Yet? Tell us then King Brutus, how did you come to have Forste in your company?" Ringo asked.

"Some that were banished became the Farrador, fewer still join the Turquai. On occasion they make their way here, where they are welcomed as allies."

"An ally? You have scarred him horribly. Those wounds…"

"He consented to every one of them." Brutus interrupted.

"Still, would anyone calling themselves an ally scar their friend that terribly?"

"Would anyone honoring peace name their son War-render-er? Brutus replied.

Ringo walked to the wall and touched it. He had a faraway look in his eyes.

"What reason would you have to scar him, even with his consent?"

"You presume too much young king. These are matters of Alkotten, and are not subject to treaty negotiations, the pleasantries extended for the sake of favor or proof of benevolence."

Troldomen smirked as he realized the irony in what Brutus said. He finished his drink with a final gulp and slammed the mug down on the ice table. "I suppose you would have us believe you have never considered war against Alusta?" He asked with a smug tone.

"What quarrels have I with Alusta that you could say such things? I above all others on the mountain have reason, but..."

"It is forbidden for a king to lie." Troldomen reminded him.

"What lie? I have not fabricated one fact."

"Though you have omitted some."

"Of what do you speak wizard?"

"The beast that gave us chase in our journey here. In all my years on the mountain, and I would say no one has walked the mountain as I have walked the mountain, but these eyes have never beheld such a beast. This creature is not natural. This was not spawned from the mountain itself. It was crafted. Oh yes King Brutus, you are not the only one that knows of your...science."

"Have a care wizard." Brutus said coldly.

"What do you mean?" Ringo insisted. "That beast was made? Here?"

Ringo turned to Brutus. "Is it true?"

Brutus gave the slightest nod, which caused Troldomen to smile with satisfaction.

"Yes," Troldomen said confidently. "The scars on Forste's body," Troldomen added. "This is why it pursued us without pause. It was taught to hunt Alustans. They used the blood of an Alustan to train the beast to kill Alustans."

Ringo looked weary. "How can there be peace when you and Mecca plan each other's destruction at every turn? It makes sense now," he said looking at the table. "This crystal... I've seen it before; Brutus' scepter. It was made from the same crystal I encountered in the caves. You can hear everything in Alusta and Mantoo because the sound from a single piece passes all of the sound around it to its host. You have the crystal core somewhere near, and the fragments will pass the sound around it from as far away as... the chandelier in the Alustan throne room. Or wherever Mecca carries his scepter," Ringo removed the crown from his head and stared at it. "And of course my father's crown," He said looking at the jewel in the middle. "This is how you know everything that has taken place up to now. He wears the old crown that belonged to Willard, the king before him, while I have his to complete my quest. That one has no jewels," Ringo said reflecting on his own words. Ringo stiffened up and turned to him. "You know everything, and it's not because of Forste, or his hearing."

"My, my, my you really are well taught." Brutus said in the most condescending tone he could muster. "Whatever shall I do with you?" As he spoke, the guards filled the chamber pointing their swords at Ringo and Troldomen.

"Your plans to kill all the Alustans failed, and your beast is dead." Ringo boasted as they bound them.

Brutus laughed. "I don't plan to kill all of the Alustans, just one. The Hoynarr is far from dead. He is making his way back up the mountain as we speak."

"Nothing could survive that fall."

"Nothing that fell did."

"I saw it, this... Hoynarr. I saw it fall."

"Just because he went over the side of the mountain does not mean he fell to the bottom my young Mantoo king."

"He may not have hit bottom, but the Alusta royal guards it killed are not so well equipped. Once the Alustans find the bodies of their warriors they will come looking for the Prince and Princess." Troldomen warned.

Brutus laughed again. "Yes they will."

Ringo looked horrified as he realized the truth. "You are using them as bait."

"So now we understand it all, do we? Don't look so surprised King Ringo. In war nothing is beyond your enemy."

"You mean to break the treaty."

"I honor the treaty. It is Mecca who will break the treaty when he arrives and declares war against Alkotten."

"You expect Mecca to come marching in here to rescue his children? And because they are prisoners, he will not attack. And when he is close enough, you will feed him to your Hoynarr."

Brutus laughed. "That was hardly the plan, but I like what you suggest."

"Your biggest threat was not Mecca it was Warrendr and the war stones he was carrying. And you have used Forste to take the fight right out of him. So now you hope to use the one weakness that Mecca has against him, the love for his children. Do you really think Mecca is without a plan? Do you think he is without the means to declare war upon Alkotten?"

"Mecca sought to destroy us all once, but even he would not risk destroying the Prince and Princess." Brutus said confidently.

"Unless...?" Ringo said slyly.

"Unless what? There is no unless young Mantoo. I have thought out every detail."

"You assume too much. Things have changed since your last war. You have no idea what Mecca is capable of; the fury he will unleash at your doorstep."

Brutus laughed aloud "We will know soon enough young Mantoo. He is already on his way here."

Troldomen approached him slowly. He looked at Brutus from head to toe. "The Brutus I know would never commit to such treachery."

"Perhaps then, you did not know Brutus at all." Brutus sneered. "Lock them away!" He commanded. A dozen guards quickly removed Ringo and Troldomen from the royal chamber. Brutus followed closely behind the guards until his prisoners were secure in a cell. He walked down a long hall to another cell far from the others. The hall was the only dark place in the palace. He nodded at the guard who quickly opened the door for him. He stepped inside the darkened cell, and stared at a lone figure sitting quietly in the corner.

"You think yourself clever?" He snapped. "There exists some code between you and the wizard. Something I overlooked, but no matter…they are in a cell not unlike this one," he said looking around. "Where they will stay until your enemies have reached your doorstep."

"Alkotten has no enemies." The prisoner said quietly.

"It does now. I have seen to it. Even now one of your witless friends is engaged in war in Mantoo and the other approaches from the west passage on his flying carriages of war to destroy Alkotten."

The dark figure rose to his feet. "I do not pretend to know the things you have done to cause this. You have betrayed your people, and your Lord," he said walking into the light. Like all of the guards throughout the palace, he looked exactly like his jailer.

"And you have betrayed me…Brutus. My revenge is almost complete. When I am done all you have worked for your entire life will be destroyed, and you will know my pain before your end."

"Then tell me." The prisoner pleaded. "Tell what I did to deserve this? Tell me what Alkotten has done to you that you seek to destroy it? I did nothing more than give you life. What have I done?" He yelled.

King Brutus walked to the cell door and stopped in the doorway. He turned around to face his prisoner and took a single step toward him. He moved into the light and tilted his head slightly.

"You've had plenty of time to reflect in here, but you still do not understand, do you? But you said it, I heard you say it."

"Say What? What did I say?" the prisoner asked.

Brutus turned to walk away and stopped at the door once more. With his back turned to his prisoner, he turned his head to the left and looked over his shoulder. He took a deep breath and said, "You gave me life. That's what you've done. That is your crime, and that is why everything you hold dear will be destroyed! You gave me life."

The prisoner looked at him in despair. "You're mad!" he began. "Do you think that I gave you life so that you could destroy everything I built, everything I've worked for?"

"Everything you've built is a crime against nature. You're so vain you even made all of us look like you. And you were so vain that even in the midst of your greatest failure; you didn't know when to stop. It is your vanity that will cost you everything. And I truly mean it when I say this Brutus; you have no one to blame, but yourself."

26 MISTAKEN IDENTITY

The battle in Mantoo was fierce. The Mantoo army was very skilled and seemed to be holding their position against the dark army of Aubaultmor. The dark army did their best to press the attack, but each time they tried to move in accordance with Aubaultmor's will, they were held off. Aubaultmor waved his hand and the Tikats began to attack from the right. Norfas grabbed one by the tail and used his tremendous strength to swing it into other Tikats.

Dionne and Wyler were positioned on the small rise overlooking the battle.

"We are losing too many soldiers father."

"They fight bravely."

"They are outnumbered. The soldiers of the dark army cannot die. We need to blow the horn."

Norfas continued to do his best to destroy the creatures called to serve Aubaultmor's dark purpose. He grabbed a crocodon by its tail and threw into a cluster of the dark army. The soldiers of the dark army that were hit exploded into dust, but were almost instantly remade with a wave of Aubaultmor's hands.

Wyler shook his head. "We must give your brother time to complete his task. We must not fail to hold them."

Suddenly, a running crocodon changed direction toward them. Dionne moved her horse to the left of Wyler. "I do not know how much longer we can wait. What sense does it make to ..." She jumped from her horse and quickly slew the crocodon as it moved close to them. "I do not know how much longer we can hold them."

"We will hold them. We are all that stand between them and Mantoo. We will hold the line." Wyler looked out at the chaos and took a deep and long breath.

He turned his head away from Dionne and whispered "We have to."

A horn blew in the distance and an army of mud-men arrived on the field. Wyler nodded in disbelief, and quietly uttered "No."

A Mantoo soldier shot an arrow into the chest of one of the mud-men. The mud-man pulled out the arrow and threw it to the ground. He stepped on it and broke it under his foot.

The Mantoo army began to retreat when a voice in the distance yelled "hold the line." Without turning around, Wyler smiled. Wesley pulled the singing sword from its sheath and raised it high in the air as he rode toward the battle.

"It's Wesley!" Dionne yelled excitedly.

"Indeed it is." Wyler said very pleased.

Wesley hit the side of his thigh with the blunt end of the sword and it began to ring out with a tone that seemed to get louder as he rode on. He rode close to the mud-men and pointed the sword at them. The vibrations and high tone coming from the singing sword created a wave of energy that blew apart the mud-men as Wesley pointed it in their direction. He quickly destroyed all of the mud-men and rode his horse next his father and Dionne. She jumped off of her horse to greet him. Wesley dismounted and gave her a hug. "You did well captain," he smiled.

"Yes, the real captain is here now. Now we have a chance." She said.

A Roar from the distance quickly grabbed their attention. Wesley looked across the field as Aubaultmor breathed fire into the air with roar.

"What is that?" He said nervously.

"That is Aubaultmor," she said matching his tone.

Wesley looked at his father and smiled. "He is smaller than your stories told us father."

"No less dangerous I assure you." Wyler quipped.

Aubaultmor looked at Wesley and managed a smile. He nodded and said "Mantoo king! You have finally shown yourself. I have waited two hundred years to kill you and your brother. I will have my revenge this day."

Wesley looked puzzled and said "Is he speaking to me? How does he know me and Ringo?"

"He doesn't," Wyler answered. "The last time he saw me, I was a young man. He thinks you're me. He's ignoring the crown because of Devonsire. Oh great spirit, he thinks you're me."

27 FREEDOM AND FOLLY

Troldomen looked at Ringo, who was looking out of the small opening cut into the center of the door. "So this is the only place in Alkotten where light does not shine." Ringo said. He looked toward the ceiling and walked to the rear of the cell. "I didn't want to come, you know. I thought it a fool's errand at first. I was in the great hall winning and…taking advantage of those I called my people."

"And now you see the error of your ways I suppose?" Troldomen asked dryly.

"What does that mean?" he asked angrily.

"We all have gifts young master. Some are uniquely ours, some we share with others, but we each poses a combination of talents that no one else does. It's what makes us unique. I don't know what's more tragic, the person that never realizes his gifts; the person that realizes his gifts, but uses them to take advantage of others; or the person that realizes his gifts, but never uses them."

"Am I really that bad Troldomen?

"Who am I to say young master?"

"What of the person that uses their gift for the benefit of others?"

"Well, well, he can be taught after all. You're not so unlike your father."

"My father always had a way of looking forward. I don't have that gift"

"Perhaps, but it may be possible that you just have not tried yet. In any case, you have other gifts that your father believed would see you through this."

"And yet here we are." Ringo said sadly. He turned toward Troldomen pulling on his own ear playfully. "I hear what they say about me. I pretend not to care, but it does bother me at times."

"Who? The nay-Sayers? The people that truly don't care for you and may in fact pray for your demise? Ringo when you were young, you used to climb up the column next to your bed and jump to the pillows. It nearly killed your mother to see you jump from that height, but you kept doing it," he said laughing with Ringo. "Oh she begged and begged, but you just kept on doing it," he continued. "One day, when no one was watching, you just stopped."

"Why did I stop?"

"If I had to guess, I would say that you simply outgrew it. After a while we all forgot about it and concentrated on the next big thing you decided to do. That's how you tell your friends from your enemies."

"What do you mean?"

"Your enemies will never forget, or let you forget the smallest things you did that were… less than glorious. The people who love you may remember, but pretend to forget because they are concerned with the good. Love allows people that care to look past your faults to the person the know you to be. If you value anyone's opinion of you, it is theirs," Troldomen reached into his pocket and pulled out an apple seed. "See this? He continued. An apple seed is the smallest thing, but it will grow into a large tree that feeds many. If it is planted and given a chance to take root, it will grow into a wondrous thing indeed. But it will never sprout a mango. The people who love you know what you could be if given the chance. Your enemies would still have you to believe you are just a seed and nothing more. Yes, folks will talk, as they always have. But what you become is much more a result of what you believe, and not because of what others say about you."

"Then who am I Troldomen? The son of King Wyler?"

"Well, you have done your share of work to ensure others see you as much more than your father's son. In fact, some of those things were scandalous, and a there are at least two specific things that may not actually be legal. But your father and I both understood why you did things like that back then. It was to gain your own identity; to become Ringo Wantoo and not simply Wyler's oldest boy. But it is a hearty question young master, and one that must be answered. Who are you?"

Ringo looked to the ceiling of the cell, and then to the floor. "I thought I knew," he whispered. "If you would have asked me before I left Mantoo, I would have been proud and boastful. I would have talked about my skill as a gambler and the…"

"And the what?

"Nothing. I've just realized that out here, in the rest of the world, all of the things I would have bragged about mean very little."

"And so who are you?"

"I am… a work in progress, I suppose. I have found that I have a need to see this through to the end. I need to know Dinatru and Warrendr are well. I need to make sure this Vad is won by my father. I need to ensure this evil upon us is stopped."

"Well there you have it. You are tenacious, clever, brave, and loyal; all the attributes of a good king."

"Humph, he sighed playfully. "Just now, I would think you were describing my father."

Troldomen laughed. "Well it's not difficult to see why. After all, you are your father's son."

Ringo stopped laughing and nodded. "You are truly wise Troldomen.

You have a talent for hiding it at times." Ringo joked.

"It is a good thing too otherwise someone might see what I was about to do." Troldomen teased.

Ringo looked puzzled. "I thought they took your pouch?"

Troldomen rubbed his hands together. "They did."

"Then what are you doing?"

"What I must," he said with a smile. Troldomen pushed one of the stones in the far wall and a portion of the wall opened up to reveal a small passage behind it. "Hurry," he said walking into the passage.

"How did you know that was there?' Ringo asked, while walking in behind him.

"I helped build it," he said running. Ringo forced the stone panel closed and followed him. They came to a section in the passage with four ways to go, but they turned in the same direction Brutus walked toward after leaving them.

"What is down here? I see light on the other end." Ringo asked.

"A different kind of light is down here young master. A light that must be shed on the dark mystery before us."

"Dark mystery?'

"Yes. The kings of the great mountain and I have a bit of a covert language that is to be used whenever one us is in peril. It was made when we were close friends, before the last visit from Aubaultmor. Let us say I was addressing your father. I would say, The Wyler I know would never do that, and he would respond by saying "who knows Wyler better than I," but when I asked that of Brutus earlier, he ignored the code completely."

"Well, it is more than possible, given what my father told me about him, that he is quite mad Troldomen." Ringo said looking around for guards.

"True, but I am betting that he is not who he claims to be." Troldomen said feeling the wall.

"You mean that he is not the real King Brutus? How could you tell? They all look alike."

"It is far more important that the other Alkotten know who he is, than for us to."

"What? What does that mean?"

"Even with their remarkable sight, the Alkotten are all too similar to tell one apart from another. They tell each other apart by scent. Ah, here it is," he said tapping a spot on the wall.

"Here is what?"

"These stones are crafted to absorb all sound. While you can hear me, the sound is trapped by the outer wall, hence the need for this passage. This way the conversation would not be picked up by any nearby Alustan."

"Clever."

"Quite. The problem with that is they were crafted to hold Alustan prisoners, not prisoners from Alkotten." Troldomen removed dust from his pocket and blew the dust down the hall. He watched as it slowly reached the prison door and wrapped around the guard's head. Within seconds the guard fell unconscious. They walked toward the door and tapped on the wall again until he found the right stone. Troldomen took dust from his back pocket, and outlined the large stone. He blew on the dust and it made sparks in the shape of the large rectangular stone. When the sparks stopped, the stone inside the rectangle was gone.

A voice from the other side of the wall asked, "Who is there?"

Troldomen smiled and said, "Your rescuer."

The voice said, "The Troldomen I know would have used the door."

"Who knows Troldomen more than I? He would make his own door," Troldomen laughed as he extended his hand through the wall and into the darkness.

The thin white hand grabbed his and the tall Alkotten male slipped through the small rectangular hole in the wall. He hugged Troldomen immediately and thanked him. They both stood in front of Ringo and smiled. "Master Ringo Wantoo, allow me to introduce Brutus of Alkotten."

Ringo gave the traditional nod that king's exchange, and looked to Troldomen.

"How did you know?' he asked.

"I gambled that if the real Brutus was still alive, he would be held in the lowest and darkest cell possible. It was a gamble," Troldomen said proudly.

"Indeed. So, who is the other...Brutus; the one wearing the crown?" Ringo asked.

"A replicate, one of many." Brutus started. "Although he is altogether different than the others; I put more of myself in that one. Not one of my better decisions, but we must make haste." Brutus said as he pointed down the long hall on their right. "This way," he said excitedly. "We must free the royal family."

28 BRED FOR DECEPTION

Forste stood outside the room and watched through a glass as a guard served drinks to Dinatru and Warrendr. The crowned Brutus walked up behind him.

"Mecca is on the way. We no longer need to delay in our plan for the rest of the royal family," he said.

Forste gave a single nod and entered the room. The guard walked out and closed the door. Forste smiled and took a seat in the room across from Dinatru and Warrendr. Dinatru was doing her best to remain calm as Forste spoke. He told her and Warrendr stories of their youth that each of them remembered. While his stories seemed to solidify his identity, neither was absolutely certain. Warrendr listened to his breathing and his heart beat as he spoke. Forste was either telling the truth, or he was convinced that what he was telling them was.

Despite that, Warrendr refused to let his guard down. The room they were in was not like the other rooms in the palace. The walls of ice hid something behind them. There was a chemical within the ice that made the room they were in sound proof. When Warrendr realized it, he raised his concerns.

"The walls absorb our voices. I cannot hear anything beyond the walls." Warrendr said placing his finger in his ear.

"It is the cold." Forste insisted. "It weakens our gifts. Soon it will be as though you never had them. This is why Brutus had to augment my hearing; to retain my hearing while I live here."

"No! This is something else. We are being deceived." Warrendr insisted.

"Warrendr sit down." Dinatru demanded.

"See! We should each hear the sound bouncing off the walls when you yell, but there is no other sound beyond the first." Warrendr said.

She turned to Forste. "Have you been in this room before?" She asked.

"Many times. King Brutus brings me here whenever we have council."

"Then it is a room designed for private conversations. No one outside can hear the conversations inside the room."

Warrendr looked at the door. "Or perhaps no one inside the room can hear the conversations outside of it."

"Warrendr you are wise to be cautious, but King Brutus has only ever showed me respect and kindness."

"My father cast you out to make you own way on the mountain. You were dubbed a traitor and prove that now living here in the home of his enemies." Warrendr snapped.

"I am your father! Mecca is a traitor to the family values our people have held dear for as long as we've existed."

"You are not my father!" Warrendr yelled. "Do not presume you will be allowed to blaspheme against your king and have his captain stand idly by."

Forste walked slowly toward him. "Mecca stopped being my king when he cast me from my home and my children. And while he may have raised you as his own, it is my blood that runs through your veins."

"And this is true because you say it? The things you say about our youth would be known to anyone in the royal service. And although you claim to be my father, I do not know you. Perhaps it is no fault of your own, but it changes nothing. I am Warrendr, son of Mecca and Prince of Alusta. And you…you are a traitor in the house of my enemy…"

"Warrendr." Dinatru pleaded as he walked toward Forste.

Warrendr acted a though he did not hear her. "You have allowed them to strip you of your honor, and even your very skin like some animal. Where is the once proud guard that stood and the right hand of the king?"

"You are correct in stating that I do not know you, but that truth has two sides for you also do not know me. You do not know the horrors I endured on the mountain or the battles I waged to survive."

"Leave him alone Warrendr." Dinatru whined.

"I represent Alusta and the house of Mecca. I did not come here to be deceived by the likes of a traitor pretending to be.."

"I am your father!" Forste yelled.

Warrendr grabbed him and pinned him to the wall.

"Say it once more and I will rip you head from your shoulders. Say it!" He yelled.

Dinatru quick moved to Warrendr's side and touched him lightly on the arm. He quickly loosened his grip and turned away.

"The stories were intriguing I must admit, and I believe that you think you are telling the truth, but of all Alustans, I have a special gift." Dinatru said.

She walked toward him and extended her arm. Her hand started to vibrate slightly then she leaned against the chair next to her. "Something stops me. I don't understand it has never failed me before." She said softly.

"What has not failed you before?" Forste asked.

"I'm an empath. I can see where you been, what you've felt, but it's not working. All I feel is cold. It's almost as if…"

"As if he had no past?" Warrendr said staring at him.

Before Warrendr could move, Forste took a blade hidden in his belt and stabbed Warrendr in the stomach. Warrendr managed to push him away, but fell to his knees. Dinatru screamed and pounded on the door. Despite her screams for help no one came, and Forste looked at her as he stood over Warrendr.

"How?" Warrendr asked in agony.

"How did I pierce your skin?" Forste asked as he wiped the blade on a cloth. He dropped to one knee next to him and slowly waved the blade over Warrendr's chest. "This room is designed to take away all of our precious gifts including the impenetrable skin and amazing hearing. You've never felt a blade pierce your skin before, but I had to endure this over and over and over again to test this room and the Hoynarr. It was made to be the negotiating room for the new treaty with your father, but Brutus made a new plan once you left Alusta. The new plan begins with Alusta's strongest warrior, the great Warrendr. I knew you would eventually see through my ruse, but I only needed to keep you in here long enough for the room to take effect on your gifts."

Warrendr tried to get up and fell over. Dinatru cried out, but only heard Forste's laughter in response. Forste tightened his grip on the knife and walked toward her slowly.

"My father will bring this mountain down around your ears." She cried as he approached.

He smiled once more and bowed. "My dear princess, one with nothing to lose, certainly has nothing to fear."

29 THE ALMOST WAR

The real Brutus , Troldomen and Ringo were running along the secret passage behind the walls of the palace when Troldomen stopped.

"What is it?" Ringo asked.

"Screams. I hear screaming. It sounds like Dinatru. It's coming from your pocket," Troldomen said pointing to it.

Ringo took the small piece of crystal from his pocket, and placed it next to his ear. "It is her. Where are they being kept?" He asked Brutus.

Brutus thought for a moment and said, "The inner sanctuary. We are close by. Come."

He ran a few yards to a wall and tapped on the third stone from the bottom. A portion of the wall shifted to his left and revealed Forste standing over Dinatru with his knife. Troldomen quickly threw freeze dust on him and shouted "Espsomeelr Rondthar!" With Forste completely frozen, Dinatru ran into Ringo's arms. Troldomen ran over to Warrendr and tried to stand him up straight.

"How is Warrendr?" She asked

Troldomen nodded. "He'll be fine if I can stop this bleeding. Something gives pause to your gifts," he said.

As Brutus walked through the entrance, Dinatru gasped.

"This is the real Brutus." Troldomen assured her.

"Then who is the other? The one that did all of this? She asked.

"He is now Brutus."

Ringo looked around. "More than one of us is confused. I know I am."

"He who wears the crown is named Brutus. Rasendor was his name before he stole the crown. He was one of my replicates. I banished him ages ago for his treacherous ways. Not long after we defeated Aubaultmor, and trapped his essence in the heart of one the Komari crystals, we hid the core in the deepest region of our lands. The core of the crystals is the hardest substance known to us and cannot be destroyed, so we hid it. The banished Rasendor took shelter in a cave within the crystal caverns and came upon a voice speaking to him through one of the crystal cores. There the dark and sinister voice of Aubaultmor was upon him day and night. And with no food or sleep, he went quite mad. Rasendor's will gave way to the will of Aubaultmor. He labored for years to build the mystic bridge, which would draw energy from the crystal orb serving as Aubaultmor's prison. But Rasendor could not wait for Aubaultmor to return. With the magic Aubaultmor taught him, he was able to steal a larger portion of my life essence, that which tells us who Brutus in Alkotten really is. I awoke one morning, imprisoned in my own palace. I was made different. After a time, I did not believe I was Brutus myself. Had he not come in my cell to mock me, I would have believed myself mad."

"So what do we call you?" Dinatru asked.

"You are very much like your father young Alustan. I have every intention of collecting my crown. You may call me Brutus, as I have only that name to mention."

Ringo turned to Troldomen. "You knew?"

"Knew what?"

"You knew that the Brutus we met was not this Brutus before we arrived."

Before Troldomen could say anything, Forste broke his spell and attacked the group. Ringo managed to push Dinatru away and hit Forste with his other hand simultaneously. The force of the blow knocked Forste into the waiting arms of Warrendr, who quickly forced the bladed hand of Forste into his own stomach.

"Now we die like Alustan warriors, in battle and with honor." Warrendr said still holding him close. Forste fell at his feet and clutched Warrendr's hand.

"I have no memories of Alusta. Only what they gave me to deceive you."

Warrendr stared at him and stood him up.

"We are the sum of our memories and beliefs, the sum of our actions and fears, and the sum of our loves, desires, and hatred. Passion moves you and fear keeps you. Are you bound by fear or moved by passion? A passion for life, for glory, for honor. You are never what someone else makes you. You are neither what you would like to be, and rarely ever what you dream of. You are almost always what you need to be. The Alustan warriors that wear my stripes know of what I speak."

Forste stood up tall. "My brother I am sorry," he said. "I have no honor. It was stripped from me a long time ago. If you will permit me..," he said stumbling to the door. "I hope to restore it now." Forste tapped on the door and closed his robe. A small panel open up and a pair of white eyes looked in. "It is done?" A voice from behind the door asked.

"Yes. They are dead." Forste said trying to sound normal.
The door opened slowly and Forste blocked the door way with his body. He waited until Rasendor came into the room, then quickly shut the door.

"What is this?" he said looking at Brutus. "Guards!" He yelled. But he would say no more as Forste stabbed him in the back. He turned and fell into Forste's arms and reached into a fold inside his robe. Then, unseen by the others, took a small amount of dust into his hand. He smiled and said "I never should have trusted you." and with his last breath, blew the dust on Forste. Forste fell to his knees and looked to Warrendr.

"When I thought I was nothing and had nothing, I felt no pain about taking everything from you. I wanted you also to have nothing. You hold my former post with more honor than I could ever muster. No more lies, no more deceit. I die in the house of my enemy, but not as one of them. Not an enemy to my people. I die as I was …Forste of Alusta." He turned to Dinatru. "Please forgive me for my deception."

"You were not yourself." Dinatru said taking one knee at his side. She held him as he fell back and closed his eyes.

Rasendor was bleeding heavily, and walked toward Brutus. "You will all die soon enough. But you…" He said pointing at Brutus. "I will leave you as you left me; homeless and destitute with your enemy outside your gate. You will die the death you intended for me."

Brutus walked over to him and lifted his crown from Rasendor's head. He placed it on his head and stepped back. "Many years ago, in my desire to live forever I created you and your brothers. You are but a shadow of who I am. No, I can never be you, and you can truly never be me. I will live as I always have, among friends and family."

Rasendor managed one last small laughed. "Alone and homeless," he said as he dropped to the ground. They were all amazed as a sandy mist appeared to rise from Rasendor's body and enter Brutus'.

"The life essence returns to its original host. You are indeed Brutus. Troldomen said proudly.

The group walked out toward the main chamber. Warrendr's wound began to heal the moment they left the room.

"Some of our gifts are returning," he said to Dinatru.

The group walked to the chamber where Brutus's wife and son were imprisoned and found their bodies. A saddened Brutus turned to Ringo. "The Alkotten, produce no tears in our eyes; I cannot cry as you would. Today your father wins a wager we made over one hundred years ago. He bet me that one day I would wish to be a Mantoo. I am the proudest of my people, and believed that I could never feel that way. Today I lost that wager because I wish I were Mantoo so that I could cry for what I have lost this day."

"What did you wager?" Ringo softy asked.

"Humph. I pledged my hand in service for one day to the king of Mantoo."

"You thought you would never lose." Ringo said.

Brutus studied him for a moment and looked up to the ceiling. "Yes, I did believe I would never lose."

"As the Mantoo king I must now collect that debt," Ringo smiled.

Just then a loud explosive sound pierced the air. The palace shook as the rumbling continued. Warrendr walked out of the room and said, "This is an Alustan cannon."

The Alusta were attacking the Alkotten palace, and Mecca was leading the charge. The army of Alkotten prepared to fire upon them. The palace itself took on a completely white look. This made it difficult for an enemy to lock into a specific target. Brutus hurried to a section in the main chamber and pulled open a tiny panel in the wall. He spoke clearly into the metal cone that slid out from the opening.

"Do not fire. We have all been deceived. The Alustans are not the enemy!" He said.

The message could be heard throughout the entire kingdom. Upon hearing it, Mecca held his hand up, which immediately stopped the firing.

"Brutus. Come out and face me!" He yelled. "Where are my children?" He yelled louder.

A few moments later Dinatru came out from behind the large white doors
and ran to her father. He held her close and looked at her clothes in horror.

"Blood? Are you bleeding? How is this possible?" He said in a panic.

"It is not my blood father. I am fine."

"Then who? Where is Warrendr?"

"I assure you Mecca, they are both fine." Brutus said as he, Ringo and Troldomen walked through the large door. "We had a…ah… internal matter that I am sorry to say was only resolved through violence. The traitor conspired to bring us to war. He wanted to destroy us both and used your children to lure you here. Warrendr was wounded in the crossfire. My personal physician is seeing to him."

Mecca looked at Ringo. "How did all of this come to pass so quickly? And tell me why I should believe any of this?"

Ringo looked at Dinatru, and then looked to Mecca. "The kings of the mountain cannot lie. What Brutus says is true. The threat came from an Alkottenian name Rasendor and an Alustan named Forste."

Mecca looked at Dinatru, then back at Ringo. "What does he have to do with any of this?"

"Alkotten did not have the only traitor in this plot to bring war." Brutus answered.

"Where are the traitors now? Mecca sneered.

"Their plot was undone, but not without cost. My family was murdered Mecca, but let their deaths be the last. Come my old friend," Brutus said kindly. "It has been far too long since we stood in the great hall together. We have much to discuss."

Before anyone could move, the sound of a horn in the distance filled the air.

"That faint sound in the distance…is that the Slagmark…. horn of Mantoo?" Brutus asked.

"How is it possible to hear it this far up?' Dinatru asked.

"There are three such horns my dear. All designed with a specific pitch that will resonate across the entire mountain," Brutus said.

"We must answer," Ringo said worried. "They are under attack…"

Troldomen also despaired. "The last time the great horn sounded, Aubaultmor was upon us. Mantoo does not have the means to defeat him alone."

Brutus looked to Mecca. "Aubaultmor seeks to destroy all life on the Great Mountain once again, and both our armies are already clad for battle. What say you Mecca? The kings of the mountain have ever answered that horn."

"And we will not fail to answer it now." Mecca looked to Dakahn. "Turn the warriors about! Our war awaits us in Mantoo!"

Ringo turned to Brutus. "We need to get there quickly. All of the secret passages you have, or the air riders; is there a quick route to Mantoo?"

"Our riders have frozen over." Mecca said gesturing toward one of them. "We had enough energy to get here, but now we are all on foot."

Brutus thought for a moment and smiled. "What is it?" Troldomen asked.

"Filenor pass." Brutus said calmly. "We will be close to Mantoo if we go that route."

Troldomen gave him a strange look "Are you mad? The ice is impassable, and the mountain too steep. You cannot march us through there. We'll fall off the mountain."

Brutus leaned over to get to Troldomen's height. "Who said anything about marching?" He snickered.

30 THE WAR WITHIN US

Isantor looked to Gallra in disbelief. "Tell me why again we cannot feast on the dead Hunden," he asked.

"Their meat is poison to us. See the stains on their teeth? It's from the box berry they have eaten. They knew it would not harm them, but once they ate it, it would be in their meat and would make us sick and probably kill all those that ate it." Gallra responded.

Isantor looked at the bodies of the dead Hunden and sighed. "Onkeel have the warriors pile the bodies and burn them. No one is to eat from them. Burn them until there is nothing left but dust."

"Have we begun already?" Fetter asked. "The smell of fire is in the wind."

Suddenly, the sound of the Mantoo horn reached the Farrador camp. Everyone in the camp stood up and looked to the north in silence.

"What is that?" Onkeel asked. "I have never heard such a horn."

"There is war in the high lands." Isantor answered. "The sky grows dark when the new sun rises. The air is thick with smoke, but there is no fire. This is the foretelling of the evil one's arrival; the one who will destroy the mountain, and claim us all."

"That was a child's tale." Fetter suggested.

"I thought that way too Fetter, once a long time ago. But all the prophecies leading up to his arrival have come to pass. The blue star passing in the sky, the Hunden attacking without cause, no food in a time when the storehouses are normally full are all things that would mark his coming." Isantor added.

"What do we do?" Fetter asked. "If the stories are true, then we must fight. Are we to sit idly and wait for death to find us?"

"No Fetter, we are warriors. Our numbers are small, but our hearts are tall young one. We have no food, but food will not matter if we are all dead."

Isantor looked at Onkeel who seemed to be unsure of his next move. "What troubles you brother?" He asked.

Onkeel looked to the sky then toward the north once again. "I have never questioned your leadership, nor have I ever run from a battle, but death is in the wind. Would you risk all of our lives for a myth told to us as children?" he despaired.

"Your father told you of the great demon of fire from the lifeless land of the east. Even after his defeat many seasons ago, his evil remained. So burned was the land, that nothing ever grew there again. My father told me too of the horn that would fill the sky when he returned and that everything that breaths must answer its call."

"I remember Isantor." Onkeel began. "I also remember what happened after that battle was over. I remember there was a fight in Alusta. I remember being banished. I remember walking endlessly. We walked for years until we found this place. I remember burying my father in the days of the great hunger, and buying my mother in the days of the great cold. I could not bear to bury my wife or my children."

"There will be nothing left to bury if we do not fight." Fetter interjected.

"I too was told of this great beast. I believe we were told so that we could prepare ourselves when it arrived. Our families were banished from Alusta a long time ago, but before that, they negotiated peace to end the war with Alkotten. Because of that, they left Alusta with pride as soldiers. And so the children of banished soldiers have made their way in the wilderness and have become something more. They have become warriors. We are those warriors. When have we not defeated our enemies?" Isantor asked proudly.

Onkeel gave him a strange look. He collected his thoughts for a moment before speaking. "When you were small you cared for nothing besides a warm place to lay your head and a full belly. The young are ever without fear. They care for nothing save adventure. The old attach themselves to others and to places where they dwell. They crave companionship, peace, a warm place to lay their heads and a full belly."

"You are neither too young nor old." Gallra said.

"This is true, and yet I desire as though I were. When our people left Alusta they could take no weapons, and so we learned to make some from rock and wood and stone. We have weapons to fight Hunden, and Turquais, and to hunt for food, but a beast of fire and stone? We do not have a weapon to destroy it. The soldiers of Alusta had swords of fire, and sling-bows that threw the firewater at the enemy. We have nothing." Onkeel despaired.

"We have weapons." Gallra said. "How do you think I killed so many Hunden? Come Fetter. Gather some of the warriors to help us."

"Hey, where is the large sling you told me about?" Fetter asked excitedly.

They walked toward Gallra's tree house, leaving Isantor and Onkeel alone. Isantor studied Onkeel closely. "You are my second in command. They cannot see you in such despair."

"I despair for my wife and my younglings Isantor. My head tells me to fight, but my heart commands me to take them and run."

"Onkeel, if we fight we stand a chance. We may live to tell our children our own story of bravery. We could tell them that they live because we fought. Their land and their mothers are safe because we fought two great battles this day. We could tell them how we fought and defeated our fears, then we fought and defeated our enemy, and we won the day. But if we do not fight, we will all die, and when you get to the great beyond, you will have to face your children and your forefathers. And what would you tell them then? Where do the Spirits send cowards? I will never know, my captain will never know, our people will never know because we are Farrador. We are warriors. We fight, we die if we must, but we will never run from battle."

Onkeel smiled. "Dunau killed seven Hunden before they took him. The last time I saw anyone that brave was when you killed six. They stayed away for years thinking we were all so skilled. I thought that if I had a drop of that bravery I could be as great a warrior as my father," he said.

"I remember that day Onkeel. I remember killing the six, but I also remember never being more afraid in my life."

"You were afraid? Onkeel said looking surprised. "How did you overcome it?"

"I didn't. It made me fast. It made me angry. It made me strong. Anyone can rush headlong into battle, but those that are truly brave do not fight without fear, they fight in the midst of being afraid," Isantor said.

"If this is the fight our fathers foretold Isantor, it is one we will not win."

"Onkeel we have always won, even now with only a small band of young warriors against many Hunden, we won. Do you know why we win?" Isantor asked.

"We win because we are skilled and we fight bravely," Onkeel said, confident in his answer.

"No the answer is simpler than that my old friend. The reason we win when there is no chance of success is because we allow the warrior within us to be greater than the warrior upon us. There are two parts of you in conflict right now, but you cannot face your enemy having two streams of thought that contradict each other. You must first be at peace with yourself, if you expect to bring peace to others. You now fight a war within you, but your heart, and not your thoughts will decide which part of you wins the day my captain."

Onkeel nodded in agreement and smiled. He turned toward Gallra's tree house and looked on proudly as he saw the fire in the eyes of the young warriors. "Come Isantor. The young ones gather weapons for the battle. Let us teach them how to use them."

31 ALL IN

In Mantoo, the war was taking its toll on the army. Wesley looked at the western passage, hoping to catch a glimpse of his brother. As the dark army finally broke through the last line, the Mantoo army move back to the last hill on the battlefield. Vannet Falls was now in plain sight, and if the last hill was taken, the secret passage would be in jeopardy. Many of the Mantoo citizens gathered in the highest towers could see the battle from their vantage points. Troldomen's spell only allowed anyone looking toward Mantoo to see the falls and jagged rocks. Aubaultmor looked toward Mantoo and saw passed Troldomen's spell. He commanded his army to press the attacked and nodded his head in confidence.

Wesley sighed in frustration. From his place on the battlefield, he turned to his father, smiled, and then drew his sword.

"Wesley!" Wyler shouted and made a large gesture with his hand.

Wesley moved his horse next to his father and waited patiently for him to speak.

"You fight well my son. Our enemy has a new respect for you and your sword, but do not mistake that respect for fear. We need to push the dark army back near Lurikai drop."

"How father? The men are exhausted, and for each one of these creatures we destroy, another three takes its place," Wesley said sounding tired and frustrated.

"I still have a trick or two in my old head my boy," he said smiling.

Suddenly a large crashing sound emanated from the Mantoo-side of the hill. The sound of drums and cymbals and horns filled the hillside. The dark army was confused, and the vibrations felt across the field were causing the mud men to break apart. Wesley smiled as he saw Dionne leading a small group of soldiers playing the musical instruments, and advancing forward. He positioned a group of archers behind the musicians and had them periodically shoot arrows into the mud men as the vibrations caused them to discorporate. As the dark army slowly retreated back toward Lurikai drop, Wyler summoned Wesley once more.

"Have your sister retreat to the gate before Aubaultmor makes an adjustment. Use the honor guard to hold the line and the singing sword to keep him from reforming those ghastly creatures. And whatever you do, avoid engaging Aubaultmor directly until your brother arrives."

"You are still certain he is coming father?"

"I would wager that he would arrive when the moment to strike our strongest blow is at hand. Remember, help your army, but do not engage Aubaultmor."

Wesley rode directly into the oncoming Mud men warriors and sliced them in half with a swipe of his sword. The soldiers of the dark army instantly crumbled into ash and dirt when he struck them. His sword made a ringing sound as he hit them, which prevented them from being reassembled. Aubaultmor took notice and snorted with anger. The fire from his nostril drew Wesley's attention.

As Wesley turned to face him Aubaultmor spoke. "Clever Mantoo. You wield the singing sword of Hooglieed. Bring it to me," he bellowed.

Wesley used the sword to cut a clear path from where he began to the honor guard. Aubaultmor waved his hand and one of the Fricke giants fell deep into his spell. The giant stepped in front of Wesley and roared. The giant stood easily four feet taller than Wesley's horse. He struck the horse with his open hand, which sent both Wesley and his horse to the ground. Norfas saw the commotion and ran toward his prince. The Fricke giant grabbed the horse by the neck and threw him thirty feet in the air. He picked up a large stone and lifted it above his head with the intention of dropping it on the young prince. Wesley quickly rose to his feet and cut off the giant's right arm above the elbow. The large rock the giant was holding immediately slipped from his left hand and landed on its head.

A group of mud men quickly surrounded Wesley, but he spun in a full circle, while extending the sword and quickly reduced them to dust. The sword continued to sing as he slashed away. It sang even louder as he cut down two Crocodons. Wesley held the sword close to a large, advancing dark soldier and the ringing alone, caused it to explode into dust.

This angered Aubaultmor, and he summoned more Fricke giants to attack the young prince. Wyler was also being attacked on all sides, and he too was fighting for his life. He was able to look across the field at his youngest son, and watched as they closed in around him. Realizing the true power of the sword, Wesley swung the sword around himself as the giants reached for him, which cut off their hands. Without pausing, he lowered his swing, which took off their lower legs. As they fell, he raised his next swing, which took off their heads. Some of the remaining Fricke giants ran when they saw this, but one leaped in the air and was about to land on top of him. A large rock knocked the giant out of the air and a good distance from the battle. Wesley looked in the direction of its origin and saw Norfas smiling and waving at him. Aubaultmor threw a ball of fire at Norfas and caught him unaware. The fire ball lifted him off of his feet and carried him almost fifty yards from the battle before burning out. Norfas quickly rose to his feet and dusted himself off. He ran back toward the battle as fast as he his feet could carry him. A chill came over him as he realized the great distance to cover and that suddenly there was no one between Aubaultmor and the Prince.

On the west road of Alkotten near Filenor pass Brutus led the combined armies of Alusta and Alkotten to a strange icy wall. He walked up a ledge along the wall pulled a thick sheet of ice from it, and then he held it up for all to see.

"The Ice on this part of the mountain is very light, but very dense. It can be broken off into planks. We use them to make many of our walls. Today we will use them to take us down the mountain faster than has ever been done before!" He yelled. Brutus walked up to Ringo and handed him the ice plank. Ringo studied it for a moment.

"Is this safe?" Ringo asked.

"War is not safe." Warrendr said taking the plank from him. He moved to the edge of the steep slope and looked down. Brutus walked up to him and looked over the edge too. "I did this as a child," he whispered. "You can sit on the plank as it goes down the mountain. There are no trees here, but the wind will be treacherous."

Warrendr took a few steps back and threw the plank over the edge. He ran to the edge and quickly jumped off. Half of the combined armies moved to the edge to see what he was doing. His leap was amazing, and to Ringo, it appeared as though Warrendr was flying. He bent his knees as he drew closer to the ground and landed steadily on the moving board of ice. Ringo looked on in amazement and watched as Warrendr rode the plank down the icy passage at amazing speed. Immediately, everyone grabbed an ice plank, and followed Warrendr down.

The side of the mountain quickly filled up with soldiers from Alusta and Alkotten speeding down it. Ringo was focused on the task at hand, and looked straight down the mountain without fear. Troldomen took notice and maneuvered close to him. They were moving so quickly down the mountain that the wind rushing past them was deafening. Neither of them noticed the hawk behind them trying desperately to catch up. Troldomen waved to get Ringo's attention.

"How are you young Master?" He asked loudly.

Ringo gave him a nod. He noticed the smile on Troldomen's face and returned a puzzled look. "What is so amusing?" Ringo yelled back.

"Look around you Ringo. You have done it! They are united for a single cause!"

"By no effort of mine! It was a matter of circumstance!"

"But the Maisha-Vad was won once they united. It did not matter how it came about. They will sign a treaty when this is over!"

Ringo studied the darkness at a distance beneath them "We have to survive it first," he said.

32 THE FALLEN PRINCE

Wesley stood only a few yards from Aubaultmor. Despite a reduction from his original size, Aubaultmor was still over twelve feet tall and seemed larger than the Fricke giants in Wesley's eyes.

Wesley was surprised by the difference in their height. He thought to himself "Aubaultmor did not seem that tall from a distance".

Aubaultmor drew his sword, which was actually bigger than Wesley and raised it over his head. From a distance, Wyler saw what was happening and moved toward them as quickly as his horse could carry him. Aubaultmor sought to destroy the prince with his first strike. He brought his sword down mercilessly, but missed as Wesley dodged to the right. Wesley took advantage of the sword hitting the ground next to him and struck it with the singing sword. Aubaultmor looked puzzled for a moment, as he did not understand why Wesley would take the time to strike his sword. He pulled his sword from the ground and raised it high once more as Wesley turned and lifted his sword. Wesley's singing sword was vibrating louder than ever from the hit Wesley gave it against Aubaultmor's sword. The loud cry it gave out caused Aubaultmor to drop his sword and cover his ears. The vibration was so great that Aubaultmor's body began to fall apart as Wesley moved it closer to him.

Wesley hit the sword against a nearby rock to maintain the sword's song, and thrust the sword into Aubaultmor's stomach. Aubaultmor cried out in pain as his body blew apart into dust and ash. Everyone stopped fighting for a moment in amazement of the sight. Wyler made his way to Wesley and placed his hand on his son's shoulder. He smiled proudly at his son, and hugged him tightly.

Wesley pushed Wyler's hands from around him and moved him aside as the dust and ash that was once Aubaultmor began to move and take form.

The half-formed Aubaultmor lifted his sword and lunged forward toward Wyler. Wesley ran in front of his father and pushed him out of the way, and the dark blade of Aubaultmor ran him through instead.

Aubaultmor withdrew his blade, and Wesley fell before his father. Wesley rose to one knee and handed Wyler the singing sword. He smiled and placed his right hand on his father's shoulder. He looked to the sky in the west, and strained to speak. "Ringo...." was all he managed to say before he fell.

Wyler was stunned for a moment, and became enraged. He tightly gripped the singing sword and attacked Aubaultmor with a fury that no one expected. Aubaultmor took a few steps back to avoid the singing sword. His body was quickly rebuilding itself from the surrounding ash and rocks as he fought. He lunged forward, but Wyler sidestepped and swung his sword at Aubaultmor's thigh. Aubaultmor's leg crumbled into dust, as the sword passed through it. Aubaultmor cried out in pain. He fell to the ground and landed on his right side. Wyler moved in to strike, but paused as he met eyes with his enemy. Aubaultmor took a deep breath and breathed out fire. Upon seeing Wyler, one of the Fricke giants charged at him. The giant ran in between Wyler and Aubaultmor and inadvertently took the brunt of the flames.

Wyler watched as the fire intended for him quickly reduced the giant to a pile of ash. Another Fricke ran over to the pile and bent down in front of it. He moved his hand through the ashes and let out a frightening cry as he turned toward Wyler. The Giant took a swipe at Wyler and knocked the singing sword from his hand. He grabbed Wyler and lifted him with one hand, and Aubaultmor smiled with delight.

The giant pulled Wyler close to his face a roared. The giant's breath blew Wyler around like a piece of paper in his hand. Eight soldiers from the dark army paraded wildly on the ground below. Aubaultmor was able to reform his injured leg and made his way to his feet. He stabbed the ground with his sword and walked over to them. He used two fingers to pull the crown from Wyler's head, and placed in on the nail of his index finger. He playfully twirled it around and laughed in triumph.

"I now see you for who you are. I have waited many years to destroy you Mantoo. Your friends in the high and low regions will follow you to your grave," he looked at the Fricke Giant and said, "Eat him!" in a menacing voice.

Once again the giant roared. Wyler tried to wiggle himself free, but the giant's grip was too tight. The giant positioned Wyler above his mouth while he tilted his head back. He opened his mouth wide, and stuck his enormous tongue out to take in his catch. A loud and growing swishing sound disrupted the proceedings. "Wait! What is that sound?" Aubaultmor asked.

Aubaultmor turned to face the mountain and took a step back to look up. The moment he lifted his head, a sheet of ice slid off the mountain and bounced off his helmet. The ice sheet landed on top of the dark soldiers crushing them into dust. It stopped directly in front of the Fricke giant that was holding Wyler. It was Ringo. Without hesitating, he fired an arrow from his position directly under the giant. It pierced the giants' lower jaw forcing its mouth closed, and killing it in one blow. The giant immediately released Wyler as it fell backwards. Ringo caught his father and placed him gently on the ground. He moved Wyler behind him and drew another arrow. He fired at Aubaultmor, who managed to snatch the arrow out of the air and snap into pieces with the same hand.

"Your Mantoo weapons are no match for me." Aubaultmor boasted.

Ringo smiled at him. "Actually my weapon is behind you," he grinned.

Warrendr jumped off of his ice board as it came off the edge of the mountain and jumped onto Aubaultmor's neck. Dust and ash flew from them as they struggled. Aubaultmor let out a cry that called every dark creature from the mountain to him, but the armies of Alusta and Alkotten slid down from the mountain and met them. Each soldier followed Ringo's lead and landed their boards on the heads on the approaching dark soldiers. After landing, each soldier pulled a sword, long staff, or bow and immediately began destroying the soldiers of the dark army around them.

"Fortune smiles on us my son. We now have the advantage." Wyler said.

Aubaultmor finally struggled free from Warrendr's grip and threw him half way across the field. Warrendr twisted and turned in the air and landed on his feet. He immediately began running toward Aubaultmor, who grabbed a hollow wooden tube from his belt and placed it in his mouth. It looked like a musical flute, but when he blew into it, no sound came out. Oddly enough, every Alustan covered his ears in pain.

"What manner of weapon is this?" Wyler asked Ringo.

"I'm not sure." Ringo said looking around.

He grabbed a piece of wood from the ground and stuck it onto the tip of his arrow. Ringo fired the arrow into the end of the flute and clogged the hole.

Aubaultmor looked at the end of the flute and threw it down in disgust.

"I think you've made him angry." Wyler said.

"That may not be the best strategy." Ringo answered. "By the way, he looks nothing like a dragon."

A roar in the distance sent a chill down Ringo's spine. He looked to the east and saw a tall, white, hairy figure running toward the battle in the distance. The whistle Aubaultmor blew into summoned the Hoynarr to the battle.

The creature went about destroying everything in its path en route to Aubaultmor. The Hoynarr slashed and clawed its way through the battle field and appeared even more unstoppable than before to Ringo. Ringo felt the strength leave his legs; they felt like logs under him. The creature released a bone-chilling roar as it approached. It was deadly, hungry for blood and worst of all, it was coming right at them.

33 WHEN MANTOO FALLS

Wyler looked around the field until he spotted the singing sword. He retrieved it quickly and returned to Ringo's side.

"I have faced this creature on my quest twice father. The Sword may cut him, but it won't kill him. I need more. Where is Wesley? I entrusted him with this sword."

Wyler's eyes told Ringo all he needed to know. "Where?" Ringo whimpered.

Wyler pointed to the exact spot where Wesley fell, and Ringo, seeing his fallen brother ran to him. He dropped to his knees and sobbed as he lifted Wesley's head. Ringo kissed his forehead and then squeezed his limp body.

"He is not yet departed." Troldomen said walking up behind them.

"What do you mean?" Ringo cried.

"He is close to death, but holds on with mere a breath." Troldomen answered.

"Can you save him?" Ringo said desperately.

"We are on Mantoo soil Ringo. Magic is forbidden here."

"Father you are king, you can change the law." Ringo said turning to him.

"It was decreed that the laws pertaining to magic could only be repealed by the elder council," Wyler replied sadly.

"As I recall the King can do what is needed to preserve the lives of every Mantoo on a field of battle including rewriting an age-old law," Troldomen said confidently.

As everyone looked at Wyler, he looked down at Wesley. He gave a small nod and turned toward Aubaultmor.

"I do not have a healing spell that can fix this," Troldomen said looking at Wesley's wounds.

"You must try Troldomen, you cannot let him die…not here…not like this." Ringo said filled with emotion.

"I…I don't have anything powerful enough to," Troldomen began.

"The Tikats," Ringo said excitedly. "The spell you used on the Tikats froze them in place. It won't heal him, but it will stop him from getting worse."

"I don't know if that will work." Troldomen said matching his excitement.

"Doing nothing will only ensure that the outcome you desire is evenly locked with the outcome you do not," Wyler said calmly.

"If the scales are to be tipped, it will be due to effort and not chance," Wyler and Troldomen said together.

"You would dare quote father at a time like this," Troldomen said almost angry.

"Why are you upset?" Ringo asked.

"It implies cheating is the right thing to do in certain circumstances." Troldomen lashed out.

"This is one of those circumstances." Wyler said sternly. "Death deserves to be cheated," he said, sadly looking at Wesley.

Troldomen casts his spell while Wyler and Ringo looked on. When he was finished, Troldomen gave Wyler a nod of assurance. The effort left him very tired. "I've only bought him moments," he whispered.

Ringo's head dropped as he took in the grave news. At that moment, the Hoynarr had reached Aubaultmor, and stood obediently in front of him, panting heavily. Aubaultmor pointed to Wyler without saying a word. The Hoynarr turned to face its target and charged at Wyler, who was trying to console Ringo.

Ringo's pain was evident as he pounded the ground with his fist. He cried out in anguish so loudly that everyone near them stopped fighting to watch him. When he noticed the Hoynarr charging, he gently laid Wesley's head down, and rose to his feet. He picked up the singing sword and charged the Hoynarr without fear or hesitation. Ringo ran past his father and hit the flat side of sword against the edge of large rock without stopping. As the sword sang out, Ringo jumped into the air and swung it at the Hoynarr with unbridled fury. The creature was instantly cut on its left side, and was confused, having never been injured like that before. Ringo kept swinging, cutting and dodging until the creature backed up. Warrendr and Mecca joined the fray, and began to swing and chop away with their swords.

The Hoynarr backed up as the three of them pressed the attack. The creature was immediately less interested in Ringo once Mecca and Warrendr joined the fight. It snapped at them furiously with its teeth as if trying to bite them.

Aubaultmor noticed Mecca's back turned to him and lifted his sword. He brought his hand down swiftly, but his blade was met by a long staff held by Brutus. Mecca realized what almost happened, and immediately left the Hoynarr and joined Brutus in fighting Aubaultmor. Wyler watched for a brief moment, and then pulled his sword and joined them.

The three kings swung their swords against Aubaultmor together. Aubaultmor backed up to the mountainside and managed to deflect the blows from his enemies just long enough to act. He turned toward the Hoynarr and gazed at him with his flaming eyes. The Hoynarr's body stiffened for a moment as Aubaultmor's thoughts entered its mind. The creature pulled a large rock from the soil and hurled it at Brutus. Thinking quickly, Mecca pushed Brutus out of the way, but ran straight into Aubaultmor's blade.

"No metal on the great mountain can pierce the skin of anyone born of Alusta." Mecca Boasted.

"My sword is made from the Hoynarr's tooth," Aubaultmor roared.

Mecca looked down to see that Aubaultmor's sword had indeed run him through. He grabbed the blade with his hand as Aubaultmor pulled it out. Mecca dropped to his knees and fell on his face before anyone realized what happened.

"NO!" Warrendr screamed, still battling the Hoynarr. The distraction was enough of an opening for the Hoynarr, who quickly forced his claws through Warrendr's back, killing him instantly. And in what only felt like a moment, Alusta's fiercest warriors were gone.

Ringo continued to press his attack on the Hoynarr, but Aubaultmor was gaining the upper hand on Wyler and Brutus. Aubaultmor tried again to take possession of the Hoynarr's mind, but when his bodied stiffened, Ringo did not hesitate to cut the beast below its knee. The pain broke Aubaultmor's spell and caused the creature to go limp.

With Aubaultmor slightly distracted, Wyler picked up Mecca's sword in his right hand and attacked. He wielded both swords equally well with either hand, but Aubaultmor managed to deflect every blow. Aubaultmor waved his hand and a sudden wind forced Brutus into the side of the mountain. He fell on his hands and knees as the wind let up. Aubaultmor lifted his hand, which caused both Brutus and Wyler to float in the air before him. They tried desperately to move, but could not break his spell.

"I have spilled the blood of a King on the great mountain, and now my body is made whole again. My powers are returning. I am gaining strength with each moment." Aubaultmor thundered as he looked at Brutus. "You imprisoned me. It was Alkotten crystal that made my prison. You will never again get that opportunity. Behold," he said pointing to the sky.

The skies high above their vantage point darkened and dark clouds formed instantly over Alkotten. Aubaultmor blew a smoke cloud into the air with his mouth, and an image of Alkotten appeared within the cloud.

Brutus was overcome with horror as he looked into the cloud that Aubaultmor placed in front of him. He watched as lightning ripped across the skies over Alkotten and continually struck his home. When the lightning stopped and the image cleared, Brutus' heart sank as he saw that the palace was completely destroyed. But his horror did not end there as suddenly lightning came down on each of his replicates, destroying his entire army instantly. Their essence returned to Brutus, who could do nothing but drop his head in despair.

A fiery smile lit up Aubaultmor's dark face. "I will take your hearts before I take your lives," he roared. He held out his hand again and looked at Wyler. "You took possession of my luck when I was defeated and now it has run dry. Behold the destruction of Mantoo."

34 HOYNARR AND HELLFIRE

Aubaultmor lifted his hand as he did before. The clouds began to swirl and the sky directly over them became black. The wind blew wildly and whipped across the field. Aubaultmor's demonic laugh filled the air as the magical veil over Mantoo fell, and everyone on the battle field could see the hidden gate.

Wyler looked on in disbelief as a tornado formed in front of the Mantoo gate. All that were present shielded the wind from their eyes and watched as the tornado crossed the falls and approached the outermost village. Wyler held his breath and cringed in anticipation as the tornado approached Dionne and the elite guard, but suddenly, and unexpectedly, the tornado dissipated. The winds stopped and the sky cleared, which seemed to confuse Aubaultmor. He was further confused as he watched Wyler and Brutus float gently to the ground against his will.

"What? Who dares?" Aubaultmor yelled.

The laugh coming from above him was small, but familiar.

"Troldomen." Wyler said softly.

It was indeed Troldomen. He was sitting on a rocky perch high above Aubaultmor's head.

"I am by no means fast, but I am timely," he said taking a puff from his pipe.

"Now here is an interesting thing Aubaultmor. It would seem since Wyler and I have a portion of your luck and magic, and the stronger you get, the stronger we get. And if that's the case…"

Troldomen extended his hand to the sky. A bolt of lightning immediately hit Aubaultmor where he stood. He jumped off the perch, and flew in the air around Aubaultmor's head. Lightning flew from their hands as they exchanged, and parried bolts. Lady Arna watched in amazement and took out her small hand-held telescope. She gasped at the sight of Troldomen and looked toward the heavens as a tear rolled down her cheek.

Ringo walked up to Wyler and took a knee to be eye to eye with him.

"If what Troldomen says is true father, then you hold the key to our victory," he said.

"How so?" Wyler asked.

"You have been the luckiest man on this mountain for two ages. If Aubaultmor's luck and yours are connected, you only have to reach out and take it from him as Troldomen has done his magic."

Wyler dropped his head and closed his eyes. Ringo fought off every beast and dark soldier that dared attack them. Suddenly a strange howl caught his ear. Ringo turned and saw a pack of thirty Hunden running toward him. He backed up and moved close to Wyler. The Hunden ran forward knocking over everything in their way as they moved toward Ringo. They formed three rows as they continued to advance.

Wyler kept concentrating and did not open his eyes. Ringo lifted his sword as they approached, and took a single step in their direction. Before he could take another, arrows dropped in between him and the first line, killing the entire first row of Hunden. Ringo turned to see the Farrador warriors behind him running at top speed, while loading their bows. The warriors fired another set of arrows killing most of the second line, but drew their long knives to engage the rest of them close up.

The fight was fierce, but quick. The Farrador saw it as an opportunity for vengeance, and did not hesitate to slay every Hunden on the field. A second wave of Hunden arrived, and instantly joined the battle. They attacked the Alustan army and killed many of their soldiers before four of them made their way to Dakahn. He lifted his sword and killed two of the Hunden with one blow. The two remaining Hunden attacked from opposite sides. They each bit down on one of his arms above the wrist, and began to pull fiercely. Dakahn grimaced in pain, but did not drop his sword and did his best not to cry out. He knew that it would be considered an act of weakness. He began to panic as he saw his own blood. Dakahn was never cut before, and having never faced the Hunden in battle, he knew little of the damage their teeth could inflict on his skin.

An arrow came out of nowhere and hit the Hunden on his left arm directly in the eye. It dropped to the ground immediately, which allowed Dakahn to strike the other Hunden in the head. When it dropped, he turned to face Onkeel, who was pulling the arrow out of the head of the dead Hunden.

"You have my thanks warrior." Dakahn said.

"Hunden teeth are sharp enough to cut us, but their eyes are weak." Onkeel replied.

"You are Farrador?" Dakahn asked.

"You are from Alusta?" Onkeel asked walking up to him. They stared at each other for a moment and noticed that they were the same height and build, and despite their very different clothes, were practically mirror images of each other.

"We are not that different." Dakahn said staring at him.

"We are very different." Onkeel replied. "I know not to feed the Hunden my hands."

They both smiled for a moment, but were interrupted by the growling of three very large Hunden. The two warriors positioned themselves to strike, but a boomerang wrapped round them in a tight circle and cut each of the Hunden's throats, then flew off to their right into Gallra's hand. Gallra gave them a quick nod and quickly ran to join the battle. He ran toward the lightning that Troldomen and Aubaultmor were still hailing at each other, and stopped next to Ringo. As he looked up in the sky at Troldomen, Ringo watched him studying Aubaultmor in great detail.

"You study the dark lord for weakness. What do you see?" Ringo asked

Still looking up at the battle in the sky, Gallra said "Many missing things."

"What do you mean?" Wyler said as he made his way to his feet.

"Ice for one thing," he said pointing "See, fire, ash, rock, lightning, wind; all from the mountain. But metal, Ice, crystal, and certain rocks are missing. Why just those elements, and objects? Do they make him weak, while the ones around him make him strong? The ash is burnt wood, but wood is stronger before the fire. The crystal is harder than the rock. He wields the dead things, but nothing that brings life, like the sun and the rain." Gallra cut himself off and became startled when he saw the Hoynarr. "What is this beast?' he asked.

"The Hoynarr. Be careful, it hunts your kind. It has already slain two of my friends," Ringo answered.

"What is it doing?'

Ringo looked at it with amazement. "Oh…Oh no. Aubaultmor is casting a spell even while he fights Troldomen." Ringo said turning his eyes back to Aubaultmor.

"What does that mean? What happening?" Wyler asked.

"The Hoynarr; it's healing and it's growing," Ringo said fearfully. "Aubaultmor means to use it to destroy us all."

35 MANTOO MUFFIN

The Hoynarr roared and charged at Ringo and Gallra. Tara, Wesley's falcon, suddenly distracted it. The Hoynarr swatted and hissed at the bird as it flew circles around its head. Tara clawed at the left eye of the beast. It howled it pain and lashed out with its right arm, hitting the bird out of the air. It landed a few feet past Ringo and Gallra. Gallra took a crystal tipped arrow and loaded it into his crossbow. He handed one to Ringo and said, "Aim for his left eye."

The Hoynarr roared and charged. Both of them steadied themselves and fired as Gallra yelled "Now!" Both arrows found their mark and blinded the beast who was screaming in pain as it pulled the arrows from its eyes.

Ringo ran over to the bird, and lifted it off the ground. "Tara!" He shouted at the lifeless bird. Ringo stroked the bird's broken body and noticed the note that was attached its leg. He quickly unraveled it and read it aloud.

"Alkotten crystal and Mantoo metal; Alusta stone placed in a kettle.

Alkotten ice, and Mantoo water; Alusta fire worn by kings daughter.

Silver shale, and buckskin leather. To bind him place them all together

Mix them, churn them while their hot, and cool them in the boiling pot

Add Eastern oak and Northern pine, and coal picked from the southern mines

Western sand and dragon's scale get stirred until the colors fail

Rolled and baked into a ball to bind evil once-and-for-all."

Wyler and Brutus looked at Ringo. "The king's scepters." Brutus said excitedly. "I loaded much of what you read into the scepters that I gave to each kings of the mountain many years ago."

Ringo looked at Troldomen and Aubaultmor who were still locked in battle. "We must hurry," he said. "Troldomen cannot hold him for much longer."

Wyler and Brutus removed the scepters that they were carrying from their belts. They shattered each of the scepters heads into Ringo's shield. Ringo called Dakahn and asked him for his firearm. Ringo blasted the ground under the shield and started a fire. Brutus took the poem and looked it over, while Wyler looked around the battlefield, amidst the carnage, for Mecca's Scepter. Wyler found Mecca's crushed Scepter and took off his helmet. He placed everything he could into his helmet and dumped the contents into the fiery shield.

Brutus looked at the fire. "Dragon Scale? There are no dragons on the mountain."

Ringo looked around and noticed the dead Crocodons. "There are your dragons," he pointed.

Brutus continued to read. "Silver shale and buckskin leather?"

Gallra held up two boomerangs. "My weapons. The blades are made with silver shale. This one is made with eastern oak. My arrows are made with Northern pine."

"Coal picked from the southern mines?" Brutus continued.

"The Mantoo crown is made from Mantoo metal. One of the jewels stones used to be coal." Ringo said as he threw it into the fire. Dakahn threw the feet of a crocodon into the fire, and the mixture within the shield began to turn purple.

"Alusta fire worn by kings' daughter?" Brutus asked.

The five of them grew quiet as they thought about the meaning.

"My hair Comb" Dinatru said walking toward them with two of the Alustan royal guards. She wiped a tear as she threw her fire comb into the mixture and walked over to Ringo.

"I thought you might have perished when Aubaultmor destroyed Alkotten." Ringo said hugging her.

"My father sent me home with a small group of guards. We are warriors, so I came to fight alongside them."

"Princess… I am sorry but..," he began.

"I heard them die Ringo," she said sadly. "My people need to see a member of the royal family while they defend our lands. I represent the house of Mecca, and I will not fail my people. What else is needed king Brutus?" She asked bravely.

"Buckskin leather and Mantoo water," he replied

"The boots worn by the Fricke giants are laced with buckskin leather." Ringo added. "Mantoo water is all around us."

Dinatru gave a nod and her two guards ran to get what was needed. They quickly returned with the laces and the water. They threw them into the fire, but nothing happened.

"What has gone wrong?" Ringo asked. "We've done everything. We've followed the recipe."

"No." Wyler said stroking his beard. "We are missing something."

"Wait!" Gallra started. Alkotten Ice would be made into water once it hit the flames. In fact, all of the mountains water is melted ice from Alkotten. Mantoo water has to have another meaning."

"Indeed it must, but what?" Brutus asked.

Ringo walked close to the fire and stood still. He reached under his armor and ripped a piece of his shirt near the neck. He held it out and twisted it, causing the sweat from his shirt to run unto the fiery heap. He took the singing sword and stirred the pile until everything was thick and black. The mixture quickly took on a dough-like consistency. Brutus looked at it and glanced at Dinatru.

"Could you handle the mixture princess? We need it shaped into a sphere."

Without hesitating, Dinatru quickly molded the pile into a sphere.

"It must be perfectly round." Wyler said nervously.

Gallra joined in and helped her.

"You were of Alusta once." She said to him.

"I have heard stories of its beauty, and the beauty of its people. I am happy there was truth in the stories," he smiled.

Dinatru returned a smile. "Perhaps if we survive this, you can come to see if the stories of the land your people left behind are true as well."

Gallra stood up. "It's ready," he said confidently.

"Well we can't force him to eat it, but we need to get it inside of him somehow." Ringo said looking at Aubaultmor.

Gallra looked at the blind Hoynarr who still swatting away at anything near him. As the Hoynarr's claws ripped through a portion of the mountain wall like it was butter, Gallra shook he head and smiled. He pointed to the Hoynarr and said "I think we may have a way."

.

36 THE FALL OF THE CHOSEN

As Troldomen and Aubaultmor continued to battle, Troldomen began to weaken. Lady Arna was still fearfully watching from a safe distance through her small hand-held telescope.

"Oh Trolly, you are so brave." She whispered. "Please be careful." she despaired.

Onkeel and Isantor were slashing their way through the remaining Hunden, when one of them jumped on Isantor's back. It pinned him to the ground and open its jaws wide. Just as it dropped its head and closed its mouth, Onkeel shoved his sword into the creature's mouth sideways. As it bit down on Onkeel sword, its jaw was cut off, and it ran away in pain, but only managed to get a few yards before it collapsed, and died.

Onkeel helped Isantor to his feet. "The battle favors the just," he said looking at his sword. Isantor looked at him and smiled.

"Yes. It would appear Gallra too has found the warrior within himself," he said pointing at Gallra. "But the wizard may not survive against the Dark one."

They watched as Aubaultmor hit Troldomen with a string of lightning bolts and fire balls from his hand. Troldomen fell out of the sky, and hit the ground with a thud. Aubaultmor lifted his leg to step on him, but Onkeel used his speed to run under Aubaultmor's foot and grabbed Troldomen before he could be crushed. Onkeel sped away toward Gallra and Ringo, but an enraged Aubaultmor fired lightning from his fingers hitting him in the back. Onkeel and Troldomen were smoking as their bodies came to a halt on the ground in front of Ringo.

Ringo and Gallra patted the small flames on their clothes and turned them over.

"Young Master." Troldomen Whispered. "I have done my part. Your destiny awaits you."

Ringo placed his hand on Troldomen's' chest. Troldomen's eyes closed, but he continued breathing. "He sleeps." Ringo said, looking at a worried Wyler.

Wyler nodded and began to tend to his fallen brother.

Gallra held Onkeel's head in arms. "The lightning burns the blood under my skin," he whispered in a weak voice.

Gallra pulled a metal rod from his pouch and plunged it into the ground a few feet from them. He twisted and pulled it, which caused it to triple its size as it unfolded toward the sky. He returned to his spot on the ground next to Onkeel's just as Aubaultmor released more lightning from his massive fingers. The bolts of electricity were attracted to the rod in the ground and missed them entirely. Aubaultmor huffed in frustration as he tried over and over again to strike them with the electricity and watched it dive into the iron rod.

Onkeel managed to smile through his pain. "You really are the Utvinder. You are the chosen one, and I made them leave you when you could not keep up," he said in a weak voice.

"None of that matters now Onkeel."

"Yes it does. You are destined to save our people."

At that moment Aubaultmor was being fired upon by the Alustan guards. They shot arrows and fire darts, which only succeeded in annoying him. Noticing the affect the electricity had on Onkeel, he began bombarding all of the Alustan and Farrador warriors with it.

"No!" Wyler shouted. "He's discovered their weakness."

"I don't understand." Ringo started. "Their skin is resistant to heat."

"They manage all temperatures well, if given time to adapt. A sudden change in temperature can be fatal to them. We cannot let them die Ringo."

Ringo looked at Aubaultmor and lifted the singing sword. "We won't."

Gallra moved to stand up, but Onkeel grabbed his arm.

"The weapon is formed, where are you going?" Onkeel asked in a weak voice.

Gallra smiled and patted his hand, while gently laying it at his side.

"I am Gallra of Farrador, son of Golarra, and I am Utvinder; the first in many generations of our kind. I go to save my people." Gallra stood up and began to walk diligently next to Ringo. He grabbed a metal boomerang from his belt and threw it at Aubaultmor who was blasting the Alustans and Farrador with lightning from his hands. It sailed between his arms and pulled the lightning into it as it passed them. The sharpened edge of the boomerang found its way into Aubaultmor's chest, and the lightning from his fingers quickly turned and followed. The bolts hit Aubaultmor in the chest, knocking him to the ground. The ground smoldered, and Aubaultmor made his way to his feet in a cloud of dust and ash. As he rose to his feet, Aubaultmor looked at Ringo and Gallra and studied them for a moment. There was calmness in the air suddenly, as if everyone on the battlefield was waiting to see what would happen next.

Troldomen took advantage of the moment and began to chant his spell.

"When the first son rises and swords are raised
darkness rules, but gods are praised
The mountain sees its darkest days
When Aubaultmor comes home

Ash and soot is all you breathe
You try to run but cannot leave
Death awaits we all believe
When Aubaultmor comes home
Mantoo iron, Alkotten Ice,
Alustan fire, and dead zone spice
shale, and snippets from three mice
mixed with southern stones
with Eastern oak and Northern pine,
and coal picked from the southern mines
with Crystal core you must combine
to bind his evil bones
When Aubaultmor comes home
When Aubaultmor comes home."

Ringo began to whisper to Gallra without taking his eyes off of Aubaultmor. "Do you think this will work?" He asked nervously.

"It better," Gallra quipped.

Ringo turned to look at the ball, which was now glowing after Troldomen's spell. "It would appear that the Muffin is ready," he said playfully.

"Muffin?" Gallra asked, confused by the word.

"Never mind. Let's do it, they're ready. Ready?'

"Yes." Gallra said with a determined look.

"Go!" Ringo commanded.

As they ran quickly, Gallra threw his last boomerang at Aubaultmor, and then turned in the direction of the Hoynarr, who was crouching next to the mountain wall. The Hoynarr smelled him coming and rose to his feet. At the same time, Ringo moved close to Aubaultmor's leg as he turned to avoid the metal boomerang. Ringo swung the singing sword, cutting Aubaultmor's leg and forcing him backwards, closer to the edge.

"He needs a bigger cut." Troldomen exclaimed sitting on the ground.

"You are supposed to be sleeping." Brutus whispered. And with that, Troldomen pretended to be unconscious in front of the orb and covered it with his cloak. Fetter walked over with Gallra's small catapult strapped to his back. He carefully took it off and placed it in front of them.

"It's a sling," he said proudly as he walked back toward the action.

Wyler placed the orb onto the catapult and pointed it toward Aubaultmor. He kept the cloak over it so it would not draw attention, and gave a nod to Ringo who turned to see if the plan was underway.

Ringo whispered "It's ready." The words caught Gallra's ears and he quickly ran past the blind Hoynarr. The beast swung its arms widely in an effort to catch Gallra. At the same time Ringo hit the sword against the side of a rock and swung at Aubaultmor's other leg cutting him deeply. Aubaultmor stumbled close to the edge of the mountain, next to Lurikai drop. The drop was little more than a large hole in the side of the mountain where a large piece of the mountain fell into the ocean many miles below. Gallra and Ringo hoped that the drop to salt water and razor sharp rock would kill anyone, or anything that fell from the edge.

They were doing their best to lead both Aubaultmor and the Hoynarr over the edge, but Aubaultmor quickly realized their plan. He took a deep breath and blew fire at Ringo. Ringo grabbed a nearby shield and managed to block the stream of fire. He fought against the intense heat and force created from the blast, but was blown back twenty feet.

Gallra continued to dodge the very close blows from the Hoynarr as he led it close to the edge. Aubaultmor noticed the ruckus and began weaving a spell to give the Hoynarr its eyes back. Ringo noticed the eyes of the Hoynarr healing and turned to Wyler and Troldomen. "We have to act now," he shouted desperately.

Ringo took a hollow tipped arrow and stabbed it into Mecca's lifeless body.

"You dare defile the body of a king of this mountain?" Brutus shouted angrily.

Ringo calmly pulled it out and loaded his bow.

"Mecca may yet save us all." Ringo said plainly.

As he shot the arrow he screamed "Wesley!" The arrow was shot high and far into the air. "Be ready," he told Wyler as he watched it fly toward Aubaultmor. Ringo whispered a prayer. Gallra managed to bring the Hoynarr close to Aubaultmor just as Ringo's arrow reached them. The arrow was releasing a thin stream of Mecca's blood into the air as it passed the Hoynarr's nose and landed in Aubaultmor's stomach. The scent of the Alustan blood caused the beast to go mad. The Hoynarr was driven mad with bloodlust and swung its massive arms in the direction of the blood trail. The claws from the half-blind beast found there mark, and the blood soaked arrow landed at Gallra's feet. Time stood still as everyone's eyes focused on the large hole that the Hoynarr inadvertently cut into Aubaultmor's stomach.

Without hesitating, Ringo turned to Wyler and yelled "NOW!"

Instantly, Troldomen pulled his cloak off of the sphere and Wyler released the catapult. Wyler's luck was true to him. The sphere flew through the air and landed directly into the large wound that the Hoynarr had just made in Aubaultmor's stomach.

Aubaultmor's body began to stiffen and looked like dried clay. The orb within his stomach began to glow as it absorbed his essence. Within moments, the orb turned blue and fell to the ground, leaving a clay-like statue of Aubaultmor frozen for all to see. Almost immediately, the skies began to clear and the remnants of the dark army fell apart into dust and were quickly lost in the wind.

Ringo closed his eyes and lowered his head. He blocked out all of the sound around him and focused on nothing but the water falls behind him. He slowly opened his eyes and stared in to face of the Hoynarr. Ringo raised his head and tightened his grip on the singing sword. As he walked toward Aubaultmor, he struck the side of the sword against a rock causing it to vibrate and sing. Ringo spun in a circle to gain momentum, and then threw the singing sword into the air toward the frozen Aubaultmor. At the same time, Gallra picked up the blood soaked arrow and waved it in the air. The smell drove the Hoynarr forward and positioned the beast directly behind the petrified body of Aubaultmor. Gallra backed up close to the edge of Lurikai drop as the Hoynarr approached slowly. Its vision was not fully restored and it stopped to sniff the air before it took a step forward.

Gallra quickly took a small rope from his pouch and tied it around the steel tipped arrow. He tied the other end to his ankle, but had to jump backwards as the Hoynarr took a swipe where he was standing. He smiled and tilted his head as he heard Ringo whisper "Don't move." The singing sword passed through Aubaultmor's body, which exploded into dust and smoke once the sword touched it. The sword kept traveling forward, spinning through the air as it travelled.

Fetter was watching the action and saw the sword coming toward Gallra. "Crazy flip!" Fetter yelled as the sword approached.

Gallra bounced off the side of the mountain and flipped sideways as the sword came near. The creature slashed at him with its right hand and missed as Gallra flipped and landed behind the beast. The sword hit the Hoynarr in the neck, which took everyone watching by surprise.

"It has a weak spot," Dinatru said in amazement.

The creature stumbled backwards and fell off of the edge taking Gallra with it.

Fetter screamed his cousin's name as he witnessed the Hoynarr take Gallra off of the edge with it. And Gallra's name continued to echo off of the Mountain walls within Lurikai drop long after he fell.

37 THE KING'S GIFT

Brutus, Fetter, Ringo, Troldomen and Isantor ran to the edge and carefully looked down. Fetter dropped his head in despair when he could not see anything, but he tilted his head to listen and heard a faint sound. He ran to his right and approached the edge from a different angle. He pointed and laughed as he saw Gallra hanging upside down by a rope attached to his ankle.

"Look, he shot the arrow into the side of the mountain as he fell!" he said pointing.

They quickly pulled the unconscious Gallra up and laid him on the ground. Ringo lightly tapped his face, and Gallra woke startled and excited.

"Did it work? Is it dead?" Gallra asked while trying to catch his breath.

Onkeel and Isantor walked up to him. Isantor bowed before him and smiled.

"Utvinder indeed," he said nodding in approval. He hugged Gallra and squeezed him tightly. Gallra was surprised and did not know how to react at first, but returned the hug and smiled. Onkeel and Fetter took turns hugging him as well.

"Utvinder?" Dinatru asked as she walked up behind them. "This Farrador is the chosen one; the one to reunite the lost tribes?"

"He has fulfilled the prophecies." Isantor said still displaying his pride.

"All save one." She said taking his hand. "Come chosen one, we have much to discuss." She said leading him away.

"Where are we going?" Gallra asked still trying to clear his head.

"Home." She said looking at the gathering Alusta and Farrador standing side by side behind Isantor, Dakahn, and Onkeel. "We are all going home," she said proudly.

Everyone stopped to watch Dionne who was on the ground crying while cradling Wesley's head in her arms. She looked up and took noticed to everyone around her and began to cry louder. Ringo and Wyler took a place on the ground next to her. Tears ran down Wyler's face as he began to feel the weight of the moment. Ringo placed a hand on his father and sister to comfort them.

"If it could be me in his stead father," he began.

"There will be no more sacrifices on the Great Mountain today young Mantoo," Brutus interrupted. "I gave way to this evil before we knew it was upon us, and my people, my family suffered for it. Mecca was right not to trust me," he said turning to Wyler. "But you dear Wyler, you were ever my friend and believed in me to the end. For that, and so much more, I will do what must be done." Brutus nodded and moved close to Wesley. "I've lost everything," he continued.

"No Brutus." Wyler said sadly.

"No Wyler, it's true. I have lost everything. My Family, my kingdom and all I cared about are gone. Aubaultmor wanted each of us to be the last of our breed before he destroyed us. Mecca would not give him the satisfaction." Brutus said.

"It is clear that my father's actions were not his own in his last days." Dinatru said sadly. "But he was good, and favored you all, and he truly appreciated your friendship. When you remember him in your halls, I pray that you would honor him by remembering that."

Troldomen looked at Brutus and then Dinatru. "Aubaultmor's evil filled the hearts of many on the Great Mountain. Strangers, friends, and even Kings sought to destroy one another as their hearts grew darker. We have lost much today. Let us forgive those that did not have the strength to defeat the dark Lord within their hearts before they were lost in the battle that took their lives, so that evil can claim no victory here today" Troldomen said.

Brutus nodded. "Perhaps I was too afraid. When sickness took almost all but my family, I crafted replicates to carry on in our stead. It was my pride that destroyed Alkotten long before Aubaultmor raised his hand. I would have no legacy now, but perhaps I can have one if I do this."

Brutus dropped to both knees and touched Wesley's head and chest. Both of them began to glow a soft blue.

"What's happening?" Ringo asked.

"He is giving his life essence to Wesley." Troldomen explained.

"Brutus." Wyler whimpered.

"This is my gift to you Wyler Wantoo. You are the lone king now. Remember me in your halls. Remember Alkotten. Rule well my dear friend. Rule well." Brutus said as the light surrounding him and Wesley faded.

Brutus fell backwards, but was caught by Wyler, who laid his head down gently.

"Behold." Troldomen said as he pointed at Wesley.

Wesley coughed and moaned before sitting up. Ringo rushed him with hugs and laughter. As Wesley made his way to his feet he stumbled for a moment. Ringo caught him and held him up as they walked toward Wyler.

Wesley hugged his father and looked at the destruction around them.

"Have we won? Is he dead?" Wesley asked.

"Aubaultmor has been destroyed". Wyler answered.

"How?"

"Ask your brother." Wyler said proudly.

Wesley looked past Ringo as he saw Troldomen. "Uncle," he said embracing him. "You've returned as well?"

"I figured my nephew needed me to show him a bit of the mountain to complete his journey," Troldomen said returning the embrace.

Wesley looked at his uncle from head to toe. "Your beard has gotten very long since we last exchanged hugs," he smiled

"It has a lot more grey too," Troldomen laughed.

"So, you took care of my brother on his journey eh? Did he rub his ears every night?" Wesley joked.

"Twice on the left and once on the right," Troldomen laughed.

Ringo looked puzzled as he looked around. "I don't rub my ears," he said assuredly.

Dionne, quickly ran into Wesley's arm and hugged him tightly. Her eyes were filled with tears as she looked at him, trying to find words. Wesley was distracted by the sight of the Alustans and Farrador surrounding them. "What's this?" He asked while looking at everyone in amazement.

Dionne focused on Ringo as he rose to thank his new friends.

Dinatru walked over to her and handed her a tooth from her fire comb.

"It's beautiful. Thank you…" Dionne began.

"Dinatru." She said. "I am a friend of your brother Ringo."

"Queen Dinatru," Ringo said correcting her.

"It is customary to give something of ourselves to our new friends." Dinatru said.

Suddenly all of the Farrador, Alustans and Mantoos began exchanging personal items, shields, swords, and bows with their new friends.

Ringo looked at Dinatru and smiled. "What gift do you give to new family?" He asked.

"Speaking of gifts young master, it is to you Ringo Wantoo that a great gift must be passed. Aubaultmor was defeated by your hand, what gift of his shall you have?" Troldomen asked as he gestured to the glowing blue orb.

"You and this young Farrador are the rightful heirs to Aubaultmor's gifts," Wyler said gesturing to Gallra.

Ringo looked at Gallra and smiled. "Any gift?" he asked turning to Troldomen.

Ringo's smile turned to laughter as he thought about the possibilities.

38 WOE THE WIZARD

Days later, in a large house surrounded by roses of every color, Lady Arna stood alone in her kitchen. The large front door opening slowly caught her attention. She quickly turned toward the sink and stared out the window. Troldomen walked toward her slowly without saying a word. He took off his hat as he entered the kitchen and looked around as he placed it on the table. "You painted," he said playfully.

"You did well not to come the first day Troldomen. I was too filled with emotion to speak with you," She said without turning around.

He paused to clear his throat with a light cough, and swallowed hard before gaining the courage to speak. "I also did not know what to say to you. I rehearsed a thousand speeches, and searched the mountain endlessly for some gem or trinket that would ease the pain of this moment, but realized that no spell or jewel could do that," he said softly.

"A spell? Does your spell begin with I'm sorry Arna? Or... I was selfish to make my own wife believe with everyone else that I had died on the mountain?"

"Selfish? Was it selfish of me to sacrifice everything I had to help save the lives of our people? Of everyone on the mountain?" He asked in a quiet, but angered tone.

"Why did you have to sacrifice everything?" She cried as she faced him. "Where was Wyler's sacrifice? Why did you have to risk losing everything to go along with his plans?" Arna asked in tears.

"My leaving was not his plan; it was mine," he said studying the look of horror that was on her face. "Wyler was already set to sacrifice his son, all of his children if the need arose. And no one else was prepared to make the sacrifices needed to save us all. So yes we planned and gambled, and gambled and planned; hoping against hope that we would prevail against insurmountable odds."

"You did. You won. Mantoo is safe, and everyone that went along you're your plan is safe now. Everyone won, but me."

"And what have you lost?"

"I lost us Trolly. Why couldn't you gamble on me?"

"Oh Arna, dear Arna. I could not. In my heart, as much as I wanted to, I knew you could not keep my secret, and the lives of everyone of the mountain would be in peril. For this to work, everyone…everyone had to believe I was dead."

"And so they did; myself included. Your plan worked; you helped save everyone. And almost everything," She said turning around and wiping a tear.

"I have asked Wyler to let you stay on to govern Inovia, and to keep your seat on the elder council," he said gently.

"I assumed you would want to retake your place by your brother's side."

"I will have a seat on the council. With the open seats to fill, and lands to govern, I will be busy establishing myself in the neighboring provinces," he picked up his hat and took a few steps toward the door, before stopping to face her once more.

"We also saved you Arna; though I wished I could have saved us as well."

"You gave up gambling for magic because you said that when you gamble, at least one person loses."

"I remember," he said opening the door.

"Troldomen," She called as he walked outside. "Welcome back," she said as a tear fell from her eye. As he closed the door, she turned toward the window again and cried uncontrollably. Troldomen stopped a few feet from the door and looked over his shoulder. He wiped a tear from his eye and slowly walked north toward the castle.

In the days that followed, Wyler was alone in his garden pacing back and forth. He turned and saw Ringo from the corner of his eye and smiled as he extended his arms to embrace him.

"I was waiting for you to come to me. You've rested quite a bit these many days and have recovered much of your strength."

"I am getting stronger each day father. I think I was more emotionally exhausted than physically," Ringo said hugging him.

"Come sit with me," Wyler said as he sat on a pillow.

"Father I would think with all that was at stake you would have shown up to court today. I mean today of all days."

"Was I found guilty of cheating then?"

"No, but it was said that you did not respect the high court enough to make an appearance at your own trial."

"It was out of respect for the law that I did not go. Had I gone and been found innocent of any wrongdoing in my own Vad, then they would say my presence swayed the court's decision in my favor. People will always talk my son; it's what they do when there is nothing else to occupy their small minds.

"Father I need to know something," Ringo said still standing.

"I know what is troubling you son."

"Did you truly gamble on me or was it more of a gamble on your grand plan?"

"Was your success not a pivotal part of my plan?"

"I'm sure it was, but…"

"Had you failed to bring Brutus and Mecca together Aubaultmor would have laid Mantoo to ash and rubble."

"Your plan seemed to extend beyond my efforts alone."

"When you left Mantoo to fulfill your quest, you did not believe in its purpose. You left out of loyalty, perhaps even curiosity, but in truth you were part of the larger group in Mantoo that refused to believe in Aubaultmor. So I depended on your sense of duty, and your love for your father to place you into the hands of the enemy, knowing full well what you would do once you came to believe in your quest. Alkotten is lost. And we were a hair from losing everything as well. I wagered everything and everyone on your efforts my son. Was I to do nothing?"

"No father. Doing nothing would only ensure that the outcome you desire is evenly locked with the outcome you do not, and if the scales are to be tipped, it will be due to effort and not chance," Ringo said slyly.

"Ringo Wantoo you are indeed well taught."

"I found myself tugging at my ear before I went to sleep a few nights ago. I never realized that I did that before all that happened."

"Do you know why you do that?"

"No."

"When you were small, and I would tell you stories about Aubaultmor, they gave you nightmares. Your mother would lull you back to sleep by rubbing your ears and telling you that…"

"That…" Ringo interrupted. "Her rubbing them would bring me luck. And my dreams would be peaceful. And if I could hear the waterfalls from my window, letting just the sound of the rushing water in, then nothing could ever harm me. And I believed her," he said sadly.

"Now that most of Mantoo has seen Aubaultmor with their own eyes we no longer need to convince them of his existence. It will make the next time all the easier," he said leaving the room.

"Next time? What do you mean, next time?" Ringo said following him.

39 WHERE THE CHIPS FALL

Many weeks later, all of the people of the Great Mountain gathered for the Coronation of Dinatru. Everyone gathered in pairs to greet the new queen on a very long line in Kuningas field, where the setting of the mountains deadliest battle was now the gathering place for its most joyous event.

Troldomen and Lady Arna approached and bowed before Alusta's new Queen. Wyler approached alone and gave a nod.

"The rule of the mountain belongs to our youth!" Wyler shouted. "As I have won the Maisha-Vad, I elect to claim my prize now," he turned to Ringo, who was next in line with Wesley and said "Bow my son," he said proudly.

Ringo took a knee and dropped his head, while Wyler placed his crown on Ringo for all to see. "You are all witness to the events here today. My son is now King over all the Mantoo lands. He shall reign in a time of peace unknown to all on the mountain before." Wyler made his way to the stage and stood to the left of Dinatru. "Today we have seen the crowning of a new queen. To the Farrador, my friends you are Farrador no more. Hence forth, you are all Alustans once more. War and disease has stripped us of our friends and loved ones. Let us remember that Mantoo and Alusta are brothers forever more. Long live peace and friendship; forever may they reign!" He shouted.

Cheers and applause filled the field. "Bless the day!" Troldomen shouted.

All those present shouted back, "Bless the day" which rang out across the field loudly.

Wyler smiled, rubbed his beard and lifted his cup. He gave Dinatru a hug and smiled. "You look like you mother," he said happily. "I am not the first king of Mantoo, and I will certainly not be the last. I pray that all of the new rulers lead their people in kindness, and fairness. Dinatru, provide your subjects with safety, and security within your land. Let justice and love fill your halls. My son is an honorable man. He is ah... Where is he?" Wyler asked looking around.

Ringo had given a quick hug to Gallra and fetter, and then ran to the horses with Wesley. Some of the guards that saw them pointed in their direction. Wyler jumped off the stage and took a few steps toward them.

"Ringo, Wesley where are you off to?" Wyler shouted

"The rule of the Mantoo lands remains yours until I return father." Ringo shouted back.

Ringo gave a passionate embrace and kiss to Ayana . He handed her a long-stemmed rose and said "I will return shortly my lady."

"It will never be soon enough," She said softly.

"I have a lot to come back for," he said slyly. He hugged Dionne and kissed her forehead. "See you soon rain drop," he said as he mounted his horse and hurried off.

"Bring me back something," Dionne shouted after him.

"Where are the two of you off to now?" Dinatru asked as they rode past the stage.

"We go to retrieve the singing sword." Wesley shouted as their horses picked up speed.

They whipped the reins and their horses ran toward Lurikai drop.

"We may just map the mountains again father, since it's changed so much recently." Ringo shouted as they rode toward the drop.

Troldomen moved next to Wyler and laughed.

"Were we this brash at their age?" Troldomen asked.

Wyler took a deep breath and blew out hard, and then laughed. "I think…more," he laughed.

He looked out at his two sons and shook his head. "You're heading the wrong way." Wyler shouted after them.

Ringo waved his hand in the air as the horses approached the edge. The two horses fearlessly jumped off the edge into the drop, horrifying the onlookers. Suddenly, the two horses and their riders rose from the drop. Everyone stared in amazement at the wings each horse had grown and were using like birds. Ringo lifted the reins and showed his father.

"I'm still holding the reins father. Try not to worry." Ringo said as he gave his father a nod of assurance.

Wyler proudly returned the nod as Troldomen clapped and shouted, "Well done Young master."

"How long before you return?" Wyler shouted.

Ringo looked at Wesley. "We'll be back in forty-five days," he said turning the horse away.

Both horses began to fly in a circle toward the bottom. Immediately, every Mantoo began to place bets on whether they would make it back on time, if at all. The game smith held his hand up to signal that all bets were in, which silenced the crowd.

"The odds are three to one for no return," the Game smith shouted.

Suddenly a lone voice was heard from the direction of the stage. Everyone in the field recognized the voice, but could not believe their ears. They slowly turned to see Wyler, who was holding a gold coin. He smiled and yelled. "Game smith, I'll take that bet."

EPLIOUGE

In the days that followed, Wyler and Troldomen stood in front of Lurikai drop and looked down the trench. Troldomen placed a horn near his ear to listen to the noise coming from the drop.

"What do you hear?" Wyler asked impatiently.

"Nothing," Troldomen barked as he moved toward his horse. He was annoyed with Wyler, and did not mind showing him a little anger at that moment. He placed the horn in the satchel on his horse, and walked back toward Wyler. "I cannot believe you did not tell them," he said angrily.

"Oh Troldomen you know there was no time."

"You know better than that. You had ten years to tell them."

"If they did not believe in Aubaultmor, they certainly would not believe in her Troldomen. They had to see him defeated first, and after that…the trial, then the coronation; it was too much, too quickly," he said defensively.

"Still, you should have tried. Now they will be completely unprepared, and she is a bigger threat than Aubaultmor ever was."

"I had no time," Wyler repeated.

"You knew they would go after the sword."

"Yes, but not so soon. I thought they would…"

"Would what? Ask permission? For someone who claims to have given up the fine art of gambling for so long, I am amazed at how you continue to wager the lives of those you love with the highest of stakes. Ringo has tasted adventure, and now is aware of the mountains many dangers, but he is also aware of all it has to offer. He brings his younger brother into the fold as it was with us. They will encounter her, and she will know of her father's fate, and they will have to face her wrath."

"As did we, but did we not endure? They will endure as well." Wyler assured him.

"Aye we did endure. But neither one of us was the same. She will be stronger, and more dangerous. Her lust for vengeance would have grown, so only one thing is certain. She will do her best to destroy them, and if they survive…'

"If they survive?"

"If they survive Wyler, they will never be the same."

Wyler looked out over the drop and lowered his head sadly. He took in a deep breath and swallowed hard to hold back tears. "I have indeed gambled on my children once more," he said sadly. "Blessed spirit, be with them," he whimpered.

ABOUT THE AUTHOR

Troy first began making up stories at bed time, after his mother sent him and his younger brother to bed. Without a television or radio to lull them to sleep, he made up stories based on the characters that they both loved. Those stories were the source of comfort and entertainment until they both fell asleep each night.

At the tender young age of nine, Troy's father introduced him to the world of fiction and fantasy. His love of the genre began with comic books and quickly spread to novels, movies and television. He wrote short stories in school to entertain his friends, and kept writing through college. After creating an early version of this (tale for a creative writing project in college), Troy went on to become a successful Vice President for a large Investment Bank.

While Cleaning out the garage one day, he came across a box filled with old college books and papers. When he stumbled across the creative writing project, he noticed that there were notes from several different professors. The Creative writing instructor liked the story so much, that she passed it to several colleagues (each of which wrote very positive notes on the paper). Troy immediately walked inside to the study, and made this story based on that earlier work.

Troy hopes to publish ten books dedicated to the tales from the Great Mountain; Wyler's Wager is the first in that series.

www.ingramcontent.com/pod-product-compliance
Lightning Source LLC
Chambersburg PA
CBHW061209170626
46809CB00003B/1305